SNOWJOB

SNOWJOB

TED WOOD

CHARLES SCRIBNER'S SONS • NEW YORK

Maxwell Macmillan Canada
Toronto
Maxwell Macmillan International
New York   Oxford   Singapore   Sydney

Copyright © 1993 by Ted Wood

Charles Scribner's Sons   Maxwell Macmillan Canada, Inc.
Macmillan Publishing Company   1200 Eglinton Avenue East
866 Third Avenue   Suite 200
New York, NY 10022   Don Mills, Ontario M3C 3N1

Macmillan Publishing Company is part of the Maxwell Communication Groups of Companies.

Library of Congress Cataloging-in-Publication Data
Wood, Ted.
Snowjob/Ted Wood.
p. cm.
ISBN 0-684-19563-1
1. Bennett, Reid (Fictitious character)—Fiction. 2. Police—Vermont—Fiction. I. Title. II. Title: Snowjob.
PR9199.3.W57S65   1993   93–18042   CIP
813'.54—dc20

Macmillan books are available at special discounts for bulk purchases for sales promotions, premiums, fund-raising, or educational use. For details, contact:

Special Sales Director
Macmillan Publishing Company
866 Third Avenue
New York, NY 10022

10 9 8 7 6 5 4 3 2 1

Printed in the United States of America

Book design by Liney Li

*For Bob and Betty Russell
with great affection.*

SNOWJOB

The bar was called Brewskis, which said it all. A typical Vermont après-ski place for people trendy enough to use pet names for a drink. And they were out in force, in their stretch pants and puffy sweaters, laughing together about T-bars and moguls and the spectacular tumbles they'd seen on the hill that day.

The bartender was a pretty blonde, around twenty-five. "A brewski?" she asked me with a smile that looked like she meant it. "We have Budweiser or Bud Light on tap and just about everything in the world in bottles."

I ordered a draft Bud and she brought the beer and stood talking, part of her job, I guessed, to get the customers relaxed to the point they feel delighted to spend three times the going rate on a beer.

"Just arrived?"

"This afternoon." I nodded.

"Thought so. You've got a tan but not the same as a skier." She sketched the area on her face as she explained. "You know, real leather brown on the face, fish-white where the toque covers your ears and forehead."

"It'll develop," I said. A new customer came to the bar and she bobbed her head at me and moved off up the bar. I looked at him. He wasn't a skier either. Night worker's pallor and a dark suit. I studied him, trying to figure out what he did for a living. The owner of the place? No. He'd have had an innkeeper's snap-on smile.

He saw me looking and asked, "Do I know you from somewhere?"

"I don't think so," I said politely. "I was just figuring that you didn't look like a skier any more than me."

"I'm not," he said shortly and turned to take his beer, not laying down any money. Then he asked, "If you're not a skier, how come you're here?" No more need to guess. He was a cop.

"Visiting friends," I said. Perhaps the next morning I would be in his office looking for assistance. Right now he didn't need the whole story.

He turned away, leaning one elbow on the bar, nursing his beer in his left hand, studying the crowd. I wondered if he was asking himself the same questions that were going through my mind. Had any of these people seen Cindy Laver the night she was murdered? Probably not. Resorts like this are repopulated every week by new people. Maybe ten percent of the crowd would be weekend regulars. The others had been far away from this corner of Vermont the night Doug Ford was supposed to have strangled the woman, a thirty-six-year-old bookkeeper.

I did my own looking around, getting the feel of the place and the crowd as the cop finished his beer and dropped a buck on the counter. The waitress stuck it in her tips glass and gave him a big smile as he left.

I went on people-watching. Nobody looked like a murderer, but then, nobody does until he's been charged. These were all healthy, cheerful people, either paired up already, like animals in the ark, or working on it. There were a couple of pairs of men alone. The gay contingent, I assumed. But there was one bunch of rowdies, a table of guys on their own.

They were well down the slippery slope to being hammered, laughing too loud, heads together over the table, swapping comments probably about the women in the bar. A tableful of nerds, acting superior.

A waitress came over to them and one of them beamed at her like an aging uncle, and stuck his hand up the back of her skirt.

She gave a little squeal and backed away but he hung on to her and she went red, slapping at his hand.

There was too much noise for anyone else to notice what was going on but I watched, waiting to move. Sir Galahad I'm not but I don't like to see anybody getting a hard time. She was trying to get away and then he put his other hand on her waist and I moved.

I sauntered over to the table and spoke to him. "Hey, George, isn't it?"

He looked at me, keeping his hands where they were. "Piss off," he told me, and his buddies all roared. I smiled at him and punched him, not hard, in the upper arm, my middle knuckle projecting to strike him on the nerve. It paralyzed his arm and his hand fell away from the woman's skirt. She took a quick step back and scurried to the bar. He sat there, nursing his injured bicep in his other hand. One of his buddies said, "Hey. 'd he hit you?"

I had the advantage of height and readiness and I stood staring down the first guy's eyes and into his moldy little soul until he folded. "Screw this place," he said. "Let's head over to the Glauwein."

"I was having a good time," one of them protested but the mauler stared at him coldly and one by one they got up. I stepped back, out of range of a sucker kick, and let them go, the groper last. He said, "I'll get you for this."

They left and I went back to my beer. The bartender was waiting for me. "Thank you," she said, without the smile. "We owe you one. What would you like?"

"Another Bud'd be good, please," I said and when she brought it I asked, "Don't you have a bouncer?"

"Don't need one generally." She flicked her hair back with one hand. "It sounds kind of snobby, I guess, but most of the clientele keep their hands to themselves. We don't get rough stuff in here. That creep is the exception. Thanks for taking care of it."

I raised my beer to her. "You're welcome. Just a drunk. He'll feel bad when he gets over it, likely stay away."

"For a while anyways. He pulls stunts like that sometimes and the boss kicks him out but they're buddies really. He knows he can come back another time."

I just smiled and said nothing and she pushed on, making friendly. "Are you staying somewhere around?"

"For a while."

She looked at me, narrowing her eyes. "You're not a skier, are you? A skier would have said, 'Yes, I'm at such and such until whenever.' "

"I'm here on business," I said. "And maybe you can help me."

A customer came to the bar and she raised one hand to me and went to serve him, then came back. "Shoot."

"I'm interested in what happened to Cindy Laver. You know about her?"

"I sure do," she said in a rush, then stopped. "You a cop or something?"

"Not here." My own little bailiwick was a hard day's drive north of the border in Canada's summer resort country. "I'm a buddy of Doug Ford's. We were in the service together."

Her mouth forced a perfect O. "Then I guess you don't want to hear that I think he did it."

"Why'd you think so?"

"He used to meet her here, every night. He's a cop, right? And she worked at Cat's Cradle, the ski place."

"And they were an item?" Doug was married. I would be staying at his house, with his family.

"They held hands under the table," she said. "He'd always order the same things. A Black Russian for her, a scotch for him. One drink. They'd sit there for half an hour.

Then she'd leave. Then, around five minutes later, he'd go out like they weren't heading back to her place or somewhere."

"Were you here the night she died?"

She looked at me levelly. "I've already talked to the police about that. I told them the truth."

"I'm going in to talk to them tomorrow. But I'd really like to hear it firsthand, from you."

She left to fill the waitress' tray with beers, then came back and stood in front of me with one hand on the bar. "They had a fight. Joyce was serving them. She didn't hear what all they said but even from here I could see they were arguing. Ms. Laver didn't finish her drink. She just got up and walked out, and he followed her."

"Thank you for telling me. And thanks for the beer." I finished it and turned to go.

She called me, softly. "What's your name?"

"Reid Bennett. What's yours?"

"Carol Henning." She stuck out her hand. "I wish you luck."

"Thanks, Carol." I shook her hand which was strong. "I'll likely be back in before I leave town."

"I'll be looking for you," she said and the invitation hung there. I wasn't about to take it up but it pleased me.

It was bright outside with the parking lot lights glinting on six-foot banks of snow on every side. My car was at the far end and I walked to it the long way, going around the first double row of parked cars. Instinctive, I guess. It's been a lot of years since I was on the sharp end in Vietnam but I still stay away from any place I could be ambushed. It could have happened too easily if I'd walked between a mess of parked cars.

I was halfway down the aisle toward my own car when the four guys from the bar got out of a parked Oldsmobile and came toward me.

"Well. It's the big man," one of them said. "Still feeling big?"

I said nothing but gave a shrill whistle between my teeth. Instantly Sam, my big German shepherd, squirmed out of the open window of my car and came bounding up from behind them. They turned as he whisked past.

I bent and patted Sam's head. "Good boy, easy," I whispered and kept on walking.

The guy I'd stopped in the bar said, "So the big man's got a big dog. We'll have to tie a can to his tail."

Sam sensed the hostility and raised his big head, gazing steadily at the one doing the talking. One of the others said, "That thing's huge, fer Chrissakes. I'm not getting myself bit."

The talker was losing them, I could see that. "There's plenny of time," he said. "That thing's not bulletproof."

"Neither are you," I reminded him and walked between them. They parted for us but I expected a back attack so I hissed at Sam who checked and turned to watch them. I didn't look back but by the time I reached my Chev I heard car doors slam. They were leaving. As I took out my keys I whistled Sam. He bounded up to join me and I bent to fuss him while the Oldsmobile drove out, moving with menacing slowness. "Good thing I brought you along, old buddy," I told Sam and put him back in the car, closing the window now and heading out, following the directions I had written down for Doug Ford's house.

It was a modest place, typical of the area, two-story clapboard with a white picket fence buried to the tips of the boards in snow. The drive had been shoveled and I drove in. Almost at once the door opened and Doug's wife, Melody, came out. She's lighter-skinned than he is, and beautiful. She hadn't changed since I danced at her wedding the year I got out of the service. Looking at her made me wonder why the hell Doug had gotten involved with Cindy Laver.

Melody half ran to the car. "Reid. Thank you for coming." We kissed like brother and sister and she clung to my arm.

"I'd rather it had been under happier circumstances. How are you holding up?"

"We're holding up," she said tightly. "But I'm scared, Reid."

I patted her arm. "I knew Doug before you did. He didn't kill this woman."

Two children were at the door, a boy, around fourteen, and a girl a year or so younger. The boy came out to meet me and I shook hands with him. "Wow, Ben. You've grown since I saw you last."

"That was two years ago when Doug brought him fishing up to your place," Melody said. "But he's done most of the spurting in the last six months."

Ben grinned proudly and said nothing. I ruffled his hair. "I brought Sam with me. Remember him?"

"I sure do." He bent and rubbed Sam's head. "Hi, Sam. How's it goin', big guy?"

"Can Sam come in the house, Melody? If you prefer, he can sleep in the car just as happily."

"Nonsense," she said. "Ben, you get Reid's bag and let's get inside. It's cold out here."

I let Ben take the bag which was light, and we went in. The place was furnished inexpensively but with a lot of care. It reminded me of my own house since I'd remarried, lots of antique country pine picked up at auctions and stripped down to the original blues and grays. Not *Better Homes and Gardens* but classy without breaking the bank.

Melody's daughter was standing in the archway that led to the living room and she looked at me shyly. She was pretty, dark-skinned like her dad but with the aquiline features of a young Lena Horne. She would break a lot of hearts, I thought.

Melody said, "Say hello, Angie. This is Mr. Bennett. He was in Vietnam with Daddy."

"Hello," she said and smiled shyly.

"Hello, Angie. Call me Reid. And this is Sam."

She was more at ease with him. "Hi, Sammy," she said and patted him lightly. "You're big."

"I hope you don't mind," Melody said. "You're in Angie's room. She's doubling up with me."

"If that's okay with Angie that would be very nice," I said and the girl nodded.

"Will you get Daddy out of prison?" she asked, wide-eyed.

"I hope so. I'll do whatever I can." I didn't want to make promises I couldn't keep. Doug was a good man when I knew him, in a bad place, but that had been a lot of years ago. And it figured that there was a solid case against him.

"I brought you something," I said, to break the tension, and opened my bag. "Hope you like it." My wife had shopped for me, when she knew I had to come down here. I had a loose sweatshirt with a picture of a loon on it for Angie and a Toronto Blue Jays warm-up jacket for Ben. They were delighted and Angie went to put hers on.

Melody led me into the kitchen. "Have you eaten yet?"

"Yes, thanks. I had dinner on the road." I sat down at the table and Melody said, "Would you like a beer then, cup of coffee?"

"Coffee would be good, please, black, no sugar."

Melody gave a nervous laugh. "Didn't they serve cream and sugar in the Marines? Doug takes his the same way."

She poured us coffee, which was strong and good, and the kids came back to show us how they looked in their new gear. Then Melody sent them into the living room to watch TV and sat down at the table with me. "I hope your wife doesn't mind my asking you to come down? Freda, isn't it?"

"Yes, but she prefers Fred. Funny name for a good-looking lady, but that's her, independent as all get-out."

"You said on the phone that her mom was there." Melody looked on the point of tears, battling bravely to make small talk when all she wanted was her husband home with her and the cloud lifted from her life.

"Yeah. Her father lost a long fight with cancer last month. We went out west for the funeral and her mom came home with us. She was at loose ends and she's delighted to be around the baby."

Melody asked about the baby and we got all the politenesses out of the way before we settled down to discuss the reason I was there. It was a long story and it came out awkwardly with her having to backtrack a few times to cover points she had left out.

It boiled down to the fact that she had suspected Doug was having an affair. There was no way of checking. He was a detective, working all the crazy hours his job demanded. She didn't know whether he'd been seeing another woman, but their own lovemaking had changed. From being the centerpiece of their marriage it had dwindled to almost nothing and that mechanical, as if his mind was somewhere else. She had challenged him about it and he told her that the pressure of work made it difficult for him to relax.

"It wasn't easy for him," Melody admitted, refilling my coffee cup. "He's the only black officer in the department. This is a snow-white town, white as the slopes out there." She shook her head. "Oh, there's no racism, not out loud. Nobody calls you nigger, but you're an oddity, know what I mean?"

I nodded. "Most of these folks have been here since the year dot. They're used to pink faces around them. Then when a smart black cop from New York comes here, for the quiet life, they're surprised. But they're not rednecks. It's going to be fine."

"It's been eight years and no problems," Melody said softly. "I have my job in the library. The kids have lots of friends, we're accepted just fine but Doug figures he has to work twice as hard, be twice as smart as every white officer on the force, especially now he's made detective."

"He was always that way in the service," I said. "More guts than brains I used to tell him. Hell, he'd've volunteered to walk point every time if the lieutenant would have let him."

Melody nodded. "Well, anyway, I was on my way home

from work one evening, around nine, and I saw him and this Cindy Laver in her car, outside her apartment. He was laughing with her, the same way he used to laugh with me. And I went around the corner and stopped and got out and when I went back I saw him going up to the apartment with her."

"Did you talk to him about it?"

"I sure as hell did," she said angrily. "He didn't come in until three in the morning but I was sitting here waiting and I told him what I'd seen."

"And he said he was on an investigation," I said.

She gasped, then half smiled. "You cops are all the same. Yeah. That's exactly what he said. And I asked him 'investigating what, her birthmarks?' and he said he couldn't tell me. It was big and it was confidential."

"How long was this before the girl was murdered?"

"Three nights," she said softly, and then her shell cracked and she began to weep.

That ended our discussion for the night. She dried her eyes right away but I called off the questioning. I wanted to hear the details of the murder and Doug's arrest but I knew I could get it more clearly from the police department next day and I didn't want to cause Melody any more heartache. So I knocked off the questions and phoned home and talked to Fred. She was in raptures. Louise had started rolling over from her back onto her stomach and was moving her arms and legs as if she wanted to crawl. Fred wished I could have been there to share her pleasure but she understood. Doug and I had been close in the service and he didn't have many friends at the moment. We said our goodbyes and I let Sam out for a last run and went up to bed.

It was a little girl's room. There were posters of the New Kids on the Block; Save the Rain Forests; Reduce, Reuse, Recycle; and a little statue of the Virgin. That stopped me as I looked around. I was brought up Catholic although I haven't done much about it since Nam, but there was an inherent goodness in this house that reminded me of my mother and I went to bed oddly happy. If there was anything in the power of his family's prayer Doug was safe.

Next morning after I'd had breakfast with Melody and
the kids, I went down to the courthouse and asked to see
Doug. The guy in charge was the typical small-town tyrant.
"You an attorney?"

"No, just a friend."

He snorted. It was an appropriate sound. He was short
and stubby, wearing a ten-year-old suit with a lodge pin in
the lapel. "Ford don't have a whole lot of them right now."

I didn't answer and after a pause he asked, "You got
any ID?"

I pulled out the little plastic card with my picture and
police chief accreditation. That impressed him. "Chief of
Police," he said thoughtfully. "Don't believe I've ever heard
of Murphy's Harbour, Chief. Is it big?"

"Not as big as this place," I told him which was less than
I might have said. The Harbour isn't one tenth as big, and
I didn't bother to add that I was the only copper in the
place. Myself and Sam. In any case it put his suspicions on
hold and he unlocked a door into the secure area and led
me to the meeting room.

It was painted institutional green, bare except for a table
with a chair each side of it. I sat down on one side and
waited for them to bring Doug out. He came in with a big
uniformed guard behind him. I stood up and the guard said,
"Stay on your own side of the table, sir. Do not pass anything to the prisoner. If you have papers or anything he
must see, give them to me, I'll give them to him."

He said it all by rote. It was nothing personal and I waved
a hand at him to confirm I understood.

Doug spoke first. "Thanks for coming, Reid. I didn't know
who else to call."

"*De nada,*" I said. "How're they treating you?"

"Can't complain." He tried to grin. "It's a whole lot softer'n boot camp."

I studied him. He looked stressed, his eyes hollow, the

green work clothes he was wearing ill-fitting and rough. "I'm not in the general population. Thank God," he said softly. "My own guys managed to do that much for me. But the other prisoners keep shouting what they're going to do when I get put with them."

"Just jailhouse machismo. Any chance of bail?"

"They want half a million dollars," he said bitterly.

I guessed the District Attorney was looking to prove to the town that he didn't play favorites with policemen, so I changed the subject. "Your family's fine," I told him. "The kids are taking it well and Melody's hanging in okay."

"She's a saint, that woman," he said and I watched his face. If he had been having an affair with Cindy Laver he would have wept now. But he didn't.

"Were you balling this Cindy Laver?" I kept it rough to check his reactions.

"With what I've got at home? Come on, Reid." He sounded disgusted. "I haven't cheated on Melody. Not once in eighteen years."

"The waitress at Brewskis says you used to hold hands with this Cindy Laver."

Now he glanced over at the guard who was standing with his hands at his side, listening to every word. Doug leaned forward and lowered his voice. I had to lean in to hear him. "That was an act," he whispered. "We figured it was safer that way."

"She was acting too?"

He nodded. The guard was straining to hear us. From his frown I guessed he was having trouble. "She wouldn't have minded if it had been for real but we decided it was the best way to cover up what was really going on."

"What the hell was going on?"

He gave a breathless little sigh. "If I tell you, Reid, you're a part of all this. That could be trouble."

"You've got more trouble than you can handle. It wouldn't hurt to off-load a little."

He smiled shortly and lifted his hand as if to give me a

high five. "No touching," the guard said and Doug waved
the hand and laid it flat on the table again.

"Ever hear of Angelo Manatelli?"

I shook my head. "A rounder?"

"Mob," Doug said briefly. "He's with the Mucci family
of New Jersey. Big into gambling, prostitution, loan-
sharking. But he's not a hard man himself. He's the
bookkeeper."

"New to me." I took out a notepad and pen and wrote
the names down. "Where's this guy fit in?"

"He was here, in town. I saw him at Rosario's, that's the
best Italian place in town. He was having dinner with a
couple locals."

"Who?"

"One of them was Eric Lawson. He owns the bank. The
other owns the Cat's Cradle ski resort."

"Name?" I was taking notes.

Peter Huckmeyer."

"And what happened then? Where does Cindy Laver come
in?"

"I knew she worked as a bookkeeper for the Huckmeyers
at the Cat's Cradle. If they were talking to criminals, I wondered if she knew why." Doug looked at me very straight.
"You know how it is. You try to know everything about
everybody."

I nodded. "I'm the same."

"So," he said slowly. "I was waiting outside the resort
when she came out at six, like always, and made her right
turn without stopping at the sign, like always. And I started
writing her a citation."

"Were you in uniform?"

Doug touched his cheek. "With this skin I don't need a
uniform. Everybody in town knows who the hell I am."

"So, was she surprised that a detective would pick her up
on a traffic violation?"

"That was the idea," Doug said. "She asked me what this

was all about and I started talking to her about the guy her boss, Peter Huckmeyer, had been eating dinner with."

"How long ago was this?"

"Three weeks before she was killed."

I sat back and looked at him. I believed him, but it seemed a little pat, that a professional accountant would play along with a cop on suspicions as slim as his. "And she bought it?"

Doug nodded and beckoned me forward with one finger so he could whisper again. "She had an ax to grind. She wasn't local. She came from Chicago. I didn't find out until later, but her ex-husband had gotten into trouble with loan sharks over his gambling. It cost her the house they owned, cost him the marriage. But even then he didn't stop. He borrowed more and when the horse was slow the enforcers came after him with tire irons. One of them got too enthusiastic and caved his head in. She was apart from him by then but still cared about him."

"So then what happened? Did you go to the chief with your case or what?"

Doug pursed his lips bitterly. "If I hadn't been trying to be a goddamn hotshot I would've. But I wanted to go to him with a complete case, not a pack of worries. So I asked her to help me, to let me know what was going down at work. That way I could've laid the whole thing on his desk like a Christmas present."

The guard scuffed his feet and I glanced over. "One more minute," he said tonelessly.

"Who else knows? " I asked Doug quickly.

"Nobody," he said as the guard advanced toward him. "Nobody but me and you and the guy who killed her."

"Did you tell the arresting officer any of this?"

"No." He shook his head fiercely. "I was scared they'd come after my family while I was inside."

The guard was moving toward us so I spoke quickly. "What can you tell me about the case against you?"

"Check with Pat Hinton. He was my partner. He's a good head. A tightass but fair as they come."

The guard touched Doug on the shoulder and he stood up. "Watch yourself, Reid. This is heavy."

"Hang loose." I winked at him and stood while the guard walked him back to his cell. Doug turned at the door to wave. "Semper fi," he said and I echoed it. The Marine motto, as abbreviated by ex-grunts.

There was a diner across the square from the courthouse and I went over there and had a coffee and phoned the police department. Detective Hinton was off duty, they told me. He would be in at four. There was no Hinton listed in the phone book, which didn't surprise me. Most small-town cops have unlisted numbers. It cuts down on the midnight cursers. I guessed that Melody knew his number so after I finished my coffee I walked Sam down to the library and left him beside the steps while I went in.

It was one of the libraries donated by Andrew Carnegie in the early part of the century, a square stone building with three steps up to the front door. The woman at the front desk told me that the chief librarian was busy but Melody must have seen me from her office. She came out and thanked the girl and led me in.

She had a clutter of folders on her desk and there were piles of new books everywhere but she cleared a chair for me and I sat.

"How is he?" she asked first.

"Fine. He sends his love."

"He asked me not to come in every day," she said, almost bitterly.

"Because he loves you," I said. "He knows what it's like, having to run the gauntlet of those people."

"You think that's it?"

"He's a good man," I told her, "and there was nothing between him and that girl. It was an investigation, concerning somebody that girl knew."

"He told me that," she said. "Remember? I mentioned it last night."

"It's the truth. I believe him." I sat there, looking at her beautiful, troubled face, and eventually she got control of herself.

"What are you going to do now?"

"He wants me to talk to his partner, Pat Hinton. He's not at work, not in the book. I wondered if you had his phone number."

She reached under her desk and pulled out her purse, opening it and taking out a little book. "Yes. Got a pencil?"

I wrote down the number, then said, "I guess you know him pretty well." She nodded and I said, "It might be good if you were to call him, introduce me by phone."

"Sure." She picked up the receiver and dialed quickly. The person at the other end answered almost immediately and she said, "Hello, Alison. It's Melody Ford."

She stared at the wall blankly, then said, "He's fine, thank you. A friend of ours has just been in to see him. Says he's okay. That's why I called. This friend, Reid Bennett, he was in the service with Doug. He's a police chief now in Canada. He wanted to talk to Pat if that were possible."

She covered the mouthpiece and said, "She's calling him." I nodded and then she said, "Hello, Pat. I've got a friend of Doug's here, Reid Bennett. Doug asked him to speak to you. Will that be all right?"

He must have agreed because she passed the phone to me without another word. I took it. "Hello, Pat. This is Reid Bennett."

"Hi, Reid." It was a veteran policeman's voice, not giving anything away. "How can I help?"

"I was in to see Doug this morning and he asked me to talk to you. I'm a copper myself so you wouldn't be telling tales out of school."

"Whyn't you come on over," he said. "I don't go in until three. Melody knows where we are."

"Great, thank you. I'll be right there. Bye."

Melody directed me to Hinton's house and I left. Sam was outside with a little old lady staring at him, her string bag of library books dangling at her side. "He's never moved, not once," she said wonderingly. "Even when I patted him. However did you train him so well?"

"He was smart to start with," I told her. Then I told Sam "Easy" and this time he responded, wagging his tail when she gave his head a pat.

I went back to my car and put him in the front seat, then I found Grissom Street and left him where he was with the window down. It was beautiful skiing weather, a bright, cold morning, about five above zero on the Fahrenheit scale. Inside the car Sam would have been comfortable at 30° lower than that.

Hinton came to the door and we both did a double take. He was the cop I'd identified the evening before at Brewskis. "Well, small world," he said and shook my hand. "Come on in."

I went in, kicking off my shoes at the door, something most Canadians do automatically. The place was similar to Doug's house but furnished in a more modern way and it had an electric keyboard organ in one corner of the living room.

Hinton introduced his wife. "Ali, this is Doug's friend, Reid Bennett. He's a police chief, no less, from Canada."

Alison was a tiny woman with a head of frizzy curls. "My goodness," she said. "I don't believe we've ever had a chief in here before."

"I'm the only guy in the department," I explained. "It's a phony title but I didn't pick it. It came with the job."

She laughed. "Is that so. Then I won't bother to curtsy. Would you like some coffee?"

"Please. Black," I said and she went out as Hinton waved me to a chair.

"Take a load off," he said. I sat opposite him and he asked, "So, you've known Doug awhile?"

"We were in the Marines together. Went from boot camp

to Nam. We both did two tours, although I was out a few months earlier than Doug because of a wound."

"And you stayed in touch?" He was being careful, but I wasn't offended. I needed his help. This was his price.

"Yeah. I was best man when he and Melody got married. And he's been up to visit my patch to do some fishing. Brought young Ben with him last time. The boy caught a good-sized walleye. He was proud as punch."

That was enough, it seemed. He crossed his knees and asked, "What can I tell you?"

"I didn't get time to talk to Doug about the case against him. He said you'd fill me in. Would that be okay?"

"Sure. For my partner," he said. "But right off the top lemme say that it doesn't look good for Doug."

"What's the case, the evidence?"

His wife came back with the coffee and we thanked her and she looked at our faces and said, "I guess I'll get lunch started. Holler if you need a refill."

"Thanks, Ali," Hinton said. She went out, closing the door. "We've been married fourteen years. She understands police work," he said fondly.

"She's very tactful," I said politely and waited.

Hinton sipped his coffee. "Facts," he said. "The deceased woman, Lucinda Lee Laver, age thirty-six. Born Chicago. Found dead in her apartment at ten A.M., thereabouts, by her landlady. That was Wednesday."

Two days ago, the day I'd received Melody's call for help.

"She was nude. She'd been strangled with a pair of her own panty hose. Whoever did it was a pro. He'd knotted a quarter inside, pressed it on her Adam's apple."

"Why did the landlady go into the apartment? Was that normal?"

Hinton shook his head. "No. But her boss called the house and couldn't raise her. So he sent a coworker, woman called Ella Frazer, over to see if she was okay."

"At ten in the morning? Sounds like he was really anxious to see her."

"Yeah." Hinton looked at me bleakly. "And this is where it gets bad for Doug. She was supposed to have made a deposit at the bank the evening before. She left work at four with fifty grand in a canvas sack. And at nine that morning, when she didn't show, her boss phoned the bank and found they hadn't received the deposit. So he got worried and called her house."

"Was the money found?" After the hint he had dropped I dreaded the answer. He gave it to me straight. "It was in Doug's car. He'd taken it out of the sack but it matched the amount she had taken with her, forty-nine grand and change. It was there to the penny."

We both sat and sipped our coffee without speaking. Neither of us spoke but in my eyes this looked like a frame-up and I was trying to find a tactful way to say so. Hinton did it for me.

"Go ahead and say it. Doug wouldn't have been that dumb. If he'd killed her he'd have put the money somewhere else."

"That's the way I see it. So I'm guessing that there was more evidence than the money against him. I'm guessing they made a case against him first, then checked his car and found the cash."

"That's how it happened." Hinton nodded. "We were off duty, Doug and me, the morning it happened. The other team investigated, Lieutenant Cassidy and Sergeant Morgan."

"What happened?"

"It broke right away," Hinton said. "The first thing the landlady said was the end of it as far as Doug was concerned."

"She said that Doug and the deceased had been an item?"

He nodded. "More than that. She'd seen him going in and out of the place for a couple weeks already. And on the night before she'd seen them going in together, having a big fight. Ms. Laver didn't want Doug to come in but he'd more or less forced his way in and they'd gone on fighting over the landlady's head while she was watching TV. She said they were still at it when she went to bed, around ten-thirty. Her bedroom's in the back of the house and she couldn't hear from there."

"What time did death occur?"

"Around two in the morning, give or take. You know how it is with coroners."

"Did you find any forensic evidence in the apartment? Anything to tie Doug to the place?"

"Fingerprints on a beer can. That was it," Hinton said. "I'd figured there'd be more than that. Like if they'd been having a thing, there'd have been fingerprints in the bedroom, the toilet seat, wherever. But the only prints they found were on one lousy beer can."

"Let's get this straight. You mean they didn't find any fingerprints at all?"

"Virtually none. The place was clean and neat and they figured she must have cleaned up recently and not touched a whole lot of stuff since."

I frowned. "Surely they found prints on the fridge door and the kitchen cupboards, places she would have touched since cleaning."

"Nothing." He shook his head. "The chief said it looked like she'd gotten compulsive while they were arguing, the way some women do, gone around with a dust cloth and wiped stuff down. Hell, some women are like that, guys too." Hinton waved his hand. "You know, they can't sit still and talk."

"Sounds to me like someone may have sanitized the crime scene and it wasn't Doug or he would have gotten rid of the beer can."

"I thought the same," Hinton said. "But I was overruled and I wasn't the investigating officer so I won't get a chance to say anything in court, but Doug's defense lawyer ought to make something of it if he's smart."

"It's starting to sound phony. The beer can could have been planted," I said. "And the woman downstairs doesn't know what time he left. Could have been right after ten-thirty."

Hinton shrugged. "I agree, and the money could have been planted in his car but you know how it goes. When you hear hoofbeats, think horses, not zebras."

"Had there been any sexual assault on the victim?"

"No." Hinton shook his head firmly. "The corner said not. He also said that she had just gotten out of the shower when she was attacked."

"And where was Doug at the time it's supposed to have happened?"

"He wouldn't say," Hinton said. "He was on duty alone. It was Ali's birthday and I took the night off so we could go out to dinner."

That surprised me. Detectives work in pairs for a good reason. It gives two points of view to everything they investigate. If one man was taking the night off, the other would generally do the same. If the caseload didn't allow it, he would take some other guy with him, maybe a uniform man working a rare plainclothes shift. I asked, "Did you have many cases on your sheet?"

"Nothing important." Hinton set down his coffee cup. "We don't have much heavy stuff going down in this town. We only work nights two weeks a month. This was our second week. The only things we had were a guy who'd beat up his girlfriend and a missing person." He paused and added, "There was nothing to stop Doug taking the same night off if he'd wanted. That weighed against him as well."

"Did he follow up on those cases? Did anyone check?"

Hinton nodded. "I did that right off. He'd interviewed a couple of people through the evening but from nine o'clock on, he had nothing to prove that he hadn't been with Cindy Laver."

Hinton was uncomfortable. I could tell that much. He fiddled with his coffee cup, setting it just so in its saucer before he spoke again. "Like you're a friend of Doug's, and Melody's, right?"

"Yeah." I left it at that. He was following some train of thought of his own. I didn't want to derail it.

"Well, I figured I was, too. I mean, Doug's my partner and you know how that goes. We're like joined at the hip for eight, ten, whatever hours we work together."

"And you like Melody," I said carefully. "Everybody does. She's a special kind of woman."

"Yeah, well, that's just it," he said angrily. "Like for three weeks I've been covering for Doug while he screwed around with this divorcée of his. She was pretty, sexy. Sure. But goddamn it, she was no match for Melody."

"I agree. And if it makes you feel better, Doug says there was nothing to it. It was just business."

"Bullshit," he exploded. "He couldn't stay away from her. Hell, I'm his partner. If there was anything else going down he'd've told me."

I shrugged helplessly. "All I know is I trust Doug. I was with him in a lot of hot spots and he was solid as a rock."

Hinton shook his head. "There's a big difference between guts and honesty. I'd trust Doug with my life. Hell, you have to think that way about your partner, you know that. But it burned me up covering his ass while he was off screwing that Laver broad."

"He says he wasn't. And, on that subject, you said she hadn't been laid before she was strangled."

"No. And she'd showered, ready for bed. Like it doesn't make sense that she'd have done that if Doug had been there with her and they were fighting. She'd have booted him out, then gotten into the shower."

I thought about it. "Did Doug have her key on him when he was arrested?"

"No." Hinton shook his head. "And he would've if they'd been serious about one another. Of course, he could have slung it away after the murder."

"If he'd strangled her and thought that deeply he'd have

hidden the money better," I suggested. "Where was she killed?"

"The body was on the bed, but she wasn't killed there. The best guess is in the bathroom."

"Were there traces on the floor?"

"Yeah." He splayed his hands. "You know how it goes in stranglings. Her bowels gave out. Whoever did it to her took the time to clean it up, but the guys who checked were thorough. They found traces on the tile. And the bedclothes under her were damp. She hadn't had time to dry herself before she was attacked."

"Who investigated?" This was the important question. I didn't know how many enemies Doug had in the department and if one of them had fingered him.

"The daytime team, Cassidy and Morgan. Then, when the landlady mentioned Doug they called the chief and he went down there himself. He made the arrest, at Doug's house. Doug was in bed."

I wondered whether there was bad blood between the other detectives and Doug but Hinton didn't mention anything so I didn't push it. Instead we talked some more and he promised to show me the photographs and the forensic report when he went on duty. That ended our discussion. Hinton hadn't mentioned anything about Angelo Manatelli or the investigation Doug said he was making into Manatelli's association with the locals. I thanked him and left with four hours to fill before I could visit him at the office and see the crime scene photographs.

I found another coffee shop with a telephone and called Irv Goodman, my former partner in Toronto.

Irv was exactly the right guy for this investigation. He's a sergeant of detectives, an old-style rank that meant he was in charge of a squad of men working under a detective inspector. He's a veteran copper and he has a law degree. Right then he was working the fraud squad, using his legal knowledge to analyze the books of questionable companies.

He took my call as if he had all the time in the world, asked after my family, then got around to business.

"I'm in Vermont, checking into a killing that's supposed to have been done by a friend of mine. He's a detective here."

"Good luck, Reid," he said. "Did he do it?"

"I don't think so but there's quite a case against him. He doesn't have an alibi and he was supposed to be having an affair with the victim."

"And what was he doing? Was it something legit?"

"He was investigating the activities of the bookkeeper for a mob family in New Jersey. Guy called Angelo Manatelli, works for the Mucci family. He isn't able to tell me much more. My friend's in custody and he's scared to say too much, scared for his family's safety."

"Okay. I'll run a make on Manatelli," Irv said. "What else?"

I explained about Cindy Laver's job and the fact that there was money involved in the killing. That's when Irv's radar clicked in. "I wonder if this is some money-laundering thing?" he asked.

"The thought had crossed my mind, but it's out of my league. How's it done?"

The sun must have been shining into Irv's office. He went poetic on me. "How do I wash thee? Let me count the ways. You got an hour or two?"

"I will have. Maybe I can call you at home tonight, if you wouldn't mind."

"That'd be best," he said. "You could be on to something. It's a long way from New Jersey to the wilds of Vermont and I don't guess the volume of business at a resort town would be big enough to do much for a mob operation, but it's an idea.

"If you want to know how it's done I'll spell it all out for you later on if you'd like."

"I'd appreciate that. When would be a good time to call?"

"My in-laws are coming over for dinner. It's Friday night and they're very serious about the sabbath. Don't be too early. Make it around nine and I can sneak out for a while. You got the home number?"

"Sure." I'd brought my phone book with me. No problem there."

I hung up the phone and stood thinking for a moment. I was at a standstill, but the time need not be wasted. I decided to head over to Cat's Cradle and take a look around. If nothing else it would give me a look at the scope of the operation. I might even see whether fifty grand was a large amount of money to be deposited on a Wednesday morning. It amounted to a whole lot of ski rentals, tow fees and coffee shop snacks.

Not too high, I discovered. This was Friday, a weekday, but already, before noon, the parking lot was packed and the hills were covered with skiers gliding down the beautifully groomed slopes. I stood and looked at it all for a minute or so before heading into the cafeteria.

It was filled with skiers clattering around in unfastened ski boots, all of them high on the fun they'd been having on the hill. I got a cup of coffee and sat with it, doing some mental arithmetic as I watched the lineup at the counter. Fifty thousand dollars wouldn't have been out of line for a day's receipts. But what did I do next?

I made my decision and left the cafeteria, looking for the office. It was in a small, rustic-looking chalet but all business inside. There was a pretty redhead at a computer in the front office and I asked her if Ella Frazer was working. She looked at me quizzically, working out whether I was a boyfriend, then said, "I think she's gone for lunch. Let me check."

I waited and a moment later she was back with a woman around fifty, dressed in a business suit and carrying a purse and a down-filled topcoat. "I'm Ella Frazer," she said.

"Reid Bennett, Ms. Frazer. The young lady tells me you're just going to lunch."

"Yes." She looked at me without volunteering anything else.

"I'm an associate of Detective Hinton's," I said, stretching the truth. "I wonder if it might be possible to talk to you for a moment, please? Perhaps over lunch."

She tutted. She had a pleasant face but she looked quite sour now. "Really, I talked to him at length, and to all the rest of your people. What else is there to tell you?"

"Probably nothing at all." I smiled at her. "But it would be very kind of you if you wouldn't mind."

"All right then. I'm going to the Glauwein. Do you know how to get there?"

"Perhaps I could drive you."

The redhead was watching with interest. At her age, mid-twenties, we must have looked like a couple of dinosaurs sparring. Ms. Frazer glanced at her and the girl's amusement decided her. "No. Come with me," she said and began putting on her coat. I helped her with it and we went out to the parking lot.

She got into a bright red Toyota Corolla and leaned across to flip the catch for me. I got in. "Thank you for seeing me," I said and she pursed her lips and started the car.

"I suppose you want to ask me about poor Cindy."

"I'm afraid so. Were you good friends?"

"Yes," she said shortly and backed out of the parking space. "I'm still in shock about what happened. I hope they hang that black bastard for what he did."

I wasn't going to get any bonuses here, I realized, and it made me choose my approach carefully. I decided on "They don't hang people anymore in Vermont."

She took her eyes off the road to glance at me. "You sound like a friend of his?"

"You'd be surprised how many friends he's got." I felt like a juggler trying to keep a ball in the air while she did her best to bat it down.

"Ask your questions," she told me, her face grim.

"Thank you." I thought before I spoke again. The wrong question was going to get her back up and I'd be on the

side of the road with a long way to walk back to my car. I
kept it neutral. "Had you known Ms. Laver for a long time?"

"Since she started here, back in '87. In fact I interviewed
her when she came looking for a job."

"So you're her boss?"

"I was. And I am missing her like hell. She was a very
good, dependable person."

"She was banking some money, the night she died. Was
that the routine?"

"Yes." A brisk little nod. "We always cashed up the day's
receipts every day at four. It included the money left over
from the previous night's operations, after our office closed.
And then Cindy would drive it to town."

"She never had an escort?"

Ms. Frazer nodded grimly. "Usually the operations manager would go with her. He has a gun license and he would
take her to the night deposit at the bank."

"But he didn't on Wednesday. Why was that?"

Ms. Frazer snorted. "Walter loves to ski. He always goes
out in the lunch hour and on Wednesday he fell and twisted
his ankle. He was hobbling all afternoon and Cindy said she
would manage on her own."

"Quite a responsibility."

Now she took her eyes off the road for a dangerously long
time as she gazed at me angrily. "Not on the face of it. Her
goddamn lover boy was a cop. He should have kept her safe
as a church. Instead he strangled her."

She looked back at the road, in time to avoid going into
the man-high snowbank along the shoulder while I thought
about her answer. If Doug had been with the dead woman
from four they'd had plenty of time to make her deposit. But
instead they had gone somewhere for an hour or so. Then
they'd gone to Brewskis for their drink and fight, and after
that they'd spent an hour or two somewhere else before they
arrived at her place, still fighting. Something didn't add up.
But I kept my questions neutral, probing for more detail.

"The guy with the broken ankle. How was he the next day?"

"His name is Huckmeyer, Walter Huckmeyer. He was fine, except for a limp. He's still limping."

"Huckmeyer? Is he the owner?"

She was concentrating on slowing and turning into the parking lot of the Glauwein, a mock Tyrolean place on the edge of town, so she didn't look at me as she spoke. "You don't know much about our town, do you?"

"No, I'm a stranger here."

She parked and switched off the motor, then sat, looking out through the windshield. "Then you're not an associate of Detective Hinton, are you?"

It was time for some truth. If she got snooty I could get a cab back to the slope to collect my car. "In a minor way. My main reason for being here is that I was in the Marines with Doug Ford and I don't think he killed Ms. Laver."

She drew a tight little breath, as if controlling her anger. "I ought to tell you to go to hell but I know what friendship is. I was a friend of Cindy's. So let me tell you that you're wasting your time." She paused. "But, to answer your question, Walter is the owner's son. One of his sons. He has two. The other is an actor."

"Thank you." I looked for something to make her cooperative again. "If it makes any difference, I'm not here to make monkeys out of the police. I'm a cop myself. But when friends are in trouble, you rally round. Right?"

That sat well. She nodded. "Okay. I'll buy that. Let's go in."

We went into the restaurant which was three-quarters full, mostly skiers I guessed from the way they were dressed. We waited at the desk until the hostess came up to us and said, "Well, hi, Ms. Frazer. This way please."

"Thanks, Jane." Ms. Frazer smiled and I saw that she could be a very attractive woman. I followed her to a corner table and we took off our coats and sat down. I noticed that

she was wearing a number of rings but had none on her
wedding finger. The hostess was hovering and Ms. Frazer
said to me, "The special is always good. On Fridays it's
fish, right, Jane?"

The waitress nodded. "New Zealand orange ruffy."

"I'd like that, and a glass of white, please," she said.

"Same for me, with a draft beer, please."

The waitress smiled and left. "All right, now what can a
friend of one party tell the friend of another?" She asked it
very carefully, as if she was afraid she was going to explode
and start smashing the furniture.

I thought about all the possible questions and started with
a simple one. "Was there anything unusual about the size
of the bank deposit that night?"

She picked up her napkin and started polishing the knife
and fork. It was an almost automatic gesture. She cleaned
the whole length of both, very carefully. "No. It was typical
for this time of year."

"All cash? No Visa slips, no American Express,
MasterCard?"

"No. They're kept to week's end and submitted sepa-
rately," she said. She had finished the cutlery and now she
polished the bowl of her wineglass. A nervous, compulsive
action, I thought. But as I watched her I couldn't help remembering what Hinton had said about the absence of fingerprints at the crime scene. Had this woman been there?
And if she had, was she the one who had strangled her
friend?

I didn't find out anything more about Cindy Laver at lunch but I did learn that Ms. Frazer was a pretty serious drinker. She sank two glasses of white wine while I dawdled over a draft beer and then she fiddled with her glass and looked as if she would have liked to order another but was embarrassed to with me there.

After a while I led the conversation around to her job and the town, subjects that gave me insight into her perception of the world. She knew just about everybody, including Melody Ford, whom she described as "a striking woman." I also learned that the Lawsons and the Huckmeyers were the local heavyweights. Lawson, the mayor, owned half the local businesses, including the local radio station, the bank and one of the town's two major ski resorts, Angel's Fall. The Huckmeyers owned the rest, including the Cat's Cradle and all three major restaurants, the Glauwein, Rosario's and Brewskis. That reminded me that Doug had seen the mob guy, Manatelli, eating dinner with the pair of them. It gave more credibility to his story of working on a big case.

I had to give Ms. Frazer marks for fairness. If she was

angry that I was a friend of Doug's she never showed it. She
protested politely when I paid for lunch, then thanked me
and drove me back to my car. Sam was none the worse for
his long wait but I let him out for a stretch, and stood to
watch the skiers having their fun in the bright sunshine, then
went back to town. It was just after one o'clock and there
was nothing I could do until I saw Hinton at his office so I
took time out to go for a run with Sam. The streets were
clear of snow but the sidewalks were icy in places so we took
it easy and covered only three miles. I showered and was
waiting at the town's neat new police station when Pat
Hinton arrived at four.

He was different at work than he had been at home, more
serious and careful. "The chief's not here or I'd take you in
to see him first," he said. "He'll know soon enough that
you're in town. I don't want him thinking I'm getting outa
line. If he says no dice, that's the end of it."

"I understand. Thanks for taking the gamble." I followed
him into the detective office. It was typical of a hundred
I've seen, brightly lit, the walls covered with a clutter of
photographs and notices. There were four desks in the room,
pushed into two back-to-back groupings. A couple of other
detectives were putting their coats on, getting ready to leave.
Pat introduced me. "Guys, this is Reid Bennett. He's a chief
from Canada. Reid, this is Lieutenant Cassidy and Fred
Morgan."

Morgan stuck his hand out first. "Glad to know ya, Reid.
Is that police chief or Indian chief?" He was laughing, the
clown of the twosome. There always is one.

I shook hands. "Police, but it's a phony title. I'm the
whole department."

Now Cassidy shook hands. "Hi. You're a friend of Doug
Ford's, am I right?"

"Yeah. We were in the service together, Lieutenant. His
wife called me to come on down when this happened." I
was careful with him, giving him his rank. No cop likes to
think someone has come to question his findings. From the

look of Cassidy he was ultra-touchy. He was lean and intense, the kind of guy who has his sights set on promotion.

He looked at me, out of narrowed eyes. "Well, I wish I could say this is a crock, but it looks bad. We had no choice but to charge him."

"I understand. I'd have done the same myself, based on what I've heard. But you know how it is. We go back a long way."

Morgan asked, "Were you in Nam with him?"

"Yes. Marine Corps."

I could tell they had worked together for a long time. Cassidy asked the next question, not even pausing. "But you're Canadian, right? How come you were in the service?"

"Our country made a kind of trade-off with yours. We took in a whole bunch of draft dodgers but a lot of guys came down here for a chance to fight. It worked out even."

That completed the formalities. Morgan said, "Well, I guess Pat'll walk you through it all. I've got to take my son to his hockey practice."

Cassidy looked at his watch. "I've got a little while. What can I tell you?"

"I'd like to hear your end of the case. Pat told me you were the arresting officer."

"Right." Cassidy lifted one hand as Fred Morgan left, then sat down at his desk. "We got a call about the woman being found dead. Fred and I went over there and checked things out. The landlady, a Mrs. Vaughan, said that Doug had been calling there for a few weeks. She wasn't too happy about that, she told us. She knew that Doug was married and it didn't make it any easier that he's black. But she's kind of a live and let live old broad. Anyways, she said that Doug had been there the night before and him and the deceased had been arguing. She didn't hear the words and there was no violence, but she could tell from the tone of their voices that they weren't making nice like they usually did."

"He'd been there a lot, had he?"

"Every night he was working. Pat here was his partner, says that Doug used to take his lunch hour and disappear for a while, with the girl.

"It was more than an hour usually," Hinton said. He sounded unhappy. "I didn't like it but he said he was working on something big."

"Yeah," Cassidy said and laughed for the first time. "A big hard-on, y'ask me." Neither Hinton nor I laughed and Cassidy went on. "Sorry, Reid, is it? But that's how I see it. So, this night the landlady went to bed around ten and she couldn't hear anything from the back of the house. Then next morning a Ms. Frazer, head bookkeeper at Cat's Cradle, she came by to see why Ms. Laver hadn't shown up for work and the landlady let her in." He opened his desk drawer and pulled out an envelope which he opened, taking out a stack of eight-by-ten photographs. "This is what they found."

He handed me the photographs, one by one. The woman was ugly in death, tongue lolling, face swollen, but I could see that she would have been attractive. The body was slim and fit with good breasts.

"She was quite a looker," Cassidy said, "before this happened."

"She was strangled with what?"

"Pair of panty hose." Cassidy pointed to the victim's throat. "It was a pro. Whoever did it had slipped a quarter into one leg, then twirled them until the whole thing was thin as a string. She was attacked from behind, the quarter resting almost exactly on her Adam's apple."

I nodded. "That makes it premeditated murder."

"Yeah. The charge is Murder One," Cassidy said. He fed me each of the pictures in turn. A wide shot of the bed, revealing that she had been laid out, hands at her side, in the middle of it, as if the person who did it was showing respect for the corpse. Then there was a cover shot of the room, neat and tidy, a small shelf of books to one side with a photograph and potted plants on it, a couple of what looked like art posters on the walls. Everything seemed well cared for.

I examined each shot carefully. They showed the bathroom, with a man's hand pointing at a place on the tiles. "That's where the crime scene guy found traces of feces," Cassidy said. He seemed to enjoy using the fancy word for waste, as if he was practicing for his court appearance. "There was hair against the edge of the shower stall as well, where her head had rested, we figured, although, who knows. It could have happened anytime, I guess. Women shed hair in the bathroom. But the placing, plus the traces you can see being pointed out here, suggested that she'd been lying here."

"Did they find the cloth that had been used to clean up?"

He shook his head. "No. We figure it was done with toilet paper and flushed down the john."

"Were there fingerprints on the handle?"

"Just a smear, as if somebody had given it a wipe."

I nodded and he showed me the next photographs. First the living room, then the kitchen. They were both equally neat. Obviously Ms. Laver had been house-proud. Then there was a shot of the garbage can. At the top of the contents was a Coors beer can. "That's the can we found Doug's prints on," Cassidy said. He was grim now. "I mean, until we found this, he could have made a case that he didn't do it. But on top of the landlady's evidence, this proved he was there and that was the last but one straw."

He wanted to tell me about the last straw, the money found in Doug's car, but I interrupted. "Do you have a shot of the can, showing the placement of the prints?"

"Yeah." He riffled through the photos and pulled out the one I'd asked for. The can was almost life-sized on the big photograph and I could see the impressions of four prints of the fingers down one side, placed one above the other where Doug's hand had gone around it. There was enough of the top showing that I could see the pouring aperture. It was facing the same way as the fingertips.

Cassidy was saying, "The way we figure it, he'd had a beer while they were fighting, then something blew up and he strangled her."

"Were there any other prints on the can?"

"Yeah. We made out two sets, all over the place. They're not on record but we've got them out to the FBI lab for comparison with their files."

"From the placement, it looks like Doug poured the beer into a glass," I said slowly. "Like if he'd drunk from the can, the spout would've been across the prints, the thumb in front."

"We thought about that," Cassidy said immediately. "But there was no glass in the place with prints on it. They'd been wiped and put away. She didn't have a dishwasher so whoever washed up would've handled the glass with a tea towel."

"Doesn't make sense that Doug would have washed up and not taken the empty can away with him," I said.

"Dumb, y'ask me," Cassidy said. "But the prints indicate that he was there. And being on top of the garbage, it indicates that it was used that night. We found the grapefruit she must've eaten for breakfast and an empty cereal box underneath it."

"Were there any other beers in the house?"

"Yeah. There was a six-pack with one gone," Cassidy said. "They didn't have prints on them. Like whoever sold them must've handled 'em by the plastic strap."

That didn't sit right, not when there was someone else's prints on the beer can in the garbage. It sounded like a plant to me. But Hinton spoke now, carefully. "We wouldn't have busted him on the evidence of a beer can, Reid. But the lieutenant searched his car and found the missing fifty grand."

"Where was it? In the trunk?"

"No, in front, between the seats. Just layin' there," Cassidy said. "Ms. Frazer had told us about the night deposit. We were going to search his house for it, but there it was."

"Doesn't make sense that he'd leave that kind of bread lying in plain view in his car. Maybe somebody came by and dropped it in there. The same guy who strangled Ms. Laver and put the beer can in the garbage."

"Where did this guy get it from? Either the money or the keys to Doug's car, or the beer can?" Cassidy asked. "Come on, Reid. You're talking like a defense lawyer. We had no choice but arrest the guy. You'd have done the same thing if you'd been in charge."

I knew he would never give me any other help unless I agreed with him, so I gave in. "Of course. But coming in now, as a friend of his, I'm looking at things differently."

"I can appreciate that," Cassidy said. "But I was doing my job the way I always do my job. Looked open and shut to me. Guy has a fight with his girl, strangles her. She has some dough, he takes it, maybe to throw suspicion on somebody else. That's the way I saw it."

There were other questions to ask, like had they checked the body for fibers. Whoever laid her out must have picked her up and there would have been clothing fibers along one side of her body. If they didn't match Doug's clothes, then he was probably innocent. But I didn't push it. Instead I asked, "What did he say when you arrested him?"

"Not a whole lot." Cassidy was thoughtful. "I read him his rights but he waved me down, said he knew what they were. All he said aside from that was that he didn't do it, didn't know anything about her death or about the money in his car."

I nodded and stayed silent. On the face of it Doug had a chance at least of getting off. But at what price? He would lose everything he owned in paying for a lawyer and at the end of the case he would be out of a job. The people in town would never believe he hadn't killed the woman. He could never work again in this town, or anywhere else as a cop.

It was less terrible than a lifetime sentence but a blow his
family would never recover from. And at worst, if the jury
turned hostile, with maybe a few racists on it, he would be
in a maximum security prison with a bunch of guys who
had nothing to lose by killing him. It would be a death
sentence.

At last I said, "Thank you for the information, Lieutenant.
It's not what I wanted to hear but you had no choice. It's
up to the courts now."

That pleased him. He stood up and stuck out his hand,
creasing his face into a minimal smile. "Sorry to give you
bad news but you're right."

I shook his hand and he nodded to Hinton and left.

Hinton said, "G'night, Lieutenant," and sat where he was
until Cassidy had gone. Then he asked, "Seen enough?"

I nodded. "Enough to see that a good defense lawyer will
be able to make a case for him, but I can also see that you
had to arrest him. Thanks for the help, Pat."

"You're welcome. But now I've gotta be starting work."
Hinton stood up. "Anything else I can show you?"

I took the hint and stood up. "No. Thanks. Be all right
if I get back to you over the next day or two?"

"Anything I can do, I will." He stood there with his hands
on the desk. "Keep on digging. I want to see Doug walk
out of jail with everyone standing in line to apologize. He's
a good buddy of mine too."

It was five o'clock and fully dark, the streetlights glinting
yellow on the piled snow around the parking lot. I sat in
my car, patting Sam's head absently, wondering what to do
next. There wasn't much really, not before I'd spoken to
Doug again and tried to get him to open up some more. I
had to find out what he had been working on. If mob money
was involved it was motive enough for someone to have
killed the woman and framed him to get him off their backs.
But unless Doug opened up to me, I couldn't do much more
for him.

The only other thing I could follow up was the beer can.

It seemed the weak link in the case. From the placement of the prints it looked as if it had been served to Doug, on a tray. If he'd helped himself to a beer, the prints would have been random. And I wondered why it, alone of the six-pack, had other fingerprints on it. Anyone could have bought the six-pack, wiped it clear of prints and stuck it in the cooler at the Laver house, taking one out to account for the empty in the garbage can. No, I decided, the beer can was a good place to start investigating.

On my own patch, under Ontario law, the only place to buy beer is the government store. I could have chased the staff up to see if they remembered Cindy Laver buying beer. But here, in Vermont, booze was sold in grocery stores. I could never canvass them myself. No, I decided, I would concentrate on the can with the prints and there was one logical place to start, at Brewskis, where Doug and Cindy Laver had taken their last public drink together.

Carol Henning was behind the bar again. She pulled me a Budweiser and waved my money away. "Draft beer we can cover. It's on the house. How's your work going?"

"Pretty good, thanks." Nobody wants to hear bad news. "Thought I'd drop in and ask about the last night Doug Ford was here. Can you remember what he drank that night?"

She shrugged. "I serve around three grand's worth of drinks in a shift."

"I hope everybody tips big," I said and she snorted.

"Not bad. I make about twice my pay in tips, but don't go telling that to the boss."

"I promise." I sipped my beer. "Do you think you could ask, Joyce is it? Next time she comes to the bar."

"Will do." She tilted her head on one side, flirtingly. "Is this gonna help?"

"Lord knows. I'm just a nosy SOB, that's all."

Now she looked at me levelly. "You're married, right?"

"Yeah. How can you tell? Do I look round-shouldered, what?"

She laughed, a nice friendly sound. "I can always tell, even when the guy's coming on to me. But you don't. I figure you play it straight."

"I'm terminally married. But they didn't poke my eyes out on my wedding day."

She laughed and said, "I'll see what Joyce remembers."

Someone came to the other end of the bar and she bobbed away while I sat sipping my Bud. A minute or so later, the waitress I'd helped the night before came up to me. "Hi. Carol said you wanted to talk to me."

"Just a dumb question. I was wondering if you can remember what Doug Ford ordered the night he was in with Ms. Laver. The night she was killed."

"Yeah. I remember because she was kind of mad. She said to me, 'I suppose we'll have what we always have. That hasn't changed.' And then he said, 'No, make it a beer for me, please, a Coors.' And I found we were all out of bottles but there were cans. I served him a can of Coors."

"Thank you." I didn't let any satisfaction show but my spirits lifted. "Can you remember who else was working that night?"

She pushed out her lower lip. "The same bunch. Carol was at the bar and Ellen was working the dining room, from the bar that is, taking drinks through."

"Any management people around?"

She thought about that before answering. "Not working. But Walt was here, Walt Huckmeyer. He hurt his leg that day, skiing on his lunch break at Cat's Cradle. He was sitting over there." She pointed to a table near the big log fire. "Like that's his favorite table."

She was excited at the chance of helping me but I didn't want to give anything away so I changed my tack. "I've not met him. Is he a good skier?"

"He used to be on the national team," she said. "You should see him carve those moguls."

I wanted to get her mind off Doug so I said, "You

wouldn't get me down there, not on a bet," and laughed. "Anyway, thanks for the help. You've got one heck of a memory." Always get people talking about themselves, my father told me once. That way you're sure they stay interested.

"I took one of those courses," she said, delighted. "It's good for the tips. You take someone's credit card and see their name and next time they come in, you call them by name. Makes them feel welcome."

"And does it work, with the tips?"

She tapped me on the arm with her forefinger. "I'm a bookkeeper when there's any work going and I know figures. It's increased my take by twenty-seven percent."

I pushed the conversation into asking if she would really prefer working with money rather than doing what she was doing here and she spent a minute or two talking about herself. Then Carol waved at her, pointing to one of her tables, and she excused herself and bustled off. Mission accomplished, I thought, and I finished my beer, raised my hand to Carol and left.

Melody's car was in the driveway when I arrived and I pulled in behind it. As soon as I switched off the motor the house door opened and Melody ran out to meet me. She looked anxious and I said, "Hi. It went well today."

She wasn't listening. "Reid," she blurted, "somebody's kidnapped Angela."

"Kidnapped?"

She was weeping but she had her voice under control. "A man just called. He said something like we've got your daughter. Tell Bennett to wait for our call. Don't call the police or your kid's gonna be sorry."

"Come inside." I took her by the arm, clucking at Sam to follow me, and led her back into the house. Ben was at the door. He looked at me, eyes wide. "Shut the door," I told him, then asked Melody, "When did he call?"

"About ten minutes ago. I phoned the police station to

see if you were there but they said you'd gone. Reid, what
are we going to do?" She was trembling and I put my arm
around her shoulders.

"I'll take care of it. By the sound of it, they want me
gone, whoever they are. Tell me, when did you see Angie
last?"

"This morning when she went to school. She wasn't home
when I got back from the library but she usually stays a
while with her friend Jennie until six. They do their homework together. So I didn't worry until the phone went."

"How did the man sound? Was he a local, would you
say?"

I had led her to the armchair and she sat down, perching
on the edge of it as I squatted in front of her. She was taut
with fear, every muscle frozen rigid, but she had stopped
crying and was thinking hard. "No. He sounded like he
could have been from New York or someplace," she said.
"You know, the kind of whine in the nose."

She'd heard a white voice, I registered. "Okay, now tell
me exactly what he said." I held both her hands and she
looked at me sightlessly as she tried to remember.

"He said, 'Hi. Is Angela still not home?' and I was wor-
ried right away and asked him who he was. Then he said,
'No, she's not, because she's here with me. Now just listen.
We don't want to hurt the kid. We want to talk to Bennett.
Tell him to wait for our call, and don't call the police or
your kid's gonna be sorry.' Then he hung up."

I patted her hand and stood up. "Somebody wants me
out of town. They're not going to hurt Angela. I'll talk to
the guy and then when he tells me what he wants, I'll do
it. Try not to worry." I made sure I sounded calm but my
mind was racing, wondering which of the people I'd spoken
to that day had passed the news on to the big boys.

Ben had been listening to every word and he knelt down
beside his mother. "I'll kill the guy," he said.

I patted him on the shoulder. "You'll get your chance.
I'll find him and you can punch his lights out. But first

we've got to get Angie back. If the phone goes, let me answer it. Right now, your mom would like a cup of coffee."

Melody raised her head to protest but I winked at her and she said, "Yes, please, Ben. And get one for Reid as well."

"No problem," he said automatically, then added, "I mean it, Mom," and went into the kitchen.

I crouched beside her again. "Good thinking. It'll keep him busy for a minute or two. Tell me, do you want me to stop working for Doug?"

"I want Angela back safe, that's all. Nothing else matters," she whispered.

"I understand. Now tell me. Does Doug have a gun in the house?"

She looked at me very straight. "Yes. He didn't think I knew, but I found it in the basement. I went into his toolbox for a hammer to hang a picture and I saw it there."

"Go and get it." I straightened up and she stood and walked out to the kitchen and downstairs. A minute later she was back with a dish towel over something in her hand.

I took it from her and flipped the towel back. Inside was a standard police Smith and Wesson .38 revolver. I flipped the chamber open and saw it was loaded. I tipped the shells out and checked. They were standard police rounds. "That's not his issue gun. They took that when they arrested him. That's his backup."

It was big for a backup gun. A lot of New York cops carry a second weapon, but it's usually smaller, a .25 automatic usually, something they can holster in their sock in case somebody takes their artillery off them. "That's the one he carried in New York," Melody explained. "But here he carried the issue gun."

"Have you ever used one?"

She was shocked. "Of course not."

"But you know how? Doug showed you, I'm sure." I'd instructed my own wife, despite her not wanting to know.

"Point and pull," she said soberly. "If you're expecting

trouble, pull the hammer back first but it's double action. Doug told me."

"Pretty soon that guy's going to call again. When he does, I'll be going out. I'll leave Sam on guard here but I want you and Ben to go upstairs and wait. Take this with you. Okay?"

"You think they're going to call?"

"I'm sure of it. Doug figured there was a mob involvement in his work. That's why he wouldn't share it with you. And those are the guys who want me out of here. I'll see them and they'll let Angie go."

"What if they're hurting her?" I could see in her eyes what she meant but I didn't let my own fears show. "They won't touch her, believe me."

She closed her eyes. Her lips were moving and I lip-read her prayer. Then the phone rang. I picked it up. "Hello, this is Reid Bennett."

Melody was on her feet beside me, trying to listen. I concentrated on the man's voice when he spoke. "Just the guy I want to talk to."

"I'm listening." Melody was right, I judged. The voice had the raw edges of New York in its tone, or maybe New Jersey, somewhere around the metropolitan area. I couldn't pinpoint it closer.

"We hear tell you're askin' a lot of questions." Not "I," but "we." This was not the main man, this was some foot soldier.

"Doug Ford's a friend of mine. Do you have his daughter there?"

"The kid's fine. But we want you should go home, back to the Eskimos. Am I making myself clear?"

"Release the girl and I'll do whatever you want."

"Okay. Now you're bein' smart. Come down to the town square an' park in front of the library. The spade lady knows where it is." He was baiting me but I didn't rise.

"Then what?"

"Then we'll have a little talk an' after that you drive the kid home an' then go home yourself. You got me?"

"When?"

"Right away. An' don't bring the dog with you." It came out "dawg." New York, no doubts left.

"I'll be there in ten minutes."

"Good. An' don't waste time calling the cops. These hayseeds'll be bumping into one another. 'f we see any of them, the kid dies. Got that?"

"Got it."

He hung up and I did the same, very slowly. Melody was holding my arm. "Is she all right?"

"She's fine. He's going to hand her over to me. He wants to talk to me first, outside the library."

"I'll come with you." She was heading for her coat but I stopped her, taking her arm. "No. He wants me there on my own. I'll set Sam to watch the house. You go upstairs with Ben like I said."

She bit her lip and tears came into her eyes. "Oh God, Reid. Take care of Angie."

"They're not going to hurt her. But I'm going. You and Ben go upstairs now. Don't come down until I get back with Angie."

Ben said, "I want to come. You promised."

"You'll get a chance to clobber him, but not tonight. First we get Angie. Do as your mom says. Your dad would want you to."

His eyes widened when he saw the gun in her hand and he stood back as she got up and went upstairs, slowly. He followed her and she paused halfway up to speak to me. "Get my Angie back, Reid."

"I promise." I waited until she was out of sight, then led Sam all around the downstairs, including the basement, and told him "Guard." It's his command to attack silently and pin an intruder, on the ground usually, after he's knocked him down.

I turned off all the downstairs lights and went out to my car. There was very little traffic on the streets and I drove down to the main square in under five minutes. There were a few pedestrians on the street, stopping to look in the windows of the stores which were all closed. But I didn't see Angie or any parked cars with people in them. I left the car running and got out, pretending to be cleaning the windshield with a handful of snow from the mound along the edge of the sidewalk. A minute or so later a Lincoln slid into a parking spot opposite me. It had tinted windows and I couldn't see who was inside.

I watched as the passenger door opened and a man got out. He was short, wearing a city topcoat and a fedora. He had his hands in his pockets and he strolled across to me, elaborately casual.

I took a few steps toward him and he took one hand out of his pocket and held it up. "Stay there. We can't talk in the middle of all this traffic," he said, and laughed at his own joke.

I backed to my car and he came up to me. Latin, bad skin, thirty-fivish, five-six, around one-sixty pounds, I registered. I took a good look at his face.

"Don' bother tryin' a remember me," he said. "After tonight you're outa here."

"Where's the little girl?"

"In the car with my associates," he said.

"Turn her loose, then we talk."

"We talk first. Then she walks, 'kay?"

"What do you want to talk about?"

He hawked and spat. "We unnerstand you been askin' a lot of dumbass questions. That makes some people I know kind of mad."

"Why's that? I'm a friend of the family. What are friends for?"

He sighed. He was milking his moment, I thought. He'd seen too many movies. He took his hands out of his pockets

and spread his arms. "This is a friendly talk we're havin'
here. This ain't your beef. Go home."

"Or what?"

"Or instead of havin' any more friendly talks we take the
kid and she doesn't come back."

"I get the message. Her mother wants her back. That's
all. I'll be out of town as soon as you deliver the girl."

"Good." He tapped me on the chest. "Like it won't do
no good getting p'lice protection. All's they'll do is drive by
the house a few times. We'll pick the kids up, both of 'em.
And next time it's no more mister niceguy."

"You've made your point. I'm out of here as soon as I
get the girl."

"Smart." He spat again. "I like that."

He turned and nodded at the car and the rear door
opened. Angela got out. She was dressed in a pink parka
and toque, still carrying her schoolbooks. She ran across the
street to me and I put my arm around her. The guy took
his right hand out of his pocket and wagged his forefinger
at me. "Remember now. Next time's for keeps."

He turned his back and strolled away to his car. I wanted
to follow and kick him right up in the air but that wouldn't
have solved anything. Instead I took Angie's hand. "Are you
all right?"

"I'm scared," she said in a very small voice.

"Did they hurt you?"

"No. They were okay. They gave me a chocolate bar but
I didn't eat it."

I put her in the car, then got in as the car opposite pulled
away, its lights out. I couldn't have read the license plate
anyway from where I was but they were professionals in
their own way. "Tell me what happened," I said, putting
my car into gear.

"I was just coming out of Jennie's house and this car came
up and a man asked me if I knew where the library was. I
did like Dad told us. I stayed away from the car but the

man said he couldn't hear me. He got out, with his hand over his ear, and I figured he was deaf. So I started saying it again and he grabbed me. I dropped my books but he put me in the back seat and another man held me while the first one picked up my books."

"Nobody touched you other than that?"

"No." She shook her head, a tense little negative that showed how frightened she had been.

"You were very brave. Your dad'll be proud of you," I said and concentrated on my driving.

"Why did they do it?" she asked. "Dad said men take girls in their cars sometimes and do things to them, you know. But they didn't."

"They wanted to scare me," I said. "And they did. But don't worry, it's all over now."

She said nothing else and I drove to the house in silence, wondering what to do next.

The hall light was on when I got there and I ran up the drive and opened the door. Melody was standing on the stairs. Sam was standing on the bottom step, looking at her unmovingly. "Easy, boy. Here," I called and he broke off eye contact and came over to me. Melody ran down the stairs and put both arms around her daughter. She still had the gun in her hand and I took it from her. "She's okay. Nothing happened," I said.

"I'm fine, Mom. They didn't do anything, 'cept put me in the car," Angie said, and then the two of them wept.

Ben was standing a few feet away. "I'll kill them," he said. "I'll take Dad's gun an' blow 'em away."

I put my arm around him. "No need, old buddy. She's all right. Now go pack a bag. You three are going on a trip."

Melody fussed over Angie until she was certain the girl was fine, while I sent out for pizza for supper. Then, when she was settling down to normal again, I set out to convince her that she had to leave town and hide for a while.

It was a tough sell. The kidnapping had achieved its objective. She was scared and wanted to be sure we carried out the letter of my promise. She wanted me to leave town. I didn't bully her but I pointed out that if Doug got off, as I figured he might, then the same guys would be using the same tactics on him again. The only way to beat them was to go after them, and burn them out so they couldn't come back again and cause trouble.

I wasn't sure how that could be done, but it had to be tried, and that meant I had to do the burning. And before that could happen, she and the kids had to disappear for a while. She thought about it without talking while we drank coffee. And at last she agreed.

We made the plan in private, where the kids couldn't hear and blow security. I asked her if she had a choice of places to go and she did. Her sister lived in Chicago and Doug's mother, who had been widowed and remarried, was living in South Carolina. None of the neighbors knew the name of either family, so there could be no follow-up. She agreed with me that double protection would be best, so she called the head of the library board and told him she had a family emergency in Chicago. With Doug out of circulation, she was taking the children with her for a few days.

That was part one of the plan. Part two, which would be revealed to the children later, was that they would switch planes in New York and head south to Doug's mother. Organized crime is not well enough organized to have its tentacles down into rural Dixie and she would be safe there while I finished what I had to do.

Angie was excited about getting away so that was fine. Ben was the only one to show any reluctance. With fourteen-year-old machismo he wanted to stay where he was and fight. But he listened to me and agreed finally. So by nine o'clock the neighbors had been told the Chicago story and I was driving the family to the airport in Burlington, me with Doug's .38 in the right-hand pocket of my parka.

I sat with them until they were called through security to board their flight. Melody gave me a quick kiss on the cheek and said, "Explain to Doug. Don't let him think we're running out on him."

"No fears," I said and squeezed her hand. "Have a holiday, if you can. I'm going to do some heavy-duty digging. Doug's innocent and what happened tonight proves it. Now I just have to make it stick."

I waited in the concourse until their flight left for New York, then phoned home and talked to Fred for half an hour, giving her a quick rundown of what was happening, but leaving out the bit about Angie's being abducted. With a brand-new daughter of our own, I knew she would take that to heart too much. When I hung up I made a second call, to Peter Horn, the special constable I had left in charge at Murphy's Harbour. He's Ojibway—a Native North

American—they don't call themselves Indians anymore. He's wise and tough. I explained what I wanted done and he told me he'd get some of his buddies on it right away.

The call put fresh heart into me and afterward I went back out to the car and headed for Chambers, the Fords' hometown. But I'm a man of my word, even when I'm dealing with criminals, so I didn't go back to town. Instead I stopped ten miles out at a crummy motel and checked in under the name Collins. From the look of the place they'd had their quota of John Smiths registered there over the years.

I didn't mention Sam but it was a cold night and I wanted security, so I brought him in to sleep beside the bed. Then I took a slow hour or so going over all the things I'd learned that day and putting together a case in my mind. It wasn't until midnight that I realized I hadn't phoned Irv Goodman in Toronto. Never mind, I thought, I would speak to him the next morning. It was Saturday and he would be at home.

Except for traffic noise the night passed peacefully and I was up at seven to let Sam out and get ready for the day. After I'd showered I took Sam and headed out to find a restaurant. There was a simple country place on the highway and I had a big breakfast with enough cholesterol to last a week and then drove into town.

It was nine o'clock and the main square was lined with cars, most of them with ski racks on the roof. I found a spot and left the window down while I went in to visit Doug.

There was a different official on duty this morning, a young woman who seemed to have some sympathy for Doug as a member of a minority group. She told me I could have fifteen minutes with him and this time there was a different guard, a bored, older man who lounged against the wall and didn't act officious.

I filled Doug in on what had happened. He gritted his teeth but didn't get dramatic on me. "You did right, Reid. Now tell me, you think your own family's gonna be okay? These guys have got long arms."

"I've called the Harbour and told my assistant. He's Ojibway. He's arranging to have some guys cover the house for me. They're all hunters. They'll fade into the scenery and put on an armed guard without making a fuss to worry my wife."

"Will they do that for you?" Doug was impressed.

I nodded. "Anyway, enough about that. I need to know what you were working on. It's the only way to untie this thing and get you out of here with no comebacks on your family."

He sniffed thoughtfully, then relaxed a little. "Now that Melody and the kids are safe, I guess it's okay," he said. "Let me explain."

By the time he was finished I could see what he meant. He didn't have enough details to make a case but the bare bones were that Manatelli was using Cat's Cradle, and the local bank, to launder money for him. Cindy Laver had given him the facts. It seemed that Manatelli, or somebody, she didn't know who it was, had formed a company in Delaware, the state where most American corporations are based. The company had contracted to be a partner in Cat's Cradle. They would buy all of the credit card slips used at the resort at a discount a quarter percent better than the financial companies allowed. That way Cat's Cradle got cash, with a small markup, and Manatelli got the credits. He was paying these into the bank which would then, Doug thought, pass them on to some bank in the Cayman Islands which would issue cash drafts in nice clean untraceable dollars.

I listened and thought about it. "Couple of things. First, it doesn't sound like a major case. I mean, what are we talking about here, in credit card slips, a hundred thousand a week in peak season? Surely the mob has bigger funds than that to worry about."

"This isn't their whole take," Doug said. "I think Manatelli is skimming his boss. And anyway, the Cat's Cradle take would be bigger than that. According to Cindy there could be twice that some weeks."

"Yes. But no crime's been committed. All it proves is that Manatelli is a poor businessman. He's making a loss on every dollar."

"That's his cost of doing business," Doug explained. "And besides, it means he never has tax problems. His income is always negative."

"But where's the crime?" I persisted.

"It doesn't happen here. It happens in New York. That's where the money's made, out of teenage hookers, dying, or wearing themselves out in four or five years for creeps like Manatelli."

"But why can't you just give this out? Surely you can make it public and then the mob takes care of Manatelli and we all live happily ever after."

Doug sucked his teeth. "I've got no proof. All I know is that I saw Manatelli having dinner in town with the bank president and the boss of Cat's Cradle. The cash arrives every week, from an address in Florida. It's tallied by Cindy or the other woman, that Ella Frazer, and then the slips are cashed and the money put into a different account, for the numbered company."

"And is Cat's Cradle declaring the extra income they're making on the slips?"

"That won't be an issue until they make their tax return. I imagine the extra percentage is going into somebody's pockets, but we don't know yet," Doug said. He pressed the table very hard with both hands. "But you see where I'm coming from. There's no names. Just numbered companies playing games with money."

"I don't understand your case," I admitted. "It looks legitimate, if dumb. Why did you get knotted up about it?"

The guard against the wall looked at his watch. I knew my time was running out and I still didn't have enough to go on. If this was all Doug was working on, it wouldn't persuade a jury to free him from his murder charge and there was no chance to smoke out the guys who had kidnapped Angela.

"It goes back," Doug said. "I left the NYPD because of a problem I couldn't handle. I was partnered with a guy called Gianelli. We worked uptown where most teams are black but we were a salt and pepper team and I got on well with Gino. Then we got a break on the hookers on the street. Instead of the case choking off at the pimp, we got a pimp to roll over and give us a lead to the top."

"And then?" The guard was looking at his wristwatch. We were down to the wire.

"And then Gino's house burned down. His wife and son were killed, he and the baby survived but barely. He was burned so bad he's never going to work again. And the baby was disfigured. That's when I came looking for a job here."

The guard came to the table. "Time's up, sir," he told me.

"Thank you, officer." I stood up. "Okay, Doug. I understand."

He nodded at me, grimly. "Whatever you do, be careful, Reid."

I winked at him and he grinned. "Semper fi," he said and held up a clenched fist.

I hit the street and found a pay phone to call Irv Goodman. "Hi. What happened last night?" he wanted to know.

I filled him in on the kidnapping and he grunted. Then I skipped him through Doug's account of the money-laundering and he told me that it sounded right. "But your buddy's a long way from making a case. It's out of his league, unless he's an accountant. And even then it's hard to prove anything except that the principal is a poor businessman."

"That's not the point, as I see it. Doug wants to get Manatelli in Dutch with his boss. They don't bother with trials. Manatelli's dead if word gets out that he's skimming."

Irv didn't speak for a long while and I wondered if the line had gone dead on me. Then he said, "So I guess you need to know Manatelli's pedigree."

"Yeah. Then I can stir things up on Doug's behalf, get this sorted out nicely."

"It's dangerous," Irv said quietly. "They'll blow your head off sooner than let an outsider cause trouble."

"If it wasn't for Doug that would have happened in Nam. I owe the guy."

"Okay then. Good luck. Got a pencil?"

When I was set up he read out what he had and I made notes. It seemed that Manatelli was the brother-in-law of Antonio "Mucho" Mucci, who ran the biggest family in New Jersey. But that was all he had, no address at which I could contact Mucci, nothing else. He told me he'd get in touch with the RCMP, our federal police department, and see if they had anything more.

I thanked him and hung up, then went for a coffee and thought about it all. It seemed there was nothing I could do to stir things up at the top, over Manatelli's head. So I would have to do it from where I was. I finished my coffee and set out to start.

The parking lot at Cat's Cradle was choked with cars on this bright Saturday morning but I found a spot and left Sam inside with the window down and headed for the office. The same attractive girl was at the desk and she must have recognized me. She smiled and said, "If you're looking for Ella, she's not in. She called in sick this morning."

There's a lot of sickness on Saturday mornings among heavy drinkers but I just said, "Oh, not to worry. Is Walter Huckmeyer in his office then, please?"

"Could be. He told me he was heading out on the slopes later but I don't think he's gone. Hold on."

I waited while she clicked back down the hallway and opened an office door. Then she turned and waved to me and I came through and followed her. "Thanks," I said and went into Huckmeyer's office.

He was around thirty, tanned and lean, a good-looking six-footer with a slim, wiry build like a movie star. He was wearing ski pants, smooth and form-fitting, and a yellow sweater of soft wool. He beamed at me from his side of a desk filled with papers. "Morning. Walt Huckmeyer. What can I do for you?"

"How's the ankle?" I asked and he frowned, then said, "Oh, fine, thanks. Just a sprain. Soon fixed."

"I didn't think good skiers sprained their ankles these days," I said. "Break their legs, necks even, but sprained ankles? What are ski boots for?"

His face darkened. "Who are you?"

"The name doesn't matter. I'm a friend of Doug Ford's and I'm on to you," I told him.

"You'd better leave." He stood up but didn't come around his desk. I outweighed him by ten pounds, was broader in the shoulders and at least as fit.

"Or what?" I sneered. "You'll bring in some creep from New Jersey to steal my kids?"

He flushed but answered immediately. "I don't know what you're talking about. Get out of here right now or I'll call the police."

"Why? Scared you, have I?"

He pressed a button on his phone. "Lois. Call the police department. I want this man out of my office."

He sat back and I reached over and pressed the button. "Save your quarter, Lois, I'm going. For now."

I let go of the button and wagged the finger at Huckmeyer. "It's not over till it's over, Walt, old sport. I'm going to be in your face everywhere you go."

The girl at the desk was on her feet as I passed. She looked shocked. "Who are you?" she asked.

"The avenging angel," I told her and left, wondering if I'd done any more than stir up Huckmeyer's corpuscles for him.

That was my plan, what there was of it. The only other thing to do was to walk into the bank and start making noises to the owner. But I didn't do that. Banks have alarm systems and if I started leaning on the manager the cops would be at the door before I knew it. And anyway, this was Saturday. The bank was closed for the weekend. No, I decided, that was as far as I could go for one morning. I didn't even go into the coffee shop. If Huckmeyer had clout with the local police department he could call them in and have me taken out for causing a disturbance, anything at all to harass me, and I wanted to keep the initiative. So I went back into town and stopped at the library. They had the phone books of most major metropolitan areas in the States and I pulled out a stack of New Jersey phone books and checked the Mucci listings. There were lots of them but no A or Antonio listed. So I couldn't take any shortcuts. All I could do was stay visible and see if Huckmeyer was going to do anything more than quake in his ski boots.

The day dragged but at six o'clock I drove out to Brewskis to check if Huckmeyer was in residence. He wasn't there. Neither was Carol Henning, the bartender I'd spoken to. So, knowing I might have trouble later, I ordered a ginger ale and sat at the bar with it and waited.

Huckmeyer turned up a while later with a brunette in ski clothes. He made for his usual table and sat down before he noticed me. When he did I raised my glass to him and beamed. His face went dark but he ignored me and ordered from the waitress. I sat where I was until the waitress had served him and his date, then sauntered over. He was talking to her and pretended not to see me. I acted like the usual overfriendly drunk. "Hi, Walt. Long time no see."

The girl looked up, then at Huckmeyer. "You know this guy, Walter?"

"Sure he does," I said cheerfully. "We have a mutual friend." I reached down and picked up the beer bottle in front of Huckmeyer. "Changed your brand, I see. I thought you were a Coors man."

He looked at me now. "Why don't you take off before I have you thrown out?"

"Who's going to do it? The waitresses?" I laughed at him. "But I can see you need some privacy now. See you around."

I went back to my place at the bar and waited. He got up and went out through the kitchen. To use the phone, I guessed. I finished up my ginger ale and headed for the door, waggling my fingers at the girl who had hardly taken her eyes off me since I'd visited the table. She turned away huffily and I went out into the night. It was showdown time, I figured, at the Brewski corral.

It was cold outside but I
didn't put my parka on. It figured that Huckmeyer had
phoned someone to convince me I should move on. If there
were guys around waiting to put the boots to me, mobility
would be more valuable than warmth.

There was no immediate menace. As I went down the
steps a good-looking young couple was heading in, holding
hands and radiating the happy glow that announced they
had just made love. And I didn't see anybody else around
but still I made my way warily along the center of the aisle
between the parked cars. Sam was five seconds from me but
I didn't whistle him. I had lots of time to do that, I figured,
before push came to shove.

It did, when I was halfway down the back row of the lot.
The reception committee was waiting in the same
Oldsmobile I'd seen two nights before. They got out without
speaking. Three of them. I guessed the one who had been
nervous of Sam last time had chickened out. They were
wearing ski masks like terrorists on a mission and they
moved toward me, shoulder to shoulder. I stopped in my

tracks and waited. Their pace slowed but they came on, the biggest one making circles with his clenched fist, anticipating what he was going to do. They were ten paces from me when I acknowledged them. "Well, well, well, the return of the Three Stooges," I said.

I'd hoped it would rile them so that one of them would rush me. One at a time I figured I could take them. But they just came on, two of them silent. The big one laughed. "Still feeling smart?" he sneered. That's when I whistled Sam.

He was out of my car in a moment, bounding down behind them. The big one pulled off his glove and dug his hand into his pocket as he turned and I saw he had a gun. I shouted, "Fight," and there was the flat bang of a small-caliber round and then Sam had him by the gun hand. The other two men had stopped and turned to check on him and I charged, slamming one of them with the point of my shoulder, sending him flying against a car and into the snow.

The other one turned back and I punched him hard in the gut. He folded and I followed up with a two-handed thump on the back of his neck that put him face down in the snow. The guy with the gun was still struggling vainly with Sam and I turned to the man I'd charged first. He had scrambled to his feet but the fight had gone out of him. He stood where he was, spreading his hands in a gesture of submission. No threat. I turned to help Sam. The gunman was trying to yank his gun hand free as he batted at Sam with his left. "Drop the gun and I'll call him off," I said.

He swore and tried to lift his arm with Sam's weight hanging on it, high enough to aim at me. I stepped aside and gave him a short right-hand punch behind the ear. It knocked him down, still holding his gun. "Easy," I told Sam, and as he backed off I put my heel on the guy's gun hand and bore down while I took the pistol off him. It was a Ruger .22 automatic and I held it while I ripped the ski mask up off his face. He was the groper I'd stopped in the bar two nights earlier.

"You're in a whole mess of trouble, buddy," I told him

heartily. "Attempted armed robbery. You'll be inside for three years, minimum."

"It was self-defense," he hissed. "Your goddamn dog was out to kill me."

"Tell that to the police," I said. "Give me your car keys."

He was slow to respond and I pressed harder on his wrist with my boot. He yowled then and said, "They're in my pocket. Leggo my hand."

I lifted my foot and he lay there and dug into his coat pocket for his keys. I took them and told the other two guys, "In the car."

They got into it, helping one another painfully. Then I opened the rear seat and told Sam, "Good boy. In." He jumped in and I commanded, "Guard," and he sat up behind them.

One of them tried to turn his head to look back but Sam snarled and made a little lunge at him and he pulled his head forward with a yell of alarm. "Stay still and you're going to be all right," I told them. "Move and he'll have your head off before you can open the door." It wasn't true. Sam's a police officer. He's not trained to savage people, just to show enough force to keep them in line, but those two were prepared to believe he'd kill.

I slammed the door and went back to the third guy who was moving away up the line of cars. "Hold it," I said and he stood there while I scooped up my parka off the ground and put it on. "Right. Let's find a phone." I gave him a contemptuous shove toward the steps of the bar.

I was hoping he was demoralized. If he got noisy and a bunch of people thought I was picking on him, he would get away. I couldn't handle a crowd, not without Sam. On top of that, I was walking a high wire. This guy was known here, I wasn't. I had to keep the whole thing low-key until the cops arrived. Then I could relax a little, knowing that Huckmeyer had dug himself in a little deeper and I was closer to getting the attention of the mob.

Fortunately there was a phone booth right inside the door.

I shoved him inside and reached past him to pick up the phone and stick a quarter in the slot. I was up against him and could smell his after-shave, some cloying lime scent, guaranteed no doubt to cast some spell on women. I wrinkled my nose in disgust, just to make him feel smaller. Then I dialed the operator and asked for the police.

She put me through and I said. "My name's Bennett. I'm at the front of Brewskis. Three guys just tried to mug me. Send an officer."

The guy at the other end tried to get details but I said, "I'm holding one of them now. Just hurry," and hung up.

I hooked the guy out of the booth and pushed him toward the door. "Outside, scumbag." I don't usually talk like a TV show but this was not the way I usually did business anyway. It was a play in which this guy had a different part from the one he'd expected.

"Listen, I can explain," he said as he went ahead of me, spreading his hands like an Armenian rug dealer.

"Good. You'll get your chance when the cops get here."

There must have been a car on patrol close by. He was there in a couple of minutes, lights flashing, but mercifully no siren. He pulled up in front of me and when he got out I gave the big guy another push, just to indicate who was in charge. The cop took the hint. "You Bennett?" he asked me.

"Yeah. This guy and two of his buddies tried to mug me with this." I held up the pistol by the butt, between my finger and thumb. The cop reached for it and I let it drop into his hand.

"Three guys and a gun and you stopped 'em?" He was young and shorter than a Canadian policeman would have been, only around five-seven, and chunky. He was chewing gum.

"My dog is police-trained. I'm a police chief from Canada. I deal with punks like this all the time."

"Sheeit." The cop stopped chewing for a couple of beats. "The detectives are on their way. You can talk to them."

Suddenly my prisoner got vocal. He had an educated voice

and articulated very clearly. "This is crap," he snarled. "I don't know what this guy's been smoking. My friends and I were just coming in for a drink and he came at us with that dog of his. I figure he was holdin' us up. The dog's worse than a gun. I was scared. I'm a member of the pistol club and I had my gun with me. So I pulled it and the dog grabbed me. Then this guy laid into us. That's what happened. Ask my buddies."

Another pause on the cop's chewing gum while he weighed the story. It made more sense to him than mine, I could see that.

He asked the man, "What's your name, sir?"

"Jack Grant. I know you. I've seen you in our store."

"The hardware store, right." The cop nodded. I could see the local boys were going to have home ice advantage.

"Just because he sells nails doesn't give him the right to try and shoot me," I snapped. "He was trying to mug me. So were his buddies. Talk to them, but don't let this slime-bag talk to them first. See what line of crap they come up with."

Standard police practice, but this guy had probably never worked plainclothes, never investigated anything more complex than a rear-ender on Main Street. I hoped the detectives would hurry.

"I'll do that, sir." The cop took out his notebook, clenching the .22 pistol between his knees while he started writing. He had got as far as Grant's name and address when the detectives arrived. I was glad that it was Hinton, not Cassidy. He had another guy with him, a stranger to me.

Hinton spoke first. "Reid? What happened here?"

"I was walking out to my car when this guy and two others tried to mug me. I whistled my dog and Grant here tried to shoot him but the dog got hold of his arm and I plowed into the three of them while they were looking at the dog."

"Says he took out three guys," the cop said. "Sounds kind of far out, y'ask me."

"Mr. Bennett was in Vietnam with the Marines," Hinton

said. "He can handle himself." Good. I had one friend at court.

"The other two guys are in my car, Detective. Could you talk to them before this guy has a chance to give them some lies to tell?"

"Sure." He turned to his partner. "You read Mr. Grant his rights and see if he wants to talk to us."

The other guy nodded and pulled out a notebook. He was taking out the card with the Miranda rules on it as Hinton and I turned away. When we were out of earshot he said, "You won't make this stick. This guy's a wheel in town. His old man owns the hardware store. This kid runs it. The family's active in the Rotary, the Masons. They're connected."

"He's connected okay. The reason he started this thing was I put a burr under Huckmeyer's saddle today. He saw me in the bar and phoned these people to come and beat some sense into me."

"That's hypothesis." Hinton almost snapped it. "It's personal. You made Grant look small inside, couple nights back. Carol at the bar told me about it. He was out to get even. Nobody's going to believe he was trying to mug you. He could buy and sell you twice over."

"Have a word with his buddies. You decide on the charge. Attempted assault will do, just so some mud sticks to Grant, and through him, to Huckmeyer."

"What's all this about Huckmeyer?" Hinton sounded angry now.

"He's tied in to what happened to that woman and Doug. I'll explain it all later. Right now these guys tried to attack me and I want to have them charged."

Hinton shook his head. "I've got no idea what in hell you're trying to do, but no matter what, we can't have guys shooting in parking lots. I'll do what I can."

When we got to the car I opened the rear door and spoke to Sam. "Easy, boy." Then I reached in and patted his head. The two guys in front didn't stir. They looked as if they had been facing front like figureheads since I left them.

Hinton opened the passenger door and said to the nearest man, "Okay, out," and to the driver, "Stay there. I'll be back for you."

The passenger got out. He looked scared, shrunken. Hinton asked him, "Name?"

"Fred Phillips." He licked his lips. "Who are you?"

"Detective Hinton, Chambers PD. Why were you three trying to attack this man?"

He was scared but he'd been thinking hard. "We weren't attacking him. We saw him comin' and we thought we'd scare him a little so we walked toward him, side by side. Like he hurt Jack the other night in here. So then he set his dog on us an' then he started beating on us."

He stopped and looked at Hinton, like a small boy ratting to the teacher. Hinton snorted. "Sounds to me like this gentleman's dog saved him from a hammering."

I blessed him silently. Without him I'd be the one getting questioned. He said, "I want some ID."

The guy brought out his wallet and Hinton asked him to take out the driver's license. He did so and Hinton copied the information into his notebook. "Right," he said, handing it back. "Go stand there." He pointed to a spot down the row, out of earshot, and the man went, not speaking.

We got the other man out of the car and spoke to him. His name was Will Lord and he said he didn't know what was happening. One minute he was walking between the cars and the next I'd charged him like a linebacker, knocked him flying.

"Ask him why all three of them were wearing ski masks, rolled down," I suggested but Hinton didn't. He used it to pour contempt on Lord. "Three tough guys in masks picking on one visitor. Well, you got what you had coming, Lord. Gimme some ID."

He took down the man's name and address and sent him to join his friend. The two of them stood together, hands in their pockets, scuffing their cold feet while Hinton talked to me. "You're not going to get anywhere with this," he said.

"They'll make it sound like three good old boys going for a beer and some mean visitor setting his dog on them."

"What about the gun?"

"I'll run a check, make sure it's registered to him. But that's all I can do. If it is, I can chew him out, but no charge will stick. In fact the chief would most likely overrule me if I tried to lay one. I told you, Grant's got juice in town. That's how he can get away with groping waitresses."

"Well, thank you for what you've done," I said. "There's something big going down, right here in Chambers. The woman's murder is part of it. So is the fact that Doug's been framed."

Hinton waved one hand, irritably. "You sound like Doug now."

"You should know that a car full of heavies kidnapped his daughter last night. They sounded like New Yorkers— the one I talked to anyway."

That got his attention. "Jesus," he said, then looked around as if afraid a minister might have overheard him. "Why didn't you tell me?"

"They didn't harm Angela. Scared her some but let her go on condition I left town. It scared Melody pretty badly. She and the kids left town right away."

"But you're still here, still making waves."

"Through the day. I'm not living in town. I kept my bargain."

He puffed out a tight little syllable of laughter. "The letter of the law, not the spirit. Good for you."

"They, whoever they are, want Doug inside for the murder of that girl. That means he didn't do it, they did. I've got to prove that."

Hinton was holding his notebook and he folded it carefully and slipped it back into his side pocket. "You said New York heavies. You sure of that?"

"I know the accent. And so does Melody. She's from Brooklyn." Hinton didn't speak so I went on. "This probably means mob, Pat, you know that."

"Sure as hell sounds that way. What's going down? Any ideas?"

"No. But Doug said he was working on something big and this all ties together."

Hinton stood looking down at his toecaps, thinking. A couple of people from the bar came past us, heading for their car. He didn't look up, even when they drove out by us. I waited. At last he said, "He wouldn't tell you what it was?"

"No. He's scared for his family. He told me that much, and I've seen he was right."

Another pause. He was staring at me, sightlessly now. Then he said, "So what was all this about tonight?"

I had a quick debate with myself. He was on my side. I owed him something, but not the whole thing. "I heard that Huckmeyer twisted his ankle, the day the woman was killed. If he hadn't, he would have escorted her to the bank with the cash, like he usually did."

"So? That happens." Hinton couldn't understand.

"It doesn't happen to national team skiers. They may lose a ski and break their necks but they don't twist their ankles. I figure he set up Cindy Laver and Doug. He's a part of what's going on. I wanted to get him excited, see if I could shake anything out of him."

Hinton said, "Let me get this straight. You think that Huckmeyer killed that girl?"

"Not himself, maybe, but he's involved in the case Doug was working on. He's part of something that stretches from here to New York and it stinks, every inch of the way."

Hinton reached out and put one hand on my arm. "Reid, I know how you feel about Doug. But taking on the Huckmeyers in this town is farting against thunder. My advice, as Doug's friend, is cool it."

I said nothing and he took a slow step toward the two men, still with his hand on my arm. "Come on now, let's finish this up."

I walked behind him, leaving him to do his police business without interference. He ushered the two men toward the front door of the bar and they went, moving slowly, not speaking. He put them in the cage of the officer's cruiser, then spoke to his partner and the uniformed man. After a few seconds he turned and waved to me and I joined him. "I'm taking Mr. Grant to the precinct. You know where it is. Follow us."

"Right." I went back to my car, collected Sam and pulled around to the front to follow him out. I saw him put Grant in the back of his car. Then the uniformed man got into his cruiser and we set off in convoy for police headquarters.

I left Sam in the car and went in the front way. The cops and the three men had been taken in the back door. A uniformed officer was alone at the desk and he looked up from the paper he was studying and asked me what I wanted. I told him I was waiting to speak to Detective Hinton when he was free and he told me to sit down for a while.

About five minutes later a tall, elegant man in his fifties came in. He was wearing a fedora and an overcoat with velvet on the collar and carrying a briefcase. Grant's lawyer, I guessed. He rated a lot more interest than I had from the guy at the desk who got up at once and came to the counter. "Evenin', Mr. Garfield. What can I do for you, sir?"

"Evening, Brad. I'm here to see my client, Mr. Grant."

"Right through here, sir." The cop bustled over to the flap on the counter and swung it up. The lawyer nodded and walked through to the back door of the office. It closed behind him and the cop looked at me. "Must be heavy 'f Grant's sent for him. You here about the same beef?"

"Yeah." I gave no more away but smiled and gave a friendly nod. I had nothing to gain by antagonizing him. "Is he the Grant family lawyer?"

"Him, no. He's not into property an' the rest of that stuff. He's a criminal lawyer. If he doesn't like a cop he can make you look real small on the stand. I don' want him as an enemy."

"I understand. I'm a cop myself," I said. I didn't add that I wasn't about to brownnose anybody, lawyer or layman.

The lawyer had at least broken the ice and the cop got me a cup of coffee and we stood at the counter, chatting and sipping for another few minutes. Then Garfield came out again, shepherding Grant and the others. None of them spoke to me but Garfield gave me a withering look. I ignored him.

They all went out without saying a word and then Hinton came through the door at the back and beckoned me. "Come on through, Reid."

I went back, to the standard business end of a police station, a green-walled area that led off to the cells one way and to a couple of interrogation rooms. Hinton's partner was sitting in one of them and Hinton led me in there and shut the door. "They walked. No charges," he said simply.

"What about the gun?"

"It's his. We checked." Hinton looked harried. Garfield had been tough on him, I guessed, and he wasn't a lone wolf like me, he had a chief over him and promotion ahead, like a carrot on a string just out of reach. He wiped the corners of his mouth with his forefinger. "If you want the letter of the law he's not supposed to have it loaded when he's carrying it to the pistol club but that's a chickenshit charge and the rest of it didn't hold up when his shyster started ripping at it."

He didn't say any more but I could feel his anger, the resentment any cop feels when a lawyer shreds him on an arrest he thought was worth pursuing. It was time to give in gracefully. "Well, thanks for your effort, Pat. I'm sorry it didn't give you a nice little felony arrest for your file but I know how these things work."

He looked relieved at that. "Yeah, well. What can I say?"

"How about me buying you dinner someplace, your partner too?" I suggested. These were the only friends I had on the department. I wanted them kept sweet.

Hinton's face creased into a smile. "That'd be great. How about you, Charlie?"

His partner shook his head and spoke to me. "No thanks, sir. I've got a case in court tomorrow, drunk driver, and I want to go over it. That Garfield is the defense attorney and you know what he's like if you haven't done your homework."

"Okay then," Hinton said. "See you in an hour. Come on, Reid."

We went out through the front office, Hinton shrugging into his overcoat as he walked. "I'm going out to eat," Hinton said. "We'll be at Angelo's. Charlie's in the detective office if you need him."

"Right, Detective." The young guy on the desk smiled and opened the counter flap. He polished all the apples that came his way, it seemed.

We went in Hinton's car, the radio tuned to the police frequency which was quiet all the way. He didn't say anything until we pulled up in front of the restaurant, a plain-fronted place but with good decor visible through the window. They even had a menu in a frame outside. Pretty classy for a small town.

The owner greeted Hinton like a long-lost brother and gave us a booth, one of the few empty tables in the whole place. We ordered the special of the day, Shrimps al forno, and a bottle of red wine. The wine came right away and I poured us a glass each. Hinton sipped his and at last began to talk.

"It looks to me like you're right," he said, and when I didn't answer he gestured with his wineglass. "About something big going down."

"What makes you think so?"

"This Garfield. He's a thousand-dollars-a-day man, not the guy that Grant would have called normally. And he came right away, like he was waiting for the call or something."

He knew his town better than I did so I waited for him to go on. "Old Man Grant went to school with Maloney, the other lawyer in town. They're thick as thieves. Maloney does all his business. Yet the kid called for Garfield. That makes me want to ask questions."

"I told you, the way I see it, Huckmeyer is wrapped up in something with mob connections. He dug up Grant to scare me off. He must have told him to call Garfield if things went sour."

Hinton took another sip of his wine. "I just wish I knew what this Huckmeyer thing is all about." He put his glass down. "I'm going in to see Doug tomorrow, tell him what's happened, see what he wants me to do."

"Good. He needs your help. I can't open as many doors as you can," I said but Hinton wasn't listening. He was looking past me.

I turned to glance back and saw two tall men coming toward our table with the restaurant owner walking ahead of them nervously.

Hinton lowered his wineglass quickly, shoving it out of sight under the table, and I knew who the men were—his superiors. And they were heading right for us.

As they reached the table Hinton stood up. "Good evening, Chief."

The chief was a heavyset guy around fifty-five. He nodded at Hinton and spoke to me. "Are you Reid Bennett?"

"That's right."

The chief just nodded to the other man who pulled out a card and looked at it while he said, "Reid Bennett, you are arrested on a charge of assault." Then he started reading me the Miranda rules.

I sat there in silence until he had finished. Then he said, "Stand up, please, sir," but there was no courtesy in his tone. I stood up and he handcuffed me. I said nothing. All the patrons of the restaurant had stopped eating and were watching me in horror and delight. A real criminal, eating at the next table, just like folks.

The arresting officer got my coat off the peg and draped it over my shoulders. "Come on," he said.

"What about the check?" I asked.

"We'll take care of that." The chief was huffing slightly, as breathless as if he had run all the way from the police station.

"What about my dog? He's in the car outside."

The arresting officer was pushing me to the door, keeping a stiff pressure on my back.

"Don't worry about him," he said jovially. "He's gonna be put down."

CHAPTER 6

I didn't say anything until we got to the station and they opened the car door to haul me out. Then I said, "I want to warn you, my dog is the K9 unit of my police department. He's got three citations for bravery in making arrests. If he's injured I will sue this department for ten million dollars."

Hinton had followed us and he heard what I said. He came to my defense. "This man's a police chief, sir," he told his boss. "And the dog is a trained police dog. It's a valuable piece of police equipment."

The chief said nothing for a moment. I was wondering who he would call to check on what I was saying. Peter Horn at Murphy's Harbour would wonder what he was talking about. The only citation Sam ever got was a raw egg with his kibble. Peter knew how many times Sam had bailed me out but he was an Indian, an Ojibway, not the most talkative guy on the telephone. If these guys did ring him they would ignore anything he told them.

After a few seconds the chief said, "Take it to the pound, Hinton. We'll decide about it in the morning."

"Yessir." Hinton turned away. I gave a shrill whistle and he turned around as Sam squeezed through the open window of my car and ran to me. "Easy, boy," I told him. "Good boy, easy." I reached out to pat him with my cuffed hands. "He'll go with you now," I told Hinton. "Take care of him."

The big man who had read me my rights laughed. "They keep 'em twenty-four hours at the pound. Then they're gassed."

I said nothing and Hinton hooked his finger into Sam's collar and led him away. Then the chief opened the rear door of the police station and they led me through to the area I'd visited earlier.

"Siddown," the big cop said and I did on a chair beside the desk. He unlocked the handcuffs. He had cranked them up tight when he put them on but I didn't rub the hurt place. Another of my wife's acting axioms. Never let them see you sweat.

The chief said, "You can take it from here. I'm going home."

"Right, sir. See you tomorrow." The arresting officer stood up politely until the chief had gone. Then he turned to me. "Okay, wise guy, what've you got to say?"

"I want Mr. Maloney, the attorney."

"Yeah. Later." He got a charge sheet and took out a pen. "Turn out your pockets."

I did so and he picked up my wallet and looked inside. He stopped when he got to my ID. "Chief of Police, Murphy's Harbour, Ontario. Where's that?"

"Twenty miles south of Parry Sound on Highway 69," I said. "Now would it be too much trouble for you to explain what kind of cockamamy charge you've cooked up to harass me?"

He sat back, unbuttoning his topcoat. He was heavy and looked proud of it, the kind of guy who always has the biggest steak on the menu, with double fries and extra onion rings. "No problem," he said jovially. "At or about six-thirty

P.M. this date, you violently assaulted three men while holding them captive with that dog of yours."

I said nothing and he grinned at me. "How's it feel? Bein'
on the other side of the desk, eh, Chief?"

"I'm not saying anything until Mr. Maloney gets here.
Call him, please."

He stood up, tossing my ID on the desk. "Gimme everything in your pockets, on the desk. And your belt and your
shoelaces."

It was routine procedure and I did as I was told. I was
glad that I wasn't carrying Doug's .38. It was hidden in
my car.

Once he decided that he wasn't going to get a rise out of
me he didn't say a lot more. He put me in a cell and went
out to the front to call Maloney. That left me more worried
than I'd been before. I'd used the lawyer's name as if I knew
him, hoping it would give me some credibility. But if Hinton
had been right and the guy was a friend of the senior Grant,
he was liable to refuse the case and leave me there until
they appointed some public attorney in the morning when I
was brought before the court. And by that time, Sam would
be dead.

My watch was with my other possessions, in an envelope
in the charge room desk, so I didn't know how much time
passed but it seemed like a geological age before the door
opened to the front office and the young cop from the desk
came through with a thin little man in his fifties. He wore
rimless glasses and he didn't look anywhere near as self-
confident as Garfield had. He fiddled with his spectacles as
he came up to my cell. "Mr. Bennett? I'm Frank Maloney."

"Thank you for coming, Mr. Maloney. Could we get rid
of the officer so I can talk to you, please."

The cop took the hint. He nodded and went back out,
leaving the door open.

"You're charged with assault, three counts?" Maloney said.

"Yes, and I realize that you don't do much criminal work,

but Detective Hinton told me you were a good man." I was studying him. He was pinch-faced without looking mean, something like the guy in *American Gothic*.

"Garfield's better," he said. I liked his modesty. "My work is in property and so on, but I do take the occasional criminal case."

"Garfield is already representing the men I assaulted."

He blinked at me. "You mean they were charged?"

"Charged, but not booked. Mr. Garfield raised such a ruckus that the police dropped all the charges. Then they turned around and had me picked up."

"Were they local people?"

"Yes." I looked at him. "And this is the test, Mr. Maloney. If you don't want to take me on, I'll understand, but I hope you'll recommend someone else. I don't have any friends in this town."

"Why wouldn't I take you on?"

"Because the guy charged in the attack on me is named Grant. I understand you're a friend of his father's."

He blinked again and his eyes narrowed slightly. "My friendship with Paul Grant has nothing to do with my practice," he said. "And if it makes any difference to your peace of mind, the only disagreements we have had are over his son."

"Then you'll represent me?"

"If you can pay, yes."

I laughed. "You're a professional, Mr. Maloney. How much do you charge?"

"Four hundred dollars a day for court appearances. And I need a retainer now of one hundred dollars."

"I have money in my wallet which is with my personal effects. Can you get me out?"

"Who's the arresting officer?"

"Big guy, forty-eight to fifty, six-two, maybe two-forty. The chief addressed him as Fred."

"That's Captain Schmidt. I'll go and talk to him."

"Thanks. I'll wait here." I lay back and he looked at me

for a moment and then realized I'd been making a jail-house joke.

"Of course," he said.

He was away about twenty minutes, I judged, then he came back with the uniformed officer who was carrying some keys, which looked like a good sign. It was. He opened the cell door and I stepped out and shook Maloney's hand. "Thank you, Mr. Maloney. What happened?"

"The charges have been dropped," he said shortly. He seemed uptight so I said no more, just retrieved my belongings and signed for them, then stooped to lace my shoes. Only then I said "Thanks" to the policeman and followed Maloney out through the front.

"You seem kind of angry, Mr. Maloney," I said.

"Would you come with me?" he asked. He was holding his briefcase handle by both hands in front of him, the way schoolgirls hold their books when they're talking to a guy who's coming on too strong. I nodded acknowledgment but first reached in my wallet and took out two fifties. "One hundred dollars," I said. "Together with my thanks."

His answer surprised me. "Keep your money. I'll collect later."

"Well, thank you. But I'm able to pay."

"I'm glad to get you out," he said. "I'm sure that you, as a police chief, see the justice system from a different angle than do I."

"I just got an update that changed my perspective some."

"One reason I do so little criminal work is that I hate the insolence of office," he said, still not moving from where he was standing, under the light. "That some official can arbitrarily deprive a man of his freedom as happened to you, that makes me angry, and anger is a bad trait in a lawyer."

It looked like I had an ally, over and above his professional involvement. "That's the way it was. Those men were about to attack me. Detective Hinton charged them and that's where it should have ended."

"Captain Schmidt said your dog has been sent to the pound." He wasn't really listening to me; he was steamed.

"I'm just going to head over there and get him out."

"How?" He snapped it. His anger seemed to be boiling out of him.

"I'm not sure. If all else fails I'll break into the place and spring him. He's more than a dog. He's been my partner for years. We've been through a lot together."

"Get in your car and follow me," he commanded and turned away, letting his briefcase swing in his left hand as he strode for his car, a neat little Volvo.

He seemed to have a plan so I followed as he drove back through the center of town, then out and down a side road with only a few houses on it. He pulled up and I stopped behind him as he got out of the car. I did the same and walked toward him. He spoke as soon as I reached him. "If you do anything illegal, like stealing the dog, you'll be rearrested. The dog will be killed and you will be charged," he said.

"Maybe I can switch one dog for another in there, leave a dog in his cage."

"They have a head count, I'm sure. That won't work." He scratched his chin with quick, impatient flicks of his forefinger. "There's a better way."

"What did you have in mind?"

"The dogcatcher, pound chief officially, is a man called Calvin Perkins. He's a distant relative of the mayor. He's a stupid man, cruel and unsuited to his position, but he has a weakness."

"Which is what?"

"Greed." Maloney gave his glasses a nervous little nudge. "He drinks a good deal and he's greedy. I suggest you go in there and ask him if he has a dog to sell you. Tell him you want something vicious. He'll appreciate that."

I nodded. "Good idea. Thank you, sir. Where's the pound?"

"At the end of this road. It's a cinder block building with

an orange light in the yard. Perkins will be there until nine
o'clock. It's eight-thirty now. Go in and see what you can
do. I'll wait here."

"Thank you." I got into my car and drove around him
and down the road a further quarter mile. I pulled into the
yard and sat there for a few seconds with the headlights
playing on the window of the office, which was lighted, working out what to do. I was also nerving myself up to handle
the news if I was too late. If Sam was dead, Captain Schmidt
was going to suffer.

I saw a man's face at the window and I doused the headlights and got out. The face disappeared and the door
opened as I reached it. A big, rangy man in his thirties stood
there with the light streaming out behind him. "We're closin'
up," he said. I could smell bourbon on the night air.

"Yeah, well. I hope you got a minute. Might be worth
your while."

"What're you talkin' about?"

"Need a dog," I said. "Pounds got dogs, don't they?"

" 'doptions're done through the day, nine to five," he said
but he didn't close the door.

"Adoptions?" I laughed. "Hell, I don' wanna 'dopt no
dog. I wanna buy the biggest meanest mother you got."

"Who're you?" He was speaking low, a cunning voice. I
could see that he was a limited guy who thought he was
clever.

"Bob Little. I got a junkyard. My old dog died. Goddamn
fork-truck driver ran over the dumb sonofabitch."

He laughed heartily. "Sounds dumb all right."

"Yeah, well. The kids'll rip me off if I don't get a dog
over the weekend. I tried at Killington but they said no dice
until Monday so I figured I'd drive over here. Glad I got
here before you closed."

"Come on in." He stood back and I walked past him into
the office which was untidy and smelled of dog droppings
and disinfectant. My heart went out to Sam stuck out behind
in one of the cages.

"Got anythin' mean on hand?"

"Couple," he said. He was feeling in his pocket now and he came out with his makin's and rolled a cigarette. I watched him and when he'd finished and lit it I said, "I don't want no fag Airedale or nothin' like that. I want a big mean bastard."

"How much?" he asked, looking at me directly for the first time.

"We can talk about that when I see the dogs."

He thought about it for as long as it took him to drag on his cigarette and cough. "Sounds to me like you ain't got a lot of choice."

"Looks to me like you don' have a lot of customers standin' in line," I said and laughed.

He cracked a grin. " 's fair. Come on an' look."

He opened the rear door of the office and went into a hallway, clicking on the light. Immediately the corridor echoed with the barking of a dozen dogs. Sam's bark wasn't among them and I had a bad minute until I saw him down toward the end. But it wasn't a straight pick. Next to him was a Rottweiler, a savage-looking animal twanging at the bars of his cage with his teeth and snarling as if he wanted to eat me.

"Got a couple don't look too bad," I said.

He led me immediately to the Rottweiler. "This one here's in for biting the goddamn mailman. Lookit, meaner'n a snake."

"Yeah. That's some dog." I was right in front of Sam's cage. He was standing silently, looking at me. I pushed a little forward so that my back was to him as I looked at the Rottweiler. While Perkins pointed at the Rottweiler I snapped my fingers behind my back. The sound was covered by the barking of all the other dogs but Sam reacted at once, barking and snarling his attack message.

I ignored him for a moment while I said, "Hell. That thing looks like he could eat a whole horse every day."

"You said you wanted a mean mother. This is one mean mother," Perkins said. "She'll have your goddamn arm off soon's look at you."

"She?" I had my excuse. "A bitch? Hell, every ratbag dog in the district'll be diggin' under the wire when she comes in heat." I turned away and faced Sam who was a picture of ferocity. "How 'bout this bastard? This a dog or a bitch?"

"Dog. S'posed t' be trained. Brought in tonight by the cops. Said he attacked three guys. I'm gassin' him tomorrow."

I pulled a coin from my pocket and flipped it, trapping it on my wrist. "Heads," I said and showed it to Perkins. "I'll take this one."

Now his cunning came to the fore. "Ah, well. Like I said, that's special from the cops. I gotta gas him in the morning."

"Seems kind of a shame to gas a fifty-dollar bill," I said.

Perkins licked his lips. "What am I s'posed to say when they come askin' if I gassed him?"

"Keep his collar, looks like it's got a license. They won't wanna look at a dead dog. Just show 'em the collar."

He considered that, looking at Sam who was crouching at the wire, snarling and barking like a wild thing. "That's a pedigree dog."

"He'll be just as dead as a mutt once you gas him."

Perkins thought about it for half a minute. "Hundred bucks," he said at last. But he had no confidence. He added, "Hell, you could be losin' that much stock while you're standin' here arguin'."

"Seventy-five," I said and he grinned at me.

"Seventy-five. An' you get the bastard into your car and outa here right now."

"You got one o' them sticks with a noose on?"

"Yeah. An' mitts. Wanna borrow 'em?"

"Think I'm crazy? Sure I do."

"Money first." He held out his hand. I pulled out my wallet and snapped out a fifty and the rest in fives. He rolled it and stuck it into his shirt pocket. "It's your ass. I'll give you the stuff. You put the dog in your car, leave me the collar. Okay?"

"Sounds fair. Where's the noose?"

He walked the length of the hallway and took down a four-foot stick with a wire noose on it. He picked up a pair of leather gauntlets from on top of the last cage and handed them to me. "I'm gonna be in my office. You just drop the collar on the desk an' bring the other stuff back in when you got that bastard in your car."

"Right." I was happier with him out of the way while I did what I had to. I waited, pulling on the gauntlets while he backed the length of the hall and went into his office, closing the door.

Then I unsnapped the door of Sam's cage and told him, "Easy," rubbing his big head with one hand while I slipped the collar over his ears and dangled it around my left wrist. Then I put the noose over his head and told him, "Speak." He gave tongue again at once, a terrifying show. I urged him forward with my left hand and ran the length of the hall, throwing the door open and pausing only to toss the chain collar with its license and rabies tag onto Perkins' desk, then seeming to let Sam pull me out of the office to my car. I could see Perkins' face at the window as I put Sam into the trunk, and slipped the noose off his neck and patted him. "Good boy. Easy," I told him and he curled down and lay still. I closed the trunk lid but didn't lock it.

Perkins was at the door. "Got 'im in the trunk. That's smart. He'll likely eat your spare tire."

"I got a million spares at the yard," I said. "Thanks. I won't tell nobody where I got him." I let the words dangle as a threat.

"You better goddamn not," he shot back.

"Nice doin' business with you," I said. "So long."

He shut the door without speaking and I got into the car and drove out up as far as Maloney's car. He saw me coming and got out. I stopped and let Sam out of the trunk and knelt to fuss him. He seemed puzzled. He always obeys me but I firmly believe that he can think and right then he wasn't sure what in hell was going on.

Maloney joined me. "Well done," he said. "That's a magnificent animal."

"He's my partner. He's saved my hide a lot of times."

"How did he lose that piece of his ear?" Maloney asked, bending to look closely at Sam's old injury.

"Someone shot him. That was a while ago. But it hasn't stopped him from working just as well since."

I stood up. "Well, thank you for the help, Mr. Maloney. You were dead right about Perkins."

He straightened up and looked at me. "If you keep this dog with you someone will notice," he said.

"I guess I'll have to send him home on the train."

"You mean you're going to stay here?"

"I came to help my friend Doug Ford. He's innocent. I know it and what happened tonight proves it. I've got to get him cleared. I can't do that from Murphy's Harbour."

"Then what will you do for, what's the word, 'backup'?" He used the term awkwardly.

"I've worked solo before."

"I'm probably going to regret this," he said. "But I get the feeling that you're an honest man, honestly trying to do what's right. Would you care to talk things over with me?"

We stood there, our breath puffing out in white clouds around our heads as I thought for a while. I knew nothing about him, except that he had helped me, but he seemed straight. He had gone to bat for me and I needed help.

"Some of it is classified," I said. "But I'll be happy to walk you through the rest of it."

"All right. Come back to my house. And bring the dog with you. He can stay with me. Nobody will question his presence at my house."

"That's very kind of you, sir. Won't your family get upset?"

"I'm a widower," he said.

"I'm sorry." The automatic response. He waved it away. "Nearly four years now. Listen. Put your dog in my car, in case you get stopped."

"Thank you." I told Sam, "Come," and he followed to Maloney's car. The lawyer opened the back door and Sam hopped in. "Easy," I told him.

Maloney shut the door. "Follow me." He got in and drove past me to make a U-turn. Then I followed him and he led me back up the side road and out to the edge of town to a big brick house set back from the roadway, floodlit and beautiful with the snow layered over the evergreens like icing on a cake. He pulled up and opened the garage with a remote control device. I stopped behind him and before he closed the garage door he turned and waved to me. I came in and he rolled down the door. "Bring the dog inside," he said.

I opened his car door and clicked my tongue at Sam who got down quietly and stood by me, awaiting his next order. Maloney looked down at him and nodded his head briskly in admiration. "A splendid dog." He turned and opened the door to the house. "Come on in."

I followed him in with Sam at my left heel. We were on the stairway leading down to the basement and up three steps to the kitchen. Maloney went up ahead of me and said, "Hold it there until I draw the blinds."

I waited, looking around, while he lowered the old roll-down blind then went through to the rest of the house to do the same. Everything was neat and Spartan. There were a couple of dishes on the draining board, and cutlery for one person. A tidy single man's housekeeping—use the same things over and over and clean them as soon as they're used. He kept house as I had in the years when I was on my own. He came back in, slipping out of his coat. He was wearing a neat gray suit under it. "Come on up."

"Thank you." I stepped up to floor level and he led the way into the room next door. It was long with an antique dining table at one end, next to the kitchen, and then a sitting area with a couple of comfortable couches and an old red leather chair with a standard light next to it. Beside the chair was a table with books on it and an ashtray with a briar pipe.

Against the wall was a butler's stand with bottles and an ice bucket and glasses. Maloney went to it and said, "I was just going to have a drink when I got the call from the station. Will you join me?"

"Thank you. I'd like a rye and water, please."

"Canada's gift to the world," he said. He dropped three ice cubes into a glass and poured me a solid slug. "Water's in the kitchen."

I went and added water and when I came back he was putting the top back on the scotch bottle. "Good health," he said and we both drank. Then he took the red chair and pointed to the couch. "Sit down. Make yourself at home."

I sat, raising my glass to him and sipping comfortably. He was certainly changing my opinion of lawyers. "I want to thank you for all you've done. It's above and beyond the usual lawyer-client line of action."

He sipped his drink thoughtfully. "I may have something to thank you for, eventually," he said. I frowned and he went on, not looking at me. "There's something unhealthy going on in town. Nothing vile, not yet, but the town has changed over the last little while. I've been here all my life and I know everybody and just about everything. Who's sleeping with whom, who owes money, who gambles, who beats his wife. But lately there's something secretive going on."

He looked at me now, sadly, I thought. "There's nothing I could take into court, but I'm concerned."

"Who's involved?"

He shook his head. "No, you first. You said you feel Officer Ford is innocent. That means you think somebody staged the evidence that had him arrested. I'd like to hear why you think so, over and above the fact that you're his friend."

"I promised Doug I wouldn't repeat what he told me, but I can bring you up to date on what's been happening to me."

"That might help." He took another drink and waited.

"Last night, Doug's daughter was kidnapped by some guys who seemed to be New York heavies. She was unharmed, but the price of her release was my leaving town."

"But you're still here."

"Not staying here, just visiting through the day."

His face creased in a dry smile. "I see. And what about the Fords?"

"They've gone out of town, someplace safe, all three of them."

"Good." He nodded crisply. "But what about this evening? What started all that?"

I filled him in quickly about Huckmeyer's sprained ankle, and the response I'd got when I approached him. He listened quietly and then said, "But that's not all, is it? Didn't you humiliate Jack Grant the other night in Brewskis?"

"You do know everything that goes on. Yeah. I gave the waitress some help when he got fresh. That's all there was to it."

"It's enough to warrant his actions tonight," Maloney said, "or at least, enough to give a plausible excuse. I don't think the two incidents were connected. I think you're right about young Huckmeyer feeling threatened."

"And in your reading of the town and the people, why do you think that might be, Mr. Maloney?"

He set down his glass and picked up the pipe from the ashtray. "This is my house, you can call me Frank. What's your first name?"

"Reid."

"Well, Reid, this is a dead-ahead community. We don't have big-time wheelers and dealers. We have people who go to church on Sundays and pay their taxes. Middle America. That's ninety-nine percent of them, anyway." He picked up his pipe and fondled the bowl. "Then we have the ski lodge owners. They're the aristocracy. They've got millions invested in their facilities. But it's all out in the open. If Cat's

Cradle puts in a new spa, say, it's in the paper, along with a full report of what it's going to cost and how long it's going to take to pay it off."

He was in love with his town. He might never get around to the thing that had started him off unless I prodded him. "Then what's changed?"

"There's video game equipment in most of the bars. That's happened since last June, sometime then. And there's a new vice-president at the bank, a woman called Bernadette Corelli." He waved the pipe vaguely, then set it down. "I know this sounds like small potatoes but it's the first time they've brought in anyone from outside and her duties don't seem to affect the main thrust of the bank's operation."

"You think she's been brought in for some purpose?"

He looked at me for a long time before he spoke. It gave me a chance to study his face properly. It was a good face. High cheekbones and deep lines made him look older than he probably was, but it was an honest face, and as a long-time copper I figure I know honesty when I see it. And there was worry in it.

"I don't know why she's here, but she's a very smart dresser, in her mid-thirties. Says she's from Chicago and has a degree in economics. Peter Lawson introduced me when I was in there just after she arrived. She stands out like a bird of paradise in a flock of crows."

"Is she Lawson's girlfriend?"

"Could be, I guess, but I don't think so. She lives in an apartment over on Walmer Street. I've never seen his car there and he doesn't seem to be spending time away from his office, taking trips with her or anything like that."

"What's her job?"

"New business development, he says." Maloney snorted. "He needs her like a hole in the head. John Fisher, the manager, he handles all the loan applications. If they're major, anything over maybe a hundred thousand, Peter himself looks after them."

"Then she might be some kind of watchdog, you think. Maybe Lawson has ties to something nasty and she's there to see he doesn't take off with the cash?"

"Sounds crazy, doesn't it," he said ruefully. "But yes, I think that's it. Only Lawson isn't acting scared or resentful. He's the same as he's always been."

I debated whether to tell him what I'd heard from Doug but decided against it. He was friendly but he didn't need to know. I moved the conversation on to another track. "You said you had problems with the way young Grant acts. Is that part of the same thing?"

Maloney shook his head, almost impatiently. "Not really. The boy's spoiled. His mother always treated him as the second coming and by the time he reached his teenage years it was impossible to talk sense to him. He's a lout. I've been asked a couple of times to sort out problems he's had."

"With women?"

"Sometimes. He's made a number of local girls pregnant. Two of them had abortions, the third one settled for payment from his father. But none of it seems to touch the boy. He figures he's golden."

"And there's something else, isn't there?"

"Yes," Maloney said. "And I want your promise that this goes no further than this room."

"You've got it."

"He gambles," Maloney said quietly. "He gambles a lot and for the last two years he's been losing more than his father can afford to pay."

I sipped my drink and thought about that. It was the first link to the kind of activity Manatelli's crowd might be involved with. "What's happened about it so far?"

"Last October he sold the Thunderbird his mother had bought him. Didn't replace it, drives his father's car instead. And another time his dad held a distress sale, cleaned out most of his merchandise at giveaway prices."

It was time for a little more honesty. I looked at him

levelly. "When you sprang me you said I could perhaps be of help to you, Frank. What did you mean exactly?"

He set down his scotch and clasped his hands around one knee. "If the mess in town is sorted out I'd be grateful."

I said nothing. That wasn't all of it and we both knew. He shook his head sadly. "All right. You're an honest man and what I have in mind is an honest ambition. I believe that if I can cure the ills of this town I can be elected judge next October. Will you help me?"

"Would you take Doug Ford's case?" This was the acid test, as far as I was concerned. If he wasn't prepared to take on an unpopular case he wouldn't make a good judge, and more important, he was not an ally I needed.

"If he'll have me," he said simply. "The police have retained a man for him, Sharpe, a former DA. That cuts a lot of ice with law enforcement officers but it's my belief that you can't jump the fence like that. Either you're a prosecutor or you're a defense attorney."

"Mr. Maloney, I like your attitude. All I'm here for is to get Doug cleared of something I know he didn't do. If you're prepared to help, I'd help you run for president, let alone judge."

He set down his glass and stood up. "Thank you." He stuck out his hand and we shook solemnly, like a couple of kids swearing eternal friendship.

I didn't tell Maloney about Doug's suspicions of laundering money. I figured Doug should tell him personally. That may sound juvenile, like a kid keeping a secret. But I knew Doug was stuck in a cell with nothing to do but worry and I wasn't going to add to his burdens by breaking a promise to him.

So, Maloney and I had another drink and then he dug a couple of steaks out of his freezer and we sat and talked until midnight, when he put Sam and me into his guest room.

Next morning was Sunday and I was awakened by church bells. I got up and found Maloney putting his topcoat on. He was carrying a Bible. "See you at nine," he said and left.

I showered and fed Sam with the sack of chow I'd brought with me from home. Then I made coffee and when Maloney came back we had a light breakfast and headed for the courthouse. At Maloney's suggestion we left Sam behind. "I'll get a license for him tomorrow, change his identity. Until then he's kind of contraband," he said sensibly.

The same woman clerk admitted us, being extra respectful to Maloney, and the same sleepy guard stood back when we visited with Doug, who was first startled, then angry when he saw Maloney.

He spoke to him first. "Mr. Maloney," he said tightly, then to me, "What's going on, Reid, why's he here?"

I told him quickly about what had happened and that Maloney wanted to help us. "I've got a lawyer," he said neutrally.

"Mr. Sharpe is a good attorney," Maloney said. "And I don't want you to get the idea that I'm trying to grab your case off him. But, as Reid will tell you, I have an agenda of my own which I don't want to discuss here. I am prepared to represent you at no cost. That's to eradicate any notion that I'm ambulance-chasing by being here. And I also promise to work at finding out what's going on outside the actual investigation of Ms. Laver's death, the case that Reid tells me you were building at the time."

Doug nearly lost his cool here. He glared at me. "That was between me and you, Reid. You said you wouldn't tell anybody."

"I haven't said anything more than Mr. Maloney just told you. And I wouldn't have gone that far if he hadn't told me that there's something sour in town, something that sounds like it's tied in with what you're thinking."

Doug sat back, still angry, and Maloney took over. He led Doug through the same few facts he had given me the night before and then added a new one. "I have a feeling that the gamblers that young Grant has become involved with are taking an unhealthy interest in our town. And that interest includes involvement with the Chambers Savings and Loan Bank." He paused and looked at Doug. "Does that gibe with what you're thinking?"

Doug still didn't speak and Maloney went on in the same calm tone of voice. "Think about it, Mr. Ford. You may get off the Murder One charge without my help, without resolving the problems you believe you see in town. But even if you do, you're finished here, finished as a policeman anywhere. The only way to clear your name completely is to expose the people who set you up." He paused and then bent forward and rapped on the table forcefully. "How in God's name are you going to do that from here?"

Doug looked at me. "You trust him, Reid?"

"Completely. If it weren't for him, I'd be in jail and Sam would be dead."

"Okay." Doug leaned across the table. "In that case, Mr. Maloney, thank you. Now please listen to me."

Maloney nodded and listened without interrupting. The guard checked his watch a couple of times, but out of deference to the lawyer, I guessed, didn't cut the interview short.

When Doug had finished he leaned back and Maloney stood up. "Thank you, Doug. I'll follow this up."

The guard came forward to take Doug back and this time Doug didn't look at me. He seemed shrunken into himself and I pitied him and the lonely hours ahead of him, on his wooden bunk, wondering whether he had done the right thing in opening up to Maloney.

Maloney led the way back to his car without speaking. I respected his silence while he unlocked the car and clicked the switch to let me in on the passenger side. I got in and he still said nothing while the car warmed up and the radio played classical music very low.

At last he said, "I think we tackle this head-on."

"You mean at the bank?"

"We don't have enough for that." He engaged the drive lever and pulled out before adding, "Yet." I sat back and let him drive, not knowing what I would have done this morning anyway. My own swipe at young Huckmeyer had only got me into trouble. It was good to have Maloney coming up with ideas. Maybe he could think of something useful.

He drove to a street on the edge of town and pulled in at a low apartment block that looked as if it had been built in the thirties. "Who lives here?" I asked as we got out.

"Ella Frazer," he said. He seemed tight. "I don't know if you should come up with me."

"She knows me. I had lunch with her and she was help-ful." I wasn't going to push but I didn't want to be left out.

He paused for a moment, then gave in. "Okay. But let me do most of the talking. I know her better than you. I handled her divorce last year."

There was no security system. Maloney went in and di-rectly to an apartment on the second floor, the top floor, and knocked on the door. Nobody answered and he waited a long time before knocking again. This time a woman's voice called. "Hold on, I'm coming."

We waited and the door opened, on a chain. I saw Ella Frazer's face through the crack. It looked as if she had just got out of bed and put some lipstick on. Her hair was mussed and she looked hung over. "Frank? What on earth's so important you have to wake me up?" she asked. The door closed, the chain rattled and she opened up again. Now she saw me and she looked at Maloney sharply. "What's he doing here?"

"I'll explain, Ella, Can we come in, please?"

She frowned, looking as if the action caused her pain, then she seemed to decide it was too much trouble to argue and waved us in.

The room looked as if she'd been drinking all weekend. It was littered with newspaper, separated into sections and dropped, and there were a couple of glasses around, one on top of the television, the other on the table. There was no liquor in sight but there was a big glass jug that still held about an inch of orange juice on the floor beside the couch.

Maloney was shocked. "Good God Almighty, Ella. What's happening to you?"

"What do you mean?" She said it with the cut-glass clarity of the careful drunk.

It was no place for a stranger and I opted out. "Would you like me to make some coffee, Ms. Frazer?"

She opened her mouth to argue but Maloney cut her off. "Good idea." She sat down, not arguing. I went into the kitchen, shutting the door behind me.

The sink was full of dirty dishes and there was a half gallon of vodka sitting on the draining board. Most of it was gone. I took off my parka, found coffee and rinsed the pot and set it on. While I was waiting I ran some hot water and washed up. I could hear Maloney's voice from the other room, low and angry-sounding, like the father of a teenager disappointed with his grades. If Ms. Frazer was answering it was too softly for me to hear. I made sure to clatter noisily before going in with the coffee.

Ms. Frazer was still sitting in the same chair. She had been crying. Her mascara had smeared up over her left eye and her lipstick was smudged. The room was tidier. The papers had been picked up and folded and the jug and empty glasses were on the coffee table. I set down the tray and picked up the debris and took it into the kitchen, Then I rejoined them. Maloney was pouring coffee. He spoke first, continuing the conversation he had been having in my absence. "It's eating you up," he said.

Ms. Frazer reached for the cup he was holding out to her and spoke. "I've worked there twenty-two years. I can't just walk away. Who in hell would hire me today? I'm fifty-three years old and there's a million people looking for jobs."

I sat down, on a chair out of her line of sight. It looked as if Maloney had been right. It would have been better if I'd stayed outside. She was easy with him as she might have been with a brother.

He was very careful with his next words. "That's true. But I have to suggest that when this business blows up, because it's going to, you can count on that, when it does there's going to be dirt on everybody. As head of the accounting department, you'll be caught up in it."

Her voice was very low when she answered. "What can I do? If I make waves they'll fire me."

"I need some documentation, that's all. When did this start? How much money is involved? If possible, where does the money come from every month to pay for the credit card receipts? That will do for a start. Later we may need more detail."

She raised her shoulders and let them flop. "What's that going to do?"

"I'll worry about that. Can you do it for me?"

She shrugged again. "I guess."

"Good." He looked across at me. "I want to talk to Ella for a minute or two, Reid. Could you wait in the car, please?"

"Sure." I went to the kitchen for my coat and left, not speaking to either of them. It was cold but sunny and I paced to the corner and back while I waited for Maloney to come out. He did, after perhaps a quarter of an hour. He drove up the street to me and picked me up. He didn't say anything when he opened the door and I kept quiet. It looked to me as if he had a soft spot for Ms. Frazer and didn't like what was happening to her.

At last he spoke. "She's only been drinking since her husband walked out on her. Up until then she was outgoing, cheerful. Day like this she'd have been out on the slopes."

"You think the stress of this money business has anything to do with the way she's acting?"

He didn't answer directly. "Dammit. It's enough to make you want to go home and tip all your liquor down the sink."

"It has to be each person's choice. You can't help anyone unless they want help."

"That's why I stayed," he said, gripping the wheel very tight. "I wanted to see if she would do it, if she'd pour her goddamn vodka away." He slowed at an intersection and then made a left turn. "She said no. Said she wouldn't drink but she wasn't going to make any gestures."

He was angry and worried and there was nothing to say so I sat silent until he said. "I thought I'd go and see Paul Grant, let him know what's been happening to Jack."

"You won't want me there for that," I said. "I'd be as welcome as a shark in a swimming pool."

He managed a faint grin. "Probably. I shouldn't be long, though. You could wait in the car. Would you mind?"

"Sure. I don't know what else I could do this morning."

"Good." He picked up speed a little and drove to the center of town, pulling into the driveway of a big brick house. "Shouldn't be long," he said again and left.

He left the car running, with the heater on and the radio tuned to the same classical station. They were playing something dreary with lots of screeching violins so I pressed buttons until I found a country station and sat back listening to George Jones. Idly I checked the house. It looked as if Grant used it as a showcase for his products. There was a multileveled deck around the front door and a number of floodlights set in the snow as well as awnings on all the windows. There were two vehicles parked in the driveway, a Cadillac and a pickup truck with the name and address of the hardware store on the door. There was a garage as well but it was drifted in with snow and I guessed that Grant had his workshop in there with lots of power tools. The place looked typical successful Middle America, comfortable affluence in a sparkling clean little town. I wondered what Maloney could dig out here that would help Doug. Maybe there was something rotten at the core, but it was well hidden. He'd have to dig deep to find it.

I couldn't see the Oldsmobile that Jack Grant had been driving but that didn't surprise me. It figured he had his own pad somewhere. If he was the black sheep of the family they were probably glad to have him gone.

Maloney was in the house for about twenty minutes and when he came out a man his own age came to the door with him. They stood talking, while the other man rubbed his shirt-sleeved arms against the cold, then he closed the door and Maloney came back to the car. I readjusted the radio to his classical station as he crunched over the snow to the car.

He got in, looking thoughtful. "Paul hadn't heard about last night," he said. "Jack didn't come home."

"He lives here, with them?"

"I told you he was a spoiled brat." He looked back over his shoulder and reversed into the roadway. "Twenty-nine years old and his mother still makes his bed for him. Only this morning there was no need because he's still on the tiles."

"I'd imagine that's standard, from what you've said about his sex life." The kid was probably getting up about now, I thought, allowing some lucky girl to make breakfast for him.

"That's not his pattern. Not according to his father. Paul realizes that the boy screws around a lot but apparently he's always home for breakfast, no questions asked. He just shows up and that's it."

"You want to talk to him?"

"It might help." He backed out of the driveway and pulled off away up the street. "I've known him since he was born. He's my godson, for what that's worth. Maybe he'll open up a little."

He didn't say anything and I prodded. "Where to now?"

"Do you ski?" he asked suddenly.

"I'm not the Canadian champion but I know how."

"Then let's go out to Cat's Cradle and get some fresh air." The idea pleased him so I didn't argue, just sat back and enjoyed the ride. He didn't say much until we got there. The lot was full of cars as usual and we had to park on the roadway, a couple of hundred yards back from the gate. Maloney unlocked his trunk and took out some coveralls. "I'm not a good enough skier to dress fancy," he said with a small, neat smile. "These are warm, go over my clothes and they make me look like a farmer, which makes my skiing look better than it is." He looked at my blue jeans. "Will you be okay like that?"

"Same kind of disguise," I said. "Let's do it." We walked back to the gate and were just about to turn in when I heard a siren back down the road behind us.

"First broken leg of the day," Maloney said cheerfully as

an ambulance pulled past us. But then a car came in right behind it, driving just as fast, and I recognized Pat Hinton at the wheel.

"That's the detectives," I said. "Maybe it's something else." I wondered if there had been a holdup and somebody had been shot. Vermont is peaceful but violent crime is spreading everywhere. It might have reached as far as Chambers.

We picked up our pace up the driveway which was lined with cars and followed into the lot where the ambulance was standing with its rear doors open. A crowd had formed around it and we joined it, waiting while the ambulance men brought their gurney around the side of the building with something on it, covered completely by a blanket. Pat Hinton was following, with a couple of ski patrol people, a man and woman in neat brown outfits.

The crowd parted as the ambulance men wheeled the gurney through and then Hinton saw me. He broke off talking to the ski patrollers and took six quick steps to stand in front of me. "Come with me," he said.

I followed as he held up a finger to the ski people to wait and led the way to his car. We didn't get in but as we reached the car he stopped and asked his question. "Where were you last night after you got out of the cells?"

"I went home with Mr. Maloney. He invited me to stay over so I did."

"That's good," he said fervently. "Otherwise I'd be taking you downtown right now."

"What's going on?"

He turned and pointed at the gondola lift and then pointed higher up the slope. "See that wooded part, close to the top of the lift?"

I nodded. Just below the wheelhouse there was a false crest covered with pines which reached almost up to the gondola cars. "He was thrown out there, in the trees," Hinton said. "We might not have found him for days but some guy took somebody else's wife into the trees for a quick nibble."

"Who was thrown out? Who's dead?"

He looked at me closely, checking my face as he gave me the news. "Jack Grant. And the fall didn't kill him. He was stabbed in the heart first."

The ambulance men had closed the door by now and were heading back down the driveway, lights flashing. Hinton turned to watch them go, then flicked a glance at me. "Will Maloney back you up?"

"Go ask him." I was almost angry. I had no right to expect friendship from this man, but at least a little professional courtesy for the fact that I was a cop, like him.

He turned away. "No need," he said. "Listen, you're going to be questioned by the chief, I guess, about this. So's Maloney. But so far as I'm concerned, you're a brother officer. Seen many homicides?"

"I worked homicide for a year in Toronto."

"Good. Those clowns from the ski patrol rushed in like the goddamn seventh cavalry. They've tramped the crime scene into a shambles, but let's get up there and see what we can find."

That pleased me. "Right. I'll tell Frank."

I went to Maloney and filled him in quickly. He asked only, "Are they sure it's Jack?"

Hinton had joined me and he nodded. "I identified him."

"In that case, would you like me to break the news to the family?"

"That would be very kind, sir. I was going to send an officer, but you're a family friend. Would you go to the station first and pick up a uniform guy?"

"Of course." Maloney nodded. "Then I'll go home. Join me when you're through, Reid."

Maloney left and Hinton led me back to the ski patrol people. They got us a pair of snowmobiles and we rode up the slope, startling a whole series of skiers. On the bunny slope, a couple of them tumbled as we approached. It was a steep ride toward the top but I do a lot of skidooing in the winter at home and Hinton looked as if he'd ridden a snow machine before so we reached the scene in five minutes. It was a hundred meters or so from the mogul field that dominated this run.

We parked at the side of the ski trail and went into the trees. The ski patrol had left a man there and he was busily trying to shoo away the sightseers who were crowding in. He yelled at us as we approached, but Hinton flipped out his badge and he gave in gratefully. "I've done what I could, officer, but everybody and his goddamn brother wants to take a look."

"You did well. Thanks for the help. What's your name?" Hinton was professional. He took the name and clapped the man on the back, then reached into his coat pocket and pulled out a roll of orange tape. He flipped it to me and said, "Ten yards each way should be good."

I quickly made a circle around the place where he was standing, moving the spectators back as I tied the tape to trees at chest height. The onlookers jostled but the barrier worked. None of them ducked under it to approach us. Then I joined Hinton. He was looking up at the trees above his head. As we watched a gondola car passed over and Hinton spoke. "There's not much forward momentum. He must have fallen just about straight down. See where those branches are broken?"

"Yeah. He must have landed here." We looked down at our feet. The snow, about two feet deep, was tramped flat all around us.

"Great," Hinton said angrily. "If there's anything here we won't find it until spring. Why did the damn ski patrol move the goddamn body?"

"We'll search anyway. I'll work down the slope from the point of impact. You want to work up?"

"Right." Hinton looked disgusted. He was wearing city clothes, a good topcoat and low shoes with toe rubbers. His pants were white with snow to the knees already. He had no hat. I was wearing a toque and had a hood on my parka. "Stick this on," I said and gave him my toque.

"Thanks very much." He put it on gratefully. Then I flipped up my hood and laced the front and stepped behind the tree where Grant had fallen. Even here the snow was trampled and I reached up and cut off a small branch with my clasp knife and quickly trimmed it until I had a small rake. Then I crouched and started sifting the trampled snow.

It was laborious work and produced nothing within the area I had taped off. But below that spot the snow was untrampled and I went forward, faster, looking for holes in the virgin snow, places where things had fallen since the last snowfall. There were lots of them and I dug up twigs and pine cones with my little rake. And then, forty yards from the place where Grant had been found, right at the edge of the small grove of trees, I saw a hole that looked artificial. It was almost square. I dug into it, brushing the snow aside as carefully as an archaeologist in an ancient tomb. And deep down in the soft snow, almost to the ground, I found a billfold.

There was no need to mark the spot. My footsteps were the only impressions on the snow here, in the woods. I stood up and trudged back up to Hinton who was still working in the trampled area immediately around the body.

He looked up at me. "This is impossible. I'm going to call in a metal detector to look for the weapon."

"Found something," I said and held out the billfold on the end of my twig. He opened both gloved hands like a begging bowl and I dropped the billfold into them.

He stood there, holding it flat on his hands. "Can you open the flap with that stick?"

I did so and he indicated the second little flap on the left side. "Should be a license under there."

I lifted that one as well and we bent forward to check the name. It was Grant's own wallet. "Pity," Hinton said. "Would've been neat if this was the perp's. But that doesn't happen in real life."

"It looks thin. The guy who dropped it probably went through it and took out his money and credit cards. There may be fingerprints."

He looked at me wide-eyed. "Wouldn't that be great." He bit the fingers of his right glove and pulled it off, then dug into his coat pocket and came out with an evidence bag. I took it from him and held it open while he slipped the bill-fold into it, not touching it with his bare fingers. "Good," he said. "There could be prints, if the guy who killed him went through it. And if the sonofabitch took his gloves off to do it."

"One small step for police kind," I said. "I've gone as far as the edge of the wood. Want me to help you here?"

"Yeah. Please. I phoned for some guys soon's I saw we had a homicide but there's hardly anybody working on a Sunday morning. They'll have to round 'em up and bring them in. Meantime, let's give this our best shot."

So I got back down on my knees and went over the ground. It's the kind of unglamorous and mostly unproductive work that cops have to do. And we knew we were working at a disadvantage. The place was so public, so trampled by the skiers who had found the body, so open to contamination from the chair lift above us that there wasn't much chance we could tie anything we found to any killer. Even if we'd found the murderer's wallet a sharp lawyer would make the case that his client had dropped it while riding the lift overhead. But you don't know what you haven't got while you still haven't got it, so we probed and got wetter and colder for almost an hour. Then a couple of guys in city overcoats came ducking under the tape. It was Lieutenant Cassidy and Morgan. And Cassidy was blazing. He pointed a finger at me. "What in hell's this guy doing here?"

"He's a trained homicide officer, assisting me at my request, Lieutenant." Hinton was just as angry but was faultlessly polite.

"You've embarrassed the whole Chambers PD," Cassidy snapped. "This man's got a record in town."

Hinton was cold and weary enough to snap at this. "What he's got is a goddamn good reason to sue our ass off," he said. "His arrest last night was a phony. You know that and so does he."

"You better have this discussion with the chief," Cassidy said. "In the meantime I'm relieving you here. Take this man and get back to the precinct and report what you've done."

"Glad to," Hinton said. "Come on, Reid."

We went back to our snow machines, leaving the two detectives standing there with their hands in their pockets and puffs of righteous breath rising around their heads.

"Let him freeze his own ass off," Hinton said. "Come on, let's get down the slope, get a cup of coffee."

We drove down, dodging skiers, and left the machines at the rescue hut. Then Hinton led me to the coffee shop and we got a cup of new life and warmed our feet. He paid for the coffee and said nothing while we drank it. When we'd finished he took me out to his car and said, "So, let's go catch hell."

The chief was in his office talking on the phone. The door was open and Hinton tapped on the door frame with his knuckles. The chief looked up and waved him in, still talking. He looked less menacing this morning, neat in a gray suit, as if he'd just come from church. He finished his conversation and stood up, looking straight at me. "I was just talking to Mr. Maloney. I'm glad you came in," he said. "I want to apologize for what happened last night."

I didn't reply at once. The department was in the wrong and they should appreciate that. Not for my sake but for the sake of the next guy they didn't like the looks of.

The chief had expected an answer but when none came he went on, a little less sure of himself now. "I acted responsibly on the case that was presented to me. I'm sure you appreciate that."

This time I had to speak. "In my jurisdiction I wouldn't have arrested a man on hearsay, Chief. I'd have asked the complainant to swear a warrant against the accused and then acted on it."

He looked at me, then away, then collected his confidence and looked back at me, nodding. "I'm afraid I've put the town in a very embarrassing situation. Will you accept my apology?"

"I will if I get compensation," I said and I heard Hinton catch his breath. The chief said nothing, waiting for me to name the number of millions I had in mind. I put them out of their misery. "For my own arrest, no charge. But I had to purchase my dog back from the pound. It cost me seventy-five dollars."

He opened his mouth to speak, relief spreading across his face, but I held up my hand. "If he'd been killed, I would have sued. As it is, I'd like my seventy-five bucks, plus." I left a pause and he waited, a chastened man. "Plus I want to volunteer to act as an investigator in this murder and the murder of Ms. Laver. I think they're connected."

He reached out to shake my hand. "Thank you. We're most grateful to you, Mr. Bennett. Or should I call you Chief?"

"Reid is fine. And I want to take my dog with me on this case without Mr. Cassidy getting snotty."

"Sure. Sure." He looked at Hinton. "Can you fill Reid in our investigation so far? And get him desk space, a phone, whatever he needs."

"Yessir." Hinton's anxiety had fallen away from him, like snow from a jerked branch. "And we've already made one find in the Grant case." We, not Reid, I noticed. He would be working here after I left. He needed all the brownie points he could score.

"What's that?" The chief was all business now, gathering his authority around him again like a man putting on a uniform.

Hinton pulled out the evidence bag with the billfold in it. "We found this at the scene. It was at the edge of the trees. Must have been thrown away from the chair lift, just before the body was dropped."

The chief picked up the bag by one corner. "Any ID?"

"It's Grant's, sir," Hinton said. "I haven't checked it but it looks like the money has gone and the credit cards. If we're real lucky there could be prints on it from the perp."

"Get Wilkins in and have him dust it." The chief made a shooing motion and we turned to leave but he called me back. "Mr. Bennett, Reid, if you don't mind, could we have a word in private?"

"Of course." I waited as Pat left and the chief got up and closed the door. "I was intrigued when you said the two homicides are related." He looked at me and I studied his face. He looked intelligent. Strong features with a long, straight nose and clear blue eyes. Polish-German ancestry, I thought and remembered that Huckmeyer, one of the people I suspected, was also probably from the same gene pool.

"To start with, you've got the wrong man in jail. I knew Doug Ford in Nam. He's an honorable man. We've been in some bad places together but he never did anything to make me think he would murder anybody. Apparently he was following up an investigation of his own, something involving the murdered woman. When I started making some inquiries along those lines I soon got hassled. The first time proved to me that Doug was right. Some guys from out of town kidnapped Doug's daughter and told me to go home." He wanted to speak here but I kept on. "And when I followed up anyway Grant and his buddies tried to beat me up. And now Grant's been killed. It bears out what Officer Ford told me."

The chief held up his hand. "A bit slower, please." He frowned. "I haven't heard anything about a kidnapping."

"We didn't report it. The child was returned unharmed and Doug's family left town."

He had more questions but this time I played hardball. "Chief, Doug Ford was certain he had a big case on his hands. He was right. You can see that from young Grant's death. But he has sworn me to secrecy. The only way to get his views is to get him out of that jail and talk to him."

"I can't do that." He leaned forward and fiddled with the edges of some files on his desk, making sure they were square and parallel with the edge of the desk, which they already were. "He's charged with Murder One."

"He shouldn't be. There's no solid case against him. The most he should have been charged with was possession of the money that went missing from the lodge and even that charge is shaky."

He looked up at last. "I can't go to the DA and tell him this. It's nothing but hearsay. You think your old buddy is innocent so we should let him out, give him his job back."

"It's hard." I gave him that much. "It's going to embarrass the department, but if you do, you're going to look a whole lot better when this business is finally cleared up and people see what really happened."

He looked at me out of those ice blue eyes and said, "And what if we never find out what happened? Ask yourself. How many homicide cases ever get cleared?"

"Random killings, sex crimes and so on, not many. But when there's a lot of people involved, someone talks. They all get solved, some sooner, some later."

He sighed and tapped his teeth with his forefinger. "I'll talk to Ford," he said. "Then, if it makes sense, I'll talk to the DA. Meantime, we'll give you every assistance." He paused, realizing that this wasn't enough yet, and then said,

"And I want to thank you for your assistance and your professionalism."

"Thank you, Chief. I'll go find Pat." I stood up and so did he, reaching across his desk formally to shake my hand.

"Go get 'em," he said.

The deskman saw me and said, "Detective Hinton is in his office, sir, upstairs and third on the left."

"Thanks. The name's Reid Bennett. What's yours?" Always get the help on your side. You never know when you're going to need them.

"Wally Beeman. Glad to know you." Another handshake. I was starting to feel like a visiting senator.

Hinton was in his office on the phone saying, "So, okay. Have him come in the moment he gets home. Can you tell him that, please?"

He hung up. "Wilkins has gone ice fishing. If his wife knew where, we could send a guy to get him. As it is, we have to wait until he decides to come home."

"There's nobody else?"

"He's had special training. Hell, I can dust for prints, most of us can, but he's trained and he's good, I'll give him that." He sat back, wearily. "So, waddya think? I'd be heading over to the morgue to check with the ME if I was on my own."

"Good idea. Why not stop off at your house and get some dry pants and shoes? It'll make you feel more like working."

"Let's go." He stood up with real enthusiasm and we set off for his place.

Fifteen minutes later we were at the morgue watching the medical examiner take his first look at Grant's body. He was an anxious young doctor and he looked at me in surprise. "Who's your partner?" he asked Hinton.

"This is Chief Bennett, from Canada. He's assisting us with the investigation."

The title set the doctor's mind at ease. He nodded to me, wiggling his hands in their rubber gloves to show why he wasn't about to shake. "Pleased to meet you. My name's Weichel."

"Pleased to meet you, Doctor." I smiled formally and stood back to watch him work. In a town like Chambers he would not have examined many homicide victims, I thought, but he was pro. He gave Hinton a camera and told him how to operate it and to take the pictures he called for.

First he wanted a shot of the body and then close-ups of the face and hands and the left breast.

Hinton took two shots of each point, following the doctor's directions to the letter. The body was lying on its back, dressed in a down jacket, good mustard-colored corduroy pants and a pair of high winter boots. There was a good deal of blood on the left breast of the jacket, and a long, narrow smear on the hem. The face was scratched deeply.

The doctor bent to examine the smear. "Looks as if the assailant wiped his knife blade here," he said. "Take a close-up, please." Hinton took the shot and the doctor went on to check the face, speaking into a tape recorder in his left hand. He counted the lacerations and described their size and distribution and the fact that they had not bled noticeably. He also commented on flecks in some of them, apparently pieces of bark.

He stopped recording and spoke to us, giving us the *Reader's Digest* version of his opinion. "He must have been dead for at least a few minutes before he fell. That's why there's no blood flow from these scratches. And there's bark in them which indicates they were probably postmortem, caused by the branches of the tree he fell through."

He went on to check the condition of the hands, which were bare. "No trace of skin or anything foreign under the fingernails which are bitten down. Scratches on both hands, mainly on the backs, similar to those on the face." He stopped now and removed the down jacket. The body was stiff but we got the jacket off and laid it on a steel table nearby while Hinton photographed the bloodstain on the sweater underneath. It was very wide, reaching from the neck to below the waistband of the pants. As a layman I figured the aorta had been severed. The doctor apparently thought the same. "He was as lucky as you get in a case like this. Death must have been almost instantaneous."

"You think this was done by a pro?" I asked.

He glanced up at me. "Indubitably. He punctured the heart with a single thrust, pulled the blade out and wiped it. An amateur would have stabbed in the abdomen, I'd say."

He turned back to the corpse and called for Hinton to lay the jacket beside it. He did so and the doctor took a tape measure and checked that the holes in the jacket and the sweater lined up. "He was standing or sitting with his arms at his sides when he was stabbed," he said, then waved the jacket away and went on examining.

It took him most of an hour while he checked each layer of clothing and then the body itself, noting the signs of lividity where blood had pooled at the lowest points of contact with the earth. "Did you talk to the people who found him?" he asked before commenting on the lividity.

Hinton had. "They say he was lying on his left side, the right leg dragged up against the trunk of the tree."

"That fits," the doctor said. He didn't bother explaining any further but I've seen enough bodies to know the pattern. I could see the dark marks of pooled blood on Grant's left hip and shoulder.

"I'm going to take a blood sample to check for intoxicants," the doctor said. "I'll also check the stains on the jacket in case the man who did it cut himself as well and there's some of his own blood mixed in."

"Thank you, sir. Chief Bennett and I would like to check the clothing now."

"Go ahead." The doctor waved vaguely and we set to work on the dead man's clothes. We started with the down jacket. There were paper tissues in the right-hand pocket and in the left a pack of Tareytons with four cigarettes in it. We checked the box carefully but there were no notes written on it, nothing to help us. But there was a chance there might be other prints on it so we sealed it and the tissues in evidence bags and checked the pants next. In the right pocket we found keys and a dollar eighty-seven in change.

I stopped now and looked at Hinton. "You know what we haven't found?"

"What's that?" He was working hard, rolling everything around in his mind, but he had overlooked one thing. "His .22 pistol. Did you give it back to him last night?"

"Yeah. And his spare magazine." Hinton was thoughtful now. "He must have left it in his car, do you think?"

"Could have done. Or maybe Garfield, his lawyer, hung on to it."

"I'll go ask him when we're through here," Hinton said.

The last thing we checked was the heavy wool shirt. And here, in the left-hand pocket, under the thick crust of blood from his stab wound we found a flat folded package of the kind drug dealers use for a gram of coke. It was soaked through with blood but looked as if it had not been opened. Hinton eased it out of the pocket and put it into a fresh evidence bag. "I'll have our drug guy check this out," he said. "Looks like cocaine to me."

"Not surprising, given this guy's reputation," I ventured. "But it looks like he hasn't used any. This might just give us a rundown on his whereabouts last night. If you know who the dealers are in town and we lean on them, it could help."

"Right." Hinton gathered his evidence bags together, including separate bags with each of Grant's garments, and spoke to the doctor. "I guess it's pretty hard to guess how long he's been dead, Doc?"

"Almost impossible. But I'm going to do a postmortem and when I see the stomach contents that may give me something. I'm about to begin it. Would you like to stay?"

"No, thanks. Our time would be better spent elsewhere," Hinton said politely. "But the department would be most grateful for your report as soon as you have it, Doctor."

"Of course. I'm just waiting for my assistant. As soon as she gets here I'll proceed."

"Thank you." Hinton nodded to the door and I took the hint and led the way out.

"I guess I'll have to turn this all over to Cassidy," Hinton said. He sounded a little bitter.

"Is he in charge of the investigation?"

"We don't have any formal homicide squad," Hinton said. "Hell, we don't need one. Cindy Laver and now this are the only homicides we've had in four years. He's the chief of detectives is how it works and he takes charge of everything."

There was nothing to say except what my wife calls the "There, there, poor thing" speech so I said nothing. He went on, "We haven't got a hell of a lot but I'd like to lean on Kelly myself."

"Who's Kelly?"

"The drug source in town. He was picked up for pushing grass, not that it's much of a crime anymore but if there's illegal substances around, he's the logical guy to know where they came from."

"Where's he live? Is it on the way back to the station?"

Hinton looked across at me and grinned happily. "Why didn't I think of that?"

We stopped at the edge of town at a mobile home set up on concrete blocks. It was the kind of place the local fathers would like to burn down now that they'd built up a decent clientele for their ski slopes. Knowing what its owner did for a living, I checked it thoroughly. It needed paint and had a corrugated iron lean-to at one end that almost covered a pickup truck. The driveway had been plowed out a couple of blizzards ago. There were banks of snow each side of the drive and the snow between them was trenched with plenty of wheel marks.

While Hinton went to the door I checked the wheel marks.

None was particularly fresh but it seemed to me as if a lot of different vehicles had driven in here. It indicated that Kelly was back to business as usual.

I joined Hinton, who was talking to a tall guy with a tattooed swastika on one cheekbone. A biker type with hard jail time behind him. He had long hair and a Zapata moustache and he hadn't shaved the rest of his face for a few days. He was angry. "What's this about?" he shouted.

Hinton was pure reason. "We can do this either of two ways, Mike. One way is, you can get on your high horse and raise hell and we can get a search warrant. But I'm warning you that we've got a drug-sniffing dog in the department who will tear this sorry place apart when he gets a whiff of what you're selling. So you'll have to flush all your goodies down the can before we get back. That's the hard way. Or you can answer a couple questions and we're on our way."

Kelly looked me up and down, hanging from one hand inside the door of his home. I guessed he had a shotgun up there and he was looking at me like he'd want me to be his first skeet.

"This is our K9 officer," Hinton said. "Now let's get reasonable."

I just stood there, staring at Kelly as if he was something I'd found on my shoe. He folded. "Waddya wanna know?"

"We found some coke on a guy, a dead guy," Hinton said. "Where'd he get it?"

"Coke?" Kelly laughed. "Coke? You gotta be kidding. I've sold a little grass in my time, I admit that. It oughta be legal anyways. But I can't afford to get into coke."

"Then who can, in town?" The obvious question. Kelly caught in slyly.

"What's in it for me?"

"I told you. We don't search your shack."

"I got nothin' here." He roared now and took his hand down from the doorjamb to wave in protest. Hinton acted immediately, shoving him back into the room and stepping in after him. I followed and shut the door. I was right about the shotgun, I noticed. It was a Winchester pump, sawed off to a barely legal length. The place stank of stale marijuana smoke.

"Get the hell out," Kelly shouted. "You can't just come in here 'less I invite you."

"You just did," Hinton said easily. "This officer heard you."

I was still looking around. There was a home-rolled cigarette in the ashtray. "Just having breakfast, were you?" I asked, and picked up the ashtray.

"Gimme that." Kelly was tough enough to snatch the ashtray from me but he sat down in his chair, a tired old wingback that needed re-covering. "Look. I don't know nothing about no coke," he said wearily. "Grass, yeah. I know where to score. Coke, no."

He looked up at Hinton who extended his hands toward him and curled his fingers a couple of times, a "come on" gesture.

"Y'ask me it was one o' the skiers brought it in," Kelly said. "Hell, they come from Chicago, Boston, all over. Plenny of coke in places like that."

New Jersey, and New York too, I thought. Maybe young Grant had been talking to the guys who had grabbed Doug's daughter. Maybe the coke had been his payoff for trying to hammer me.

Hinton sneered, a professional noise; he wasn't a sneerer in private. "You mean to tell me a guy with a hungry nose has to go all the way to New York to score?"

"That's the God's honest truth," Kelly said and I believed him. He set the ashtray on the table and folded his arms. "You can bust me if you want. Shit. I don' mind. It's warmer in the joint than it is in here. But I can't tell you what I don' know."

"Thank you for your help," Pat said. He looked at me. "I think that's enough for now, don't you?"

"Yeah. Let's go." I nodded to Kelly. "Thanks for the help."

He sat there sullenly as we let ourselves out. As we walked back to the car Hinton said, "I think he's on the level. He's a pain in the ass but he made sense about coke coming in from outside. This is a hick town. If a guy had a habit he'd have to drive someplace else to get his supply. It makes sense to me that if a user came skiing, he'd bring some if he needed it."

"The guys who snatched Doug's kid were city people," I said. "Maybe he got his bindle from them."

Hinton got into the car and started it up, thoughtfully. "You know, you're gonna get me believing this conspiracy theory of yours if this goes on."

"I think young Huckmeyer is involved," I said. "Like for instance, why would they dump the body on Cat's Cradle? How did they get the key to get in and start up the chair lift? They could have dropped Grant in a ditch a lot easier. If they wanted to get rid of the body they could have taken him out and shoved him under the ice somewhere. You wouldn't have found him till the spring thaw."

"I'll bring this up at the conference. There'll be one, some-time today," he said.

"Somebody's going to have to check the lift and all the cars. We have to find if there's any bloodstains in one of them."

"Great," Hinton said soberly. "You can imagine the roar they'll make at Cat's Cradle if we close down their big lift for three, four hours in the middle of their busy day."

"That's all the more reason to do it. Check on Huckmeyer's reaction. It's starting to look to me as if the out-of-town guys are anxious to make him worry."

We pulled into the station and checked the offices. The chief was out at the ski slopes, the deskman told us. He and Lieutenant Cassidy were checking the scene of the crime.

"Fine," Hinton said and led the way upstairs to the detective office. He went through the door and then stopped in his tracks.

I was following and did the same thing. Sitting at one of the desks was a guy I hadn't expected to see there for some time yet, Doug Ford.

Hinton stuck out his hand. He looked happy, for the first time since I'd met him. "Doug. You're out. Great. What happened?"

Doug shook his hand formally. "Thanks, Pat. The chief came over and told me about Grant being offed. Then he said he was going to see the DA and get my bail reduced. They came back and let me out without bond."

He still hadn't spoken to me and I guessed he was angry at my breach of his trust even though I'd referred everybody to him for facts and had told them nothing secret. I broke the ice with "Are you glad about this, or mad?"

Doug sat down again and swung his feet up on the desk, something he must have done a hundred times when he worked here every day.

"To tell the truth, I'm still not sure. You know what I told you, the thing I was working on, now it's all going to be out in the open."

"It had to come out, Doug. You were keeping it to yourself and the mob was out to get you killed. You wouldn't have lasted five minutes in the open population of a prison.

They'd have murdered you the way they murdered Cindy Laver."

Doug looked at me bleakly. "Just because you're right doesn't make me any happier, Reid. I've got some heavy guys want me gone. They'll kill me or hurt my family to shut me up."

"You couldn't stop them doing it from jail," I said. "Maybe they'll pull out of their operation here, but even if they do, it's too late. There's enough gone on already that they're dirty. Once it's proved, they're charged and you're golden."

"That's pretty much what the chief said to me," Doug admitted. "Okay, I know you didn't tell him the whole story but he was anxious to know what I was following up. I explained it to him and he said he could see why I was keeping it quiet. He can see we don't have a case. All we've got is that somebody's being dumb, discounting credit card slips. It's not enough."

"It was enough for him to know you're innocent and get you out of that hole downtown. Now we can work on the rest of it."

Doug smiled at last, a peace offering. "Yeah. You're right. I'm a stubborn SOB. You're right."

Hinton had listened to us attentively. Now he asked, "Well, if it's all out in the open, this thing you were following up, why don't you fill me in?"

Doug looked at him for a long time before speaking. "Why not?" he said at last. "Okay, Pat, this doesn't go outside this office, right?"

"Right." Hinton put down his evidence bags on the table and sat down, slipping out of his topcoat. "Shoot."

"Cat's Cradle is laundering mob money," Doug said. "Period, end of speech."

"An' that's why you and Cindy Laver were close? You weren't balling her?"

"I don't fool around," Doug said. "Yeah. Cindy was my informant. We decided to make it look like a thing, so people wouldn't wonder why we were spending so much time together."

"Are you gonna tell Melody now?" Hinton asked eagerly. "Hell, she can come home now you're out."

"She and the kids are safer where they are," Doug said. "I'm still on bail, kind of house arrest. I wouldn't be able to guard the kids once they were out of the house and those scumbags could come back and snatch one of 'em anytime they want to."

"So what happens now?" I asked. "Do you have to wait for the chief to get back or can you go home?"

"He's going to take me home when he gets back from Cat's Cradle. Meantime he asked me to wait here," Doug said. He took his feet down. "Jesus, I hope this thing can be untangled. I've been in that cell four nights and it felt like forever. I couldn't face going inside for years."

"You're not going back." Hinton beat me to it. I let him talk. But he didn't say a lot more. He just sat and looked at Doug and slapped the table. "You're not going back," he repeated and clamped his mouth shut. He was close to tears. Then he composed himself and asked, "Are you back on the case?"

"No." Doug shook his head. "The chief and the DA said the same thing about that. I'm still suspended, still charged with Cindy Laver's killing. They're waiting for a break in the Grant case, then they'll drop the charge."

"They're making sense," Hinton said. "If you charged somebody, or even assisted in the investigation, a defense attorney'd have a field day. Your word's tainted until this is wound up."

"Yeah," Doug said. He sat with his shoulders hunched, his arms folded, weary.

He needed some space so I took the hint. "I'll get some coffee. Who wants some?"

They both nodded, glad of the diversion, and I wandered downstairs and got three cups. By the time I got back, Hinton was discussing Grant's murder and the emotional temperature was back to normal. Doug was listening but I could tell that he felt outside of himself, like a heart patient listening to the story of somebody else's treatment. He was knotted up tight. All he wanted was freedom, for somebody to come in and tell him he was out of danger, that the case against him had been dropped.

While we were finishing our coffee the phone ran. Hinton answered it and said, "Yessir, he's here with Mr. Bennett and me." He nodded. "Right, Chief. I'll bring him down." He stood up. "The chief's back. He wants you to go down and see him, then he's taking you home."

Doug stood up. "Good."

"One thing I was thinking," I said carefully. "If you're going to let Melody know what's happening, don't phone direct. Phone a cutout and ask them to pass the message. And tell her not to phone home."

Doug looked at me out of troubled eyes. "Christ," he said softly. "I hadn't thought of that. Thanks, Reid."

I sat and waited for about five minutes until Hinton came back on his own. "The chief wants us to check the guys who were with Grant last night," he said. "Let's get to it."

We went first to Lord's house. It was small and neat. There were two cars in the driveway. Hinton knocked and a woman came to the door, a pretty blonde with a harried look. Hinton nodded. "Hello, Marcie, is Will in, please?"

"What's this about?" she demanded.

"Won't take a minute. We just want to talk to him," Hinton said, still smiling his official smile.

"He was here with me all last night," she said.

"Fine. Can we come in, please, or would you rather he stood out here and talked to us where the neighbors can see?"

"Come in," she said angrily.

We stepped inside and Hinton stamped his feet on the mat and stood there. I followed his lead and kept my boots on. This wasn't a social call.

I could hear the TV playing in the living room and Lord's wife went and brought her husband out. He was walking

stiffly with his head held a little to one side, the result of
my bang on the back of his neck, I guessed.

He didn't say anything and Hinton moved in. "I guess
you've heard about young Grant."

"It was on the radio," his wife said.

"Marcie, please." Hinton sounded like an uncle. "This is
going to take a lot longer if you keep answering for him."

"I heard," Lord said. He pointed to me. "Why's he here?
He's not a cop."

"Mr. Bennett has kindly offered to assist the department,"
Hinton said. "He's a homicide specialist from Canada. Now,
tell me, where did you go with Grant after you left the
precinct?"

"We went over to the Glauwein," Lord said. "Mr.
Garfield and Jack and Fred and me."

"And what happened?" Hinton's voice was quiet, setting
Lord up for a sudden change of tone.

"Mr. Garfield bought us a drink and he said he was going
to get this guy here charged and arrested. Then I went
home. The others were still there."

"Who served you your drinks?"

"Millie. You know, the dark girl with the big—" He
glanced at his wife who was watching him coldly. "You
know who I mean."

"And what did you order?"

"I had a beer. The other guys had scotch."

"What time did you leave?"

" 'Bout quarter to ten. It's like a ten-minute walk and
I got home and Marcie was watching the news. It'd just
started."

"And he never went out after that," Marcie said. Her
voice sounded like fingernails on a blackboard.

"When did you go and pick your car up from wherever it
was?" Hinton was still calm. There was no need for anything
else here. Lord was worried but he sounded as if he was
telling the truth.

"It was here all night. Fred picked me up earlier in the

evening and then we switched to Jack's car. That's the one
we were in at Brewskis."

"Okay then. One last question? Did you see what Jack
Grant did with his gun?"

"No." Lord shook his head and then regretted it as the
stiffness struck him. He put one hand on his neck and
glanced at me. "No," he said again. "I saw him put it back
in his pocket when you gave it to him but he din' say anything about it."

"Okay. Thanks for your time," Hinton said. "I may be
back to talk to you again. Don't take any trips."

We went out and Hinton said, "He's telling the truth. His
wife wouldn't let him do anything else. She's a ballbreaker,
that one, always has been. She's the daughter of a neighbor
of mine."

"If she's that hard, how come she let him loose to howl
on a Saturday night? You think he was paid to come after me?"

Hinton was getting into the car and he paused and looked
at me over the roof. "Why didn't I think of that? Makes a
lot of sense. I'll ask the next guy."

He did ask Phillips, the second man we went to see. But
he denied it angrily, swearing at Hinton for the suggestion.
He was single and with no wife to censor his comments he
was more forceful than Lord had been. "I don' have to tell
you nothin'," he said indignantly. " 'specially with this guy
here," indicating me.

Hinton shut him up right away. "You realize you're the
prime suspect, Fred. You were the last guy seen with
Grant."

Phillips looked at him, registering the thought for a moment. Then he said, "No I wasn't. He was still there, at the
Glauwein, talking to the lawyer when I left."

"And where did you go?" Hinton was sneering now.
"You're telling me you walked all the way back here, two
miles? You know what I say to that, Fred. I say bullshit."

Phillips shook his head, anxious to disagree. "No, that's
not how it happened. How it happened was a buddy of mine,

Bill Freeman, he was there. An' when he left he said 'Hi' to me, you know. An' Garfield said, 'I still have to talk to my client, Fred. Will your friend drop you at your car?' "

"How did he know you had a car somewhere? Did you tell him ahead of this?"

Phillips frowned stupidly. "Guess I must've. Anyways, that's what he said, so Bill said 'Sure' an' him and me left the two of 'em there talking."

"Where's your phone?" Hinton demanded.

"In the kitchen. Why?" Phillips blustered.

"What's this guy's number. This good buddy of yours?"

"You gonna call him?" Phillips was shocked, but recovered. "Yeah, well, okay. His number's 555-2122."

Hinton dialed. "Is this Bill Freeman? Good. Detective Pat Hinton, Chambers PD. Listen, Bill, can you tell me if you gave anybody rides last night?"

He listened and said, "And you're sure the car was there?" He waited again and said, "Thank you. 'preciate the assistance."

He hung up and turned to Phillips. "How come you had your car out at Cat's Cradle?"

"That's where we met Jack Grant. He was out there, skiing, I guess. Anyways. He called and said to meet him there so I picked up Will and we went to Cat's Cradle to meet Jack."

Hinton had the obvious question. "What was Grant doing at Cat's Cradle? He doesn't work there."

"I din' ask him. He called me, told me he'd be there so that's where I went."

"You met him in the lot, or inside, in the snack bar?"

"Inside. He was havin' a coffee, talkin' to a guy."

Hinton didn't let his excitement show. "Did you know the guy?"

"Never seen him before." Phillips shrugged. "Hell, there's people skiing at Cat's Cradle from all over. You know how it is."

"Describe him."

Phillips had to think about it. Like most people he was unobservant and embarrassed when questioned. "Well, you know. Nothing special. He was sitting down so I can't be sure but he didn't look big. He had dark hair."

"How was he dressed? Like a skier?"

Phillips blinked. "Could've been a skier, I guess. But he wasn't wearin' ski clothes, not right then. Had a suit on, gray suit, kind of shiny. Good suit."

"Any topcoat, next to him on a chair maybe?" Hinton persisted.

"Yeah, come to think of it. Black topcoat an' a fedora hat. Don't see many guys in fedoras, do you?"

Hinton kept on at him, getting the best description he could, and the more we learned, the more the guy sounded like the man who'd spoken to me the night Angie Ford was kidnapped. I said nothing, and Hinton got all the information he could. Then he told Phillips not to leave town or talk to anybody and to telephone if he saw the man in town.

"You think he done it?" Phillips asked in amazement.

"Let's say we'd like to talk to him," Hinton said. "Right now you're as much a suspect as anybody so keep your nose clean, Fred. We'll be back to you."

When we got to Hinton's car I told him about the resemblance to the hood I'd seen and he nodded grimly. "Everything we hear makes it sound like Doug's right on this one. That guy sounds like a city hood. You don't see nine-hundred-dollar suits in Chambers. The locals don't dress that well, and even the rich skiers dress casual while they're here."

"I'd say he was the likeliest guy to have killed Grant. I spoke to him. He was a mob soldier; he'd do whatever he was told, no questions asked."

"Sounds like our boy okay," Hinton said. "The trick's gonna be finding him so we can have a chat."

He drove in silence and I asked, "Where to now? Garfield?"

"Yeah. And it might make it easier if I talked to him on

my own. He's smooth as silk. He won't give me a goddamn thing if you're there. He'll talk about legal privilege or some bullshit and clam up. He might be easier with me. He knows me from court."

"You're the boss." I would have liked to have been there, watching Garfield's reactions, but I've done enough interrogation to know that you have to play your subject like a fish. If he doesn't want to cooperate, he won't.

And so I sat in the car for five minutes while Hinton went into the big house with its gracious veranda with flower boxes around the rail, all capped with snow now but promising beauty in a few months' time when this town went back to being a quiet little place with nobody in it but locals.

Hinton came out with Garfield behind him. The lawyer stood at the door and looked out at the car and made a comment to Hinton who replied and touched his hat in goodbye.

He got in, tossing his hat onto the seat beside him. "He was pretty upset to see you with me. Asked if the department had to count on criminals for help," he said.

"That figures. Did you get anything useful?"

"*Nada,*" he said. "Says he didn't take the gun off Grant. Says Grant was calm and he didn't see any need to disarm him. He wasn't about to do anything foolish."

"Did he leave him in the Glauwein?"

"No. He says he advised the kid to go home, that he shouldn't drive after drinking. Dropped him off at his house around ten-thirty and went home himself."

"Grant didn't go home. I was there this morning with Maloney. They hadn't seem him all night," I said.

"Exactly." Hinton pulled out of the drive and headed up the street. "Make you wonder whether our good counselor is telling it like it is."

We looked at one another and left it at that. Hinton drove back to the station house and we went in. The same uniformed officer at the desk said, "They're all in the detective office, Pat, the chief, everybody. Said for you to join 'em."

"Thanks." Hinton led the way upstairs and opened the door of the office. Lieutenant Cassidy was standing at one end of the room with a flip chart and a Magic Marker. The chief, Captain Schmidt and Sergeant Detective Morgan were sitting around the two tables.

"Ah, there you are," the chief said. He waved at a couple of chairs. "Steve's just summing up what we've got so far. We'll get to you in a minute."

We sat while Cassidy finished. He hadn't got much, but he had the findings of the autopsy. The doctor's best bet was that Grant had died around midnight but because of the cold weather he could be out by as much as two hours each way. He apparently hadn't eaten in some hours before death but he had alcohol in his blood, enough to suggest he had been drinking earlier in the evening but not a high enough level to make him impaired at the time of death. Also, from the look of the lividity marks, Grant had been dumped where he was found within a few minutes of dying. Cassidy gave us these facts, then went on to talk about the wallet I'd found at the scene. It had been fingerprinted and searched. The only prints found were those of the deceased. He also had a list of the contents of the billfold.

He went over these in detail. A couple of Visa slips, one of them for gasoline. This was being checked with the gas station to see when he had bought it. A phone number which had been checked against the backward phone book which lists numbers sequentially with the names following them. This number belonged to a girl in town. She would be questioned later. Aside from that, he had a driver's license, the ownership paper for his car, a membership for Cat's Cradle and for the gun club and his pistol license. There was no money or credit cards in the wallet.

The chief munched through this for a couple of minutes, assigning Cassidy to check with the girl he'd mentioned and to report back on when the gasoline had been bought. Then he turned to Hinton. "Okay, Pat. What did you find out?"

Hinton took over the flip chart and ran through what we'd

got. He pointed out that Grant's pistol was missing and that he had reportedly been seen last at the driveway of his house at ten-thirty. "At that time he had ingested three scotches within three quarters of an hour. That suggests that his blood alcohol would have been considerably higher than it was in the postmortem. It suggests that he wasn't killed before midnight."

Cassidy took over, looking at the chief first. "He may have put the gun in his glove compartment."

"Not if he went straight home. His car was at Brewskis," Pat countered. "Maybe he left it at home and went out again."

"I was at his home this morning with Mr. Maloney," I said. "His father told us that the guy hadn't been home. Assuming the parents were still up at ten-thirty, that means he didn't go back there. He must have gone on somewhere else after Mr. Garfield dropped him off."

"Any chance that Garfield's lying?" Schmidt asked. He was avoiding talking to me but he dropped the obvious question on Hinton who shrugged. "Could be, Captain. But he isn't going to change his story to me. Maybe a senior officer should talk to him."

The chief said, "Right. I'll go over there myself. Anything else?"

"Yessir," Hinton said. "According to Fred Phillips who was with him after he was released from custody last night, he'd picked Grant up from the company of a snappy dresser, guy in good city clothes, in the snack bar of Cat's Cradle."

"Any description of the guy?" the chief asked.

"Not very accurate. But Reid says he sounds like the same man he spoke to the night Doug Ford's daughter was abducted. Reid." He turned it over to me.

"This man was five-six, one-sixty, about thirty-two years old. Latin appearance, New York area accent. I'm no expert, could have been Brooklyn, New Jersey, something like that. But he was wearing the same kind of hat and coat that Phillips described."

"Ring any bells with anybody?" the chief asked and all the others shook their heads. I waited. They were allowing me to join the investigation but there were some big egos in the room. Cassidy and Schmidt both resented my presence. I didn't want to make things worse by coming up with half-baked notions.

When nobody answered the chief said, "I'll go over to talk to Garfield, then to the Grant's, ask them if I can look through his room. See if the gun's there. Meantime, let's look for this New Yorker and for Grant's car. Pat, you and Mr. Bennett get on that. Also, take a run back to Phillips' place, see if he can add anything to the description of the guy in the suit."

"Yes sir." Hinton was ready to go but I still had a question. "One thing, Chief. I guess you've already checked it, but I'd like to know, please. What time does the ski lift stop running at Cat's Cradle?"

The chief pursed his lips. "Yeah. I checked that. It closes at ten o'clock. The ski patrol take a last run down all the slopes and they put the lights off then."

"Is the lift house locked up at night?"

"Yes." He was too professional to be angered by my question. "I've already been over this with the other officers, before you got here. It's locked but it's a Mickey Mouse lock. You could open the door with a credit card." He waved one hand dismissively. "You don't need anything more. We're a law-abiding town, normally."

Cassidy jumped in now. "And just for your information, Reid, or should I say Chief, we've sent the fingerprint guy out there. He's dusting the lock and the lift controls and he's also checking each car in turn for bloodstains. If he finds any he's going to print the car."

"Reid's fine," I said evenly. "Thank you, Lieutenant." I could see he was going to do whatever he could to make me look small. He was jealous of his own rank and the integrity of his town's department. Most cops would be the same way. I didn't expect any friendship.

"Anything else?" the chief asked. He was almost as resentful as Cassidy but covered it better.

"The only thing I wondered is, how hard is it to operate the lift? Should we be looking for someone who knows how to do it or is there a simple on-off switch?"

"It's simple. A kid could do it," Cassidy said. "That was the first thing we looked at."

"Good." I gave him a big smile. "It's a pity, but now we know the guy who dropped him off that chair could have done it alone." I wasn't going to be intimidated. "The only question left is, why did they go to the trouble of dumping him on the slopes? They could have dropped the body anywhere, left him in his car, anything. But they took the extra risk and trouble of lugging him up to the gondola lift and turning it on while they dumped him. Anybody got any ideas?"

They looked at one another and shook their heads. So I gave them my own theory. "The only reason that makes sense is that they're trying to scare the management of Cat's Cradle. The publicity won't do the place any good, will it?"

"You still think young Huckmeyer's involved in this?" the chief asked slowly.

"There's a connection. Huckmeyer was at Brewskis when I got there. I rubbed him up the wrong way and he made a phone call. Next thing I know, Grant and his buddies are waiting to beat me up."

"This is all coincidence," Schmidt said. His face was even more florid this morning. He looked as if he had spent the night with his old pal Jack Daniel's.

"It would be worth asking the help at the coffee shop at Cat's Cradle whether anybody called on the phone for Grant last night."

" 've you been in that place?" Schmidt demanded. "Hell, they must have a couple hundred people in there, different people all the time. It's not some private club where you can get a guy paged."

"I've been there. But Grant was a member at the place.

He's a local. The help probably knew him. It wouldn't be like trying to find a stranger."

"Worth a shot," the chief said doubtfully. "Fred, you take a run out there, find out who was working last night, ask them about the phone call and if they saw anybody with Grant."

"Will do," Schmidt said. He looked angry, the way you look when you know you've goofed and other people are aware of it.

He stood up. "I'll get on it right now," he said and the meeting was over.

Hinton was anxious to defuse the tension. "We'll get back to Phillips', Chief," he said. "Let's go, Reid."

We got nothing there. Phillips said he had waited in the car outside, listening to the radio. We thanked him and left.

"Not a lot else to do but search for the car," Hinton said. "I guess we'll check the center of town first, then just drive around the streets and look for it."

"How about we divide and conquer? If you drop me at Maloney's house I'll pick up my car and take a section of town."

"Okay. We're not joined at the hip," Hinton said. "Where's Maloney live?"

I directed him and he dropped me off. Maloney's car was not there and I didn't have a key to the house so I had to leave Sam inside and drive away. Hinton had given me the north end of the town with a rendezvous in an hour's time at a restaurant in the main square. He drove off and turned left at the main street. I followed a minute later and turned right.

If I hadn't been on business it would have been a very pleasant drive. The town was quiet and pretty. The houses looked like something off a Christmas card and I slipped back into remembering the town I grew up in. It was a mining town in Ontario, nowhere near so pretty as this, all the trees stunted from the relentless acid rain from the smelter stacks. But the snow was the same, and the few kids on the street were playing hockey with the same intensity.

I was half lost in my memory when I saw a familiar car parked in front of a house at the end of a long street, under a maple. The sight snapped me back to the present. I pulled in behind it and got out of my car.

The driver wound the window down and looked up at me. "Doug," I said. "I thought you were supposed to be staying home."

"I'm a cop," he said grimly. "Even with my badge lying in the chief's top drawer. They can't stop me thinking."

"What are you doing here?"

"My job," he said softly. "Grant's car is parked in the next driveway."

He was right. The Oldsmobile was there, driven up to the front of the garage as if Grant lived there. I didn't approach it but went back to Doug Ford. "Yeah, that's his car. How did you know it was here?"

"They all should have known," Doug said. "Wendy Tate lives here. She's one of his women. Was one of his women, I guess."

"How did you know his car was missing?"

"I didn't," Doug said. "I just figured I'd talk to some of his old girlfriends, see if any of them knew anything. This was the first place I came to."

"Have you knocked at the door?"

"Nobody home," he said. He seemed angry at having to say anything. "I figured as long as I was here I should stick around until she got back."

"Look, Doug. I'm glad you found the car but the chief's right. If you get involved in this case it's gonna blow it for the defense on your own problem. I'll go find a phone and call for Pat Hinton. When he gets here, you should be gone."

"Right." He sounded savage now. "Make sure the white boys get the credit."

He started winding the window up but I grabbed the door

and opened it. "Listen, Doug. You don't have to give me this crap. This isn't about black and white. This is about homicide, goddamn it. I thought you were a cop, not a Black Panther."

"I'm going home," he said. "You do what the hell you like."

I let go of the door and he slammed it shut. I waited while he made a three-point turn in the roadway and drove back out, moving slowly as if his tension was so high he was afraid to put his foot down. I watched him go, then went up to the house. It seemed quiet but with all the doors and windows shut, who could tell. I pressed the bell. Nobody answered and I tried again, then turned away.

There was a garage beside the house, an old frame building, big enough for one car. The snow was clear in front of it, looking as if the owner used it every day. I wondered if her car was in there and she was at home, ignoring my ringing. Idly I turned the handle and swung the door up a couple of feet. It moved easily and the momentum from my tug carried it up and over my head so I could see inside. One look was all I needed. There was a body on the floor, a woman, wearing blue stretch pants and a many-colored down jacket. She was lying on her back and I could see a dark stain on the front of the coat, around the heart.

I didn't need to check her pulse. Her eyes were wide and her mouth was hanging open. There was a thread of dried blood from one corner of the mouth running down her jaw onto the collar of her coat.

Carefully I backed out and closed the garage door. She had been dead some hours, maybe all night, I knew that. Doug had been locked in his cell at that time. But he had come here today and I wondered whether he had touched the handle. If he had, he would be hard put to explain it away. Knowing I might be destroying evidence I did what I had to, wiping my gloved hand over the handle until anything on it would have been smeared beyond recognition. Next I did the same thing with the front door bell and the knocker. Only then did I drive to the nearest phone and call the police department.

Hinton got to me first but before he was even out of the car Captain Schmidt was pulling in behind him. Schmidt did the talking. "Where's the body?"

"In the garage, Captain."

He opened the door, touching the handle very lightly so

as not to disturb any prints. He went and crouched by the woman. "Been dead awhile," he said. Then he stood up. "How come you were snooping around in here?"

"When I found Grant's car I rang the doorbell. There wasn't any answer so I checked the garage to see if there was a car here and whoever was inside was ignoring me."

"Is that standard practice up among the Eskimos?"

"It's called checking your options. You'd have done the same thing."

He snorted and turned to Hinton. "Get on the radio. Call the hospital, have them send the ME over, and get Wilkins down here with his camera and crime scene kit."

Hinton ran back to his car and Schmidt turned back to the body.

"Do you know who she is, Captain?" I kept it polite.

He nodded. "Yeah. Her name's Wendy Tate. She's divorced, works at the drugstore in town. Hear tell she had round heels, the kind of broad Grant would've known."

"Was it her phone number in his wallet?"

Schmidt shook his head, crouching by the body. "No. We checked that place. Neighbor says she's gone to Mexico for a couple weeks, left last Saturday."

I crouched with him. He was touching the front of the coat, probing the bloodstain with his forefinger. "Feels like a couple holes, small," he said. "Here, try."

It was amateur, messing around with evidence with your fingertips, so I didn't do it. "Take your word for it, Captain. Could it be small-caliber pistol shots?" I said.

"Could be. What caliber was that gun of his?"

"A .22 automatic. Could have been the murder weapon."

"I'll talk to the ME about testing Grant's hand for powder traces," Schmidt said.

"Won't tell us a whole lot. He fired the gun earlier, at my dog."

He snorted. "In that case," he said and left it there.

A car pulled in behind us and the chief got out. He came

up and looked at the body, not bothering to crouch. "Who found her?"

"I did, Chief."

He asked me how and I told him what I'd said to Schmidt. He looked at me angrily. "I've been chief here for eleven years. In all that time we've had one homicide. Then suddenly we get three inside a week." It was my fault, he was saying.

"This must be tied in with the Grant death. Captain Schmidt says there are holes in the coat, maybe bullet holes, small caliber."

"Any sign of a weapon?" He was speaking to Schmidt and I could see he wanted me gone. I was a jinx, a blight on his town.

Schmidt said, "Haven't looked for it. Can't see it lying around and I want Wilkins to get photographs before I start turning the place over."

The two of them looked at one another and I could see something like a plea in Schmidt's face. The chief read it and he turned to me gravely. "Can you come with me, please?" he asked and led the way back to his car. I went with him and he spoke softly. "I don't know how to put this, but you're a chief yourself, you know the pressures of the job."

I said nothing and he glanced away then back at me. "The thing is, my men are good men and they're resentful that you're here. I know you want to help. I know you're an experienced man. But I'd like it if you would back off and give my guys some space."

An honest speech. I knew he would back it up with authority if he had to. His department's morale came ahead of me. But I didn't want it to come ahead of Doug Ford's case. I compromised with him. "I understand. And I appreciate what you've done for Doug. I think you can see now that he was on to something and somebody framed him."

"That's why I had him released," he said carefully. "I

don't think the charge will stand much longer. He was obviously right in his assumption that something heavy is going down right here in Chambers. But right now I'm up to my ass in alligators and I have to get the best out of my troops. I can't do that with you looking over their shoulders."

"Okay, I'm through with Grant and this girl's death. But while you're busy with this investigation, do I have your permission to keep on checking into the Laver murder?"

"Sure," he said. "Ask around all you want. If you get any hassle from anybody, refer them to me. But stay away from my guys. Could you do that?"

"Okay. I'd like your permission to talk to you if I come up with something that makes a difference."

"You've got it. And you've got my permission to check the crime scene, talk to witnesses, conduct the investigation all over again if you want to." He reached up and stroked his nose, something he probably did whenever he was thinking hard. "It would give me the greatest pleasure to find something that cleared Officer Ford. He's efficient and quick and good. He's a credit to the department and I want him back. See what you can do to get him out of this mess and you'll have my gratitude as well as his."

"I'll tell him that. Thanks, Chief." I went back to my car and drove off, back to Maloney's house first. His car was there and I went in and found him in the kitchen, working a pasta-making machine. Sam was lying under the table and he got up and came over to me, wagging his tail. I bent down and fussed him before doing anything else. Maloney watched in approval.

"He's a great dog," he said, then, "How's the investigation going?" He was cranking the handle and turning out broad strings of lasagna.

"There's been another victim. Woman called Wendy Tate. Looks as if she was shot with Grant's gun."

He straightened up and looked at me, openmouthed. "When did this happen?"

"I found her, half an hour ago. She's been dead all night, in her garage. Grant's car's in the drive."

"What the hell's going on?" he wondered out loud.

"I'm not sure, but the chief was getting some heat from Captain Schmidt so he asked me to back out, which I've done. I'm concentrating on the Laver killing, with the chief's permission."

He wasn't really listening. "Wendy Tate. She was friendly with a lot of men. Digging into her past is going to rattle a lot of cages in town."

"That's about what Schmidt said. I didn't think about the domestic angle on the investigation. Maybe some guys are going to be embarrassed today."

"That's for sure." Maloney turned back to his pasta machine and fed another chunk of dough into the hopper. "So what will you do next?"

"They've sprung Doug Ford. He's under house arrest. Has to stay home. I'd like to go over and spend some time with him. He's pretty shook up."

"I understand." He nodded and went back to turning the handle on the machine. "Are you going to move in with him?"

"Might be better if I did. I hope you don't think I'm being ungrateful but he needs some support."

"Of course," he said. "Can he stretch the house arrest far enough to come over here for dinner? Ella Frazer will be here. Might make him feel better."

"I'll suggest it, thank you. But he's pretty fragile right now. He's been stuck in solitary for four days. That messes up your head."

"Play it by ear," Maloney suggested. He gathered up his lasagna and started cutting it into lengths. Maybe he figured I was feeling awkward, because he chatted on. "I took a cooking course after my wife died. Out of necessity at first but I've gotten to like it."

"Something I've never had the patience for, even when I was living on my own," I said politely.

He finished his cutting and laid the knife aside. "Okay. So, what can I do to help your investigation?"

"I'm not sure, at the moment. The chief knows something about Doug's suspicions. Enough to make him think Doug was right and to get him out of jail." A thought occurred to me, remembering how messed up Ms. Frazer had been. "Is that going to complicate your talking to Ms. Frazer?"

"No. I'll tell Ella. She'll be easier in her mind, knowing that it's out in the open now." He took a plate and laid the lasagna strips on it carefully. "I've been thinking since I got back here."

He looked up, waiting for a cue to continue, and I said, "What about particularly?"

"Firstly, I thought that even if we bring this money thing into the open, it doesn't do anything to clear Officer Ford. The homicide is a different investigation. All we can do is dig up a separate motive from the one the police had thought of in the first place."

"Right. I want to go into the case itself. You and the police are better equipped to investigate money-laundering anyway."

"Right. But the other thing was deeper than that."

"What was it?"

He looked at me, then bent to load more lasagna on the plate as he talked. "I was wondering, with a lawyer's perverse mind, just why Officer Ford kept his suspicions to himself, even to the extent of going to jail for a murder he obviously didn't commit."

"He was afraid for his family's safety. For himself, he wouldn't have cared about them—but when you have a wife and kids, it's different." I said. "Are you saying you suspect him of the killing?" Sam was butting his head against my knee, gaining contact after twenty-four hours of confusion about what was going on. I stroked his head absently and waited for Maloney to continue.

"No. He's innocent of the killing, I believe, and the money business doesn't seem to involve him in any way. I just asked myself what he was trying to do and why he was trying to do it."

He looked at me and I checked his face to see if it had the smugness that many lawyers show when they bring out a damaging idea. But it didn't. He looked genuinely concerned and I was certain that he was still rooting for Doug.

"I've had the same thoughts, I guess. I plan to talk to him about it," I said.

Maloney turned away to wipe his hands on a tea towel that was hanging on the handle of the stove. "Good. I wish you luck, Reid. I think your friend is innocent but the prosecution is going to ask the same question I just did. We need to know in plenty of time just what his motives were."

"I'll tell him that. And thanks for all you've done for me," I said and we shook hands and I collected my bag and left with Sam trotting gratefully at my heel.

I got to Doug's house and knocked. He came to the door, looking angry. He didn't speak to me and I asked, "Thought you'd like some company. Can I come in?"

He still didn't speak but stood back and held the door open. Sam was at my heel and I made the second request. "Okay if Sam comes in? He's family. And Melody didn't mind."

"Sure," he said and we went in and he shut the door.

I hadn't brought my bag with me. That would come later, if the atmosphere warmed up at all.

As I was slipping my boots off Doug asked angrily, "Where's my gun?"

"Melody gave it to me the night Angie was kidnapped."

"I asked where is it, now?" he said.

"It's in my car. I'll give it to you."

That seemed to appease him. He didn't say anything but turned away into the kitchen. "Sit down," he said over his shoulder. "Want some coffee?"

"Be good, thank you," I said carefully. This wasn't the man I knew, the guy who had humped through the boonies with me, taking risks without a second thought, a man I had counted on as I would have on my own brother if I'd ever had one.

He brought two cups, black, and I thanked him and we sat looking at one another.

He didn't speak and I could see no way into the conversation that wouldn't spark his anger so I drank coffee and waited for him to make the going. At last he said, "What did she say? Wendy Tate?"

"She was dead. In the garage; looked like she'd been shot but she could have been knifed like Grant was."

Now his police professionalism took him out of himself. "Go on."

I told him about the blood and the way Schmidt had touched the stain.

Doug hissed with contempt. "Goddamn Boy Scout. What's that going to prove?" He was still consumed with anger, but now it had a focus. That made it easier to deal with.

"He gave the chief the evil eye and the chief's asked me to step out of the investigation. He's given me permission to go over the Cindy Laver case, but he doesn't want me underfoot while his guys are trying to sort out what's happening with Grant and this woman."

"They haven't had a homicide here since Pluto was a pup," Doug said. "None of the guys has any idea what to do, outside of courses they've taken. They could use a pro."

"Pat Hinton seems capable."

"Pat's fine, but he hasn't covered any homicides. None of them have."

He was simmering down now. We were a couple of Marines again, cursing an incompetent officer. I milked it. "Reminds me of that Lieutenant Harris. Remember that sonofabitch?"

Now Doug looked at me with more warmth. He took another sip of his coffee and set the cup aside. "Okay, Reid. Like, I'm sorry, man. You left your family behind to come down here and save my sorry ass an' all I can do is give you shit. I'm sorry, buddy."

It was a time to do some kidding. "Didn't expect anything else. You always were a crabby bastard."

He laughed then and we stood up and shook hands first, then impulsively hugged one another. We let go and I said, "Is it part of your bail that you can't drink?"

He shook his head. "No, that wasn't mentioned."

"Good. I've got a bottle of Black Velvet in my bag."

He clapped his hands together. "So go get it in, an' bring your bag. You're staying here, aren't you?"

"I'd planned on it." I went out and got my bag, dropping it at the base of the stairs and taking out the bottle I'd picked up at the duty-free store at the border. Doug got glasses and ice and built us a couple of drinks and we toasted one another. "Semper fi," I said and he echoed it.

I don't usually drink until closer to dinner, but it went down well and Doug relaxed. He asked me about Fred and the baby and we didn't mention the case for the time it took to finish the drink. I offered another one but he shook his head. "Later maybe. Hey, did you eat yet?"

When I told him no he went into the kitchen and made us a couple of sandwiches and we had them with a beer, slowly getting back to talking about the case. I told him about the beer cans and my suspicion that Huckmeyer had picked up his empty from Brewskis and planted it. "We could clear you right away if we got prints from the waitress and the bartender at Brewskis and checked them against the other prints on the can," I suggested.

"Think those two'll go for that?" he asked seriously. "They don't have to give you diddly."

"I get on well with the bartender and the waitress. I cooled Grant out one night when he groped the waitress."

"Maybe they'd do it, then," Doug said. "Hell, they wouldn't do it for me. They didn't care for me and Cindy looking like we were playing nice. Too white bread to let it show but they were worried about the purity of the goddamn race."

"That's one way of looking at it," I said. "But there's also the fact that you happen to be married to the best-looking woman in town and everybody knows it."

He looked almost sad then. "You think that's it?"

"I'm sure of it. People don't like to see marriages going down the tubes."

Doug smiled slowly. "I guess that's it, but I've got to tell you there were a lot of heads whipped around in a hurry when I came here. Seems like the brothers don't ski. Folks here had never seen a black face except on TV. When I walk into the room everybody does a double take."

"Trust me. They're not racist. I'll take a run out to Brewskis this evening and see when I can get prints off those two women. I doubt they're working Sunday if they were there all week."

"Good," he said. He was quiet now, thoughtful. "It's liable to clear me of the homicide but not of theft of that money."

"George Horn, an Ojibway friend of mine, the son of my deputy, has a saying that applies here. He says, if you see fifty ducks take off and you fire at all of them you'll miss. You have to shoot one duck at a time."

"Makes sense," Doug said. "Yeah. He's right."

I looked at him a long time before speaking. "Doug, I've got a question to ask. It's liable to get you mad so I want you to know that any cop would ask the same question. Can I go ahead?"

"Shoot," he said and took a big bite of his sandwich as if to gag himself and not have to answer.

"You didn't tell the chief about your investigation. I'm not talking about when you were arrested, I mean before that. And yet now you're ready to talk. People are going to want to know why. Can you tell me, as a friend?"

He chewed slowly and then spoke, very softly. "You're wondering why I was keeping all this to myself, not telling even Melody."

I nodded without speaking and he went on. "All right. I told you about my partner in Harlem. That was true. But there's more than that."

"I figured there had to be."

"Yeah. Well. The thing is, I knew that guy, that Manatelli." He fell silent for a while and I waited, seeing how easily I could snuff out the news he was going to give me. "Thing is, his son, kid called Gino, was in school with Melody."

He fell silent again and this time I had to prod him. "And then what?" I asked gently.

"And she was the best-looking girl in school. Just like she's the best-looking woman in town here. All the kids were after her. The brothers thought she should have gone out with them on account of being black. But she went out with Gino."

He looked at me for a long time. "Now I ought to be glad about what happened because if it hadn't she wouldn't have married me." He set down his plate. "Anyway, by the time she was in college, the only black kid in her class to make it, she and Gino were an item. He wanted to marry her."

Most people have romances in their past. It would have been surprising if a woman as beautiful as Melody were an exception, I thought, but waited. Doug went on in the same low, passionate voice. "So young Gino, the goddamn hood in training, he goes to his old man and says he wants to marry her. And that lowlife hood scumbag tells him, and I'm quoting, 'No son of mine is going to marry any goddamn nigger.' "

"He's an ignorant prick," I said.

"Yeah," Doug said, in a low growl. "And I'm gonna teach him some manners. That's why I was working on my own. I don't care whether the case ever comes to court. I want the news to get back to the guy he's working for. They won't sue the bastard. They'll settle him for keeps."

didn't answer right away.
Doug was too full of anger to want anything but approval
and I couldn't give him that. Not that I care for organized
criminals. The grief they cause outweighs the Catholic cer-
tainty my mother tried to drum into me that we ought to
love our enemies. I don't love mobsters but I believe in
justice. Death is too severe a punishment for an insult, however hurtful.

Doug spoke first. "You think I'm wrong?"

It called for a careful answer. "Not exactly. I think you're
right, for the wrong reasons."

"The reason don't matter," he said harshly. "Think about
it, man. I get off the murder rap, maybe even the theft rap
as well. But Manatelli isn't going to go away. That's why
his guys picked up young Angie. The only way to get him
off my back is to get his boss mad at him. That way the
whole thing is cleared up and there's no comebacks."

"I know, that's what makes you right. But setting out to
get Manatelli iced, that's nasty."

"I don't have any alternatives now. Too much is going

down." He set his empty plate aside. "That's why I opened up to the chief this morning." He snorted a little laugh. "I should've done it right off. Like I know this department. Subtle they ain't. I figure if they start stomping around looking for evidence on the money-laundering they'll set off alarm bells from here to Newark. Mucci's gonna hear what Manatelli's doing and take care of business back there."

"You think Mucci will settle it and leave you alone?"

Doug shrugged. "Why not? He'll just see cops finding out things about laundering money. If it's his money I've got trouble. But I don't think it's his. The figures are too small. It's Manatelli's skimming. I think Mucci will see that and plug the leak in his money by canceling Manatelli's check."

"But hold on now." I stuck one finger in the air. "He won't have to dig far to see you're at the back of this. In fact they already know you are. That's why they snatched Angie."

"I figure that was Manatelli's palace guard," Doug said. "They work for Mucci but they take their orders from Manatelli." He shrugged. "It was the same with us. All us grunts worked for the president of the U.S. of A. but we took orders from whatever shavetail they put in charge."

It made sense and I nodded. "Okay then. So let's think about this Grant killing. Why would they knife him and throw his body on the slopes of Cat's Cradle?"

"Orders from Manatelli," Doug said without hesitation. "I guess he figured Huckmeyer wasn't fulfilling his commitment to keep the operation quiet. He wanted Huckmeyer to know he isn't dealing with the Knights of Columbus."

"But killing Grant is a bit heavy for that. Surely they'd have gone to Huckmeyer and stuck a gun in his ear just to remind him."

Doug had the obvious answer. "Grant must have done something to make them think he was going to open up. They wanted him quiet. They did it their usual way. And leaned on Huckmeyer at the same time."

"Okay. I can buy that. But I guess I should bring you

up to speed on what's been happening since I came to see you yesterday. Like for instance, Will Lord saw Grant talking to a guy who sounds to me like the one who snatched Angie. This was before Grant and his buddies came to Brewskis to jump me."

"Planning to jump you? I know something went on. You said Maloney got you out of a jam. But what in hell did happen?"

I took a couple of minutes to fill him in and he listened, asking careful questions until he was up to date on all the events of the last twenty-four hours. Then he said, "Maybe they were ticked off when Grant didn't do like they'd planned. But how did they know? Unless this guy he was talking to followed him to Brewskis and saw what went down."

"Maybe he did, but I doubt it. My guess is that somebody filled him in after."

"Wendy Tate," Doug said slowly. "I'll bet this guy had picked her up. It didn't take much. Then, he was at her place and Grant came over and he heard what had happened."

"Makes sense, if this Wendy Tate was that kind of woman. But why kill her?"

Doug threw up his hands. "Maybe she heard more than the guy wanted. Maybe she got antsy when it looked like this mob guy was going to kill Grant. Maybe he even killed Grant right there in front of her and had to shut her up. Who knows? But it all holds water."

"There's one other thing," I said, remembering what Maloney had told me. "I heard that Grant was a gambler. A couple of times he'd lost big. Once he sold his car overnight to pay the tab. Second time his father had an out-of-season discount sale at the store to raise cash. Maybe he was in Dutch again and this time they offered him the chance of paying his debt by chasing me out of town. When he screwed up they came after him for payment."

Doug stood up and walked to the window, staring out blankly at the snow while he thought. "There's a million maybes. I'm just wondering if the guys in the department will think of them."

I sat where I was, trying to be the voice of reason. "So what if they don't? What can I do to steer them right?"

We talked it over for an hour, not getting any closer to a solution. The best we could come up with, now that the chief had asked me to remove myself from the investigation, was to pass our ideas on to Pat Hinton and have him bring them up in the daily progress meetings the detectives would hold until the case was cleared up. When we'd resolved all that I said, "Okay, so if I'm going to help clear you of the Cindy Laver murder, I need to know exactly what happened between you that night. Like why was she angry? The waitress said you seemed to be having a fight."

"She was scared," he said.

"Suddenly? She'd been going along with you for a couple of weeks. Why was she scared then? Had someone threatened her?"

"Yeah. She told me that someone had left her a note. It said 'We don't like you playing around with that cop. You'll be healthier if you stop.' "

"Did you see the note?"

"No. She didn't even tell me about it for the first hour. That's why we were arguing. She told me it was over, she wasn't going along with it anymore."

"Yet she still went to Brewskis with you. She didn't tell you this when you met her?"

Doug looked miserable. "This is the bit that eats me up, Reid. When I met her she was all for saying goodbye there and then. I managed to calm her down some and get her to agree to come for a drink. If I hadn't, she would never have been murdered. I've thought about that every minute since they came and told me she was killed."

"That's just punishing yourself. They may have been waiting to kill her anyway. But in any case, you figured she was just sore, so you kept on like this was a normal night?"

He held up one hand, finger and thumb apart. "I was this close to finding out where the money came from to buy those credit card slips. Hell, Reid. You know what it's like when you're on a case and it starts to break your way."

"Why hadn't she told you already? Surely it would be a matter of record in her office. If she was going to tell you, she could have told you right off."

"She never got to see the records of where it came from. The money was delivered by a cash courier service. It was always accepted by Huckmeyer and he signed the receipt slip for the money. But he was planning to be out of town that Friday. There was a meeting of some ski group. She'd told me about it and we both knew this was her chance to get into his files and find out where the money was coming from."

"Then what? Were you planning to go there and investigate? What good would that have done?"

"No." He had trouble containing his tension and he stood up and went over to the window. "No. I was going to get the message to Mucci. Let him know that Manatelli was shipping in money to this place from wherever. Once I knew where it was coming from it would have given Mucci proof that the cash wasn't his. That would have been the end of Manatelli, the end of the whole business."

I waited so long before answering that he turned to look at me, wondering. Then I said, "That's not police work, Doug. That's no better than the mob."

"Don't preach at me," he shouted. "You know how god-damn far you get as a cop fighting them legally. Nowhere, that's how far. By the time they've bought the judges and frightened the juries they walk, all of them, always. They walk right back onto the street and round up more little kids to peddle their asses. And they go on, driving their Cadillacs, balling their high-priced women."

"This isn't a movie. This is real life. The only thing we've got going for us is the law. I know how the lawmakers and the judges and the bleeding hearts screw things up for the police. Hell, I've been a cop as long as you have. But you don't stop them with death squads or by getting them killing one another."

He was about to shout again but instead he controlled himself and sat down, rigidly, on a kitchen chair. "Okay, Mr. Bennett," he said softly. "What would you do instead?"

"I'd call in whoever's needed, FBI, I guess, and have them investigate the operations of the bank. It takes longer but all the *t*'s are crossed and the *i*'s dotted. They make their case, or even if they don't, there's enough mud flies that word of it gets back to Manatelli, maybe even to Mucci. It could be that the outcome is the same. Manatelli sleeps with the fishes. But at least I'd be able to sleep nights without feeling as much of a scumbag as he is."

His voice was just as low. "This isn't personal with you."

"You can't afford to let it get personal. If it gets down to one on one, we can tackle it the way we tackled Charlie in Nam. You kill him or he kills you. But you don't hate everybody with the wrong shape eyes."

"You've had it too soft, living in Canada," he said. "You should've come back to a war zone, same as I did in Harlem. Then you'd have known what crime is all about. It's not about some guy fishing out of season or failing to stop at an intersection. It's about welfare mothers hooked on crack, blowing their goddamn food stamps while their kids go hungry."

I waved my hand in dismissal. "You may be right, but there's a time for philosophy and there's a time for getting things done. Right now what matters is clearing you of the charges against you. First the murder. Then the money. After that we handle the big things. Okay?"

He was still sure he was right, still angry. But he bit off his reply and said, "All right."

"Fine. Then the first thing I want to do is to go check the crime scene. It may not turn anything up but it's step one. Then tomorrow I'll get the prints of the women at the bar, compare them with the beer can found in the garbage. I'll get on it now."

"Whatever you say," he said in a deadly flat voice. "I'll sit here and wait like a good little citizen."

I nodded and got up. "See you later."

"Sure," he said and I put my parka on and whistled Sam and went out to my car.

Cindy Laver's landlady was a stout little woman wearing a good blue dress that looked like it was her Sunday uniform. It took ten minutes of waiting on her doorstep while she phoned the chief but at last she let me in and showed me up to the flat where Cindy Laver had lived and died.

She came with me, talking the whole time. "It's horrible. I count on the rent from this place to supplement my pension. Nobody's ever going to rent it now. I can't even open it up yet anyway. The police haven't finished with it. I don't know what I'm going to do."

I wasn't really paying attention but just to be agreeable I said, "Rent it by the week to skiers. You can charge more and they won't know its history." We had come in through the front door and up her main staircase. If it was the only entrance the case against Doug looked that much blacker. "Is this the only way in?" I asked.

"Yes," she said firmly. She unlocked the door and bustled in ahead of me. She intended to stay there the whole time, talking, I could see that.

"Mrs. Tibbet, I'd like to examine the place in boring detail if you don't mind. I'm a trained investigator and I won't damage anything. I wonder could you let me stay here alone please."

"Are you ordering me out of my own house?" Her hackles were rising.

"Nothing so bad-mannered, I hope. It's just that I have to concentrate very hard and your presence will be a distraction."

This made her almost respectful. "Are you a psychic?"

"No, I'm an ordinary homicide detective from another jurisdiction. After I'm through I'd very much like to talk to you at length. Perhaps I could take you for a cup of coffee or something."

"Oh, I have coffee," she said. "I'll go put the pot on. Come on down when you're through."

"Thank you, ma'am. You're very understanding." I gave her a big, sunny smile and stood while she backed out reluctantly, then closed the door behind her. Score one for my silver tongue.

When she'd gone I stood for a minute in the room, Cindy Laver's living room, getting a feel for the dead woman's life and tastes. She hadn't furnished the place, that was evident, but the pictures were hers, I was sure. They were art posters. One was a gaudy poster from an exhibition of Fauvist painting, whatever that is, at the Metropolitan Museum in New York. Another was from some other gallery, Monet's water lilies. There was a book on the coffee table, more art, the Impressionists. A woman with taste, obviously.

The investigators hadn't disturbed things. There was a trace of fingerprint powder around the light switch but the couch was untouched. The cushion at one end of the couch was dinted as if someone had just gotten up from sitting there. No doubt it had been photographed but nobody had sat down since the night she was killed. Perhaps she and Doug had been the last people here, sitting arguing while downstairs Mrs. Tibbet strained her ears.

Acting on instinct, I sat down, at the right-hand end, the one where there was no cushion, the place a man would have sat. Also on instinct, I slid my fingers down the side of the couch. I was right; there were coins there, a sure sign that a man had sat here before and money had tipped out of his pocket. I probed deeper, squeezing my weight down to widen the crack, and then my fingers encountered something else. It was a pocketknife.

I got up and went through to the bedroom closet and got

a wire coat hanger. There were a number of them, one with
the plastic sheet still draped on it. I brought it through,
slipping the sheet off the hanger and setting it on the coffee
table. Then I bent the hanger into a hook and sat down,
scrunching my weight on the end of the seat again, and
probed in the gap with the folded hanger until I managed
to fish out the knife. It was a small, expensive pocketknife
with a little shield set into its bone handle. I bent closer and
looked at the shield but my run of luck was over. It had
nothing on it.

I laid the plastic wrap on the couch and flicked the knife
onto it with the hanger, then I bundled the sheet around
the knife and knotted it, making a clear evidence bag. Jack
Grant had worked in a hardware store. He would have carried a pocketknife and this was a good one, the kind he'd
have picked up from choice from the display in the store.
But it still didn't mean he had killed Cindy Laver. Chances
are he wouldn't have sat on the couch that night, not if he'd
come to murder her, but finding the knife diffused the case
against Doug and that was valuable.

I searched the rest of the apartment, finding nothing, except for the one fact that Mrs. Tibbet hadn't told me. There
was a fire escape from the kitchen window. It was a black-
painted iron staircase that led all the way to the ground, the
kind of fire precaution you find only in small towns where
there isn't the fear of burglary that stops most big-city fire
escapes a whole floor above the ground, with a drop ladder
for the last ten feet. I wondered if it had been checked as
carefully as the rest of the apartment and made a note to
ask the chief. To save discussion with Mrs. Tibbet about my
evidence I used the escape to go down and put the knife in
my car, taking a moment to fuss Sam. Then I went back up
and wiped my feet carefully free of snow before climbing
back through the window and going downstairs for coffee.

I didn't learn much from my talk, except that Mrs. Tibbet
had been upset by Doug's presence. Not because he was
black, she insisted, but because he was married to that nice

Melody who was so wonderful at the library and such a pretty girl. And such nice kids, etc. I nursed the conversation around to Cindy Laver's life before she had become involved with Doug and was told that she had been a very quiet young woman who never brought gentlemen home. She had lived there from the first month she came to town. Sometimes she had come home very late and once or twice had never come home at all but you knew what young people are. She had stayed with friends or something like that.

The only thing I did work out was that the fire escape came down beside the kitchen window of the lower floor. If Mrs. Tibbet had been in bed she would probably not have heard or seen anybody using the back entrance to Cindy's place.

I thanked her for her help and left, driving directly to the police station. A different uniformed man was on duty but I guess word of my involvement had spread. As soon as I gave my name he went into the chief's office and I was allowed in.

The chief was looking tired and I thought I could smell whisky on his breath, but he accepted my evidence gravely, handling it with the proper care, and said he would have it fingerprinted and added to the evidence file in the case.

"Any advances on his killing, or Ms. Tate's?" I asked. He shook his head and assured me that the investigation was still proceeding. He countered by asking me what I intended to do next and I told him I would be asking around for anything that might help. I didn't mention my fingerprint plan for the workers at the bar. And that was it. I was out of his office within ten minutes and on my way back to the Ford house. When I got there I found a strange car in the driveway, a black Cadillac.

Doug met me at the door. "Good timing," he said tonelessly. "You've got a visitor."

I followed him in carefully, pausing to shuck my overshoes and coat, wondering if one of Manatelli's men had come calling. But the man in the living room was a spare-looking

Norman Rockwell Yankee. I recognized him from the glimpse I'd had at his own front door. It was Jack Grant's father.

He was nursing a drink and he stood up, setting the drink aside. "Mr. Bennett." He stuck out his hand. "I'm Paul Grant."

"Sir." I shook his hand. It was cool from his glass but firm and hard, a working hand.

"Siddown," Doug said. "You like a taste, Reid?"

"Please." I sat and waited for Grant to start.

He cleared his throat first, a nervous clatter like the bolt action of an old rifle. "I'm sorry to intrude," he said.

"You're not intruding. I'm very sorry for your loss."

He squinched his eyes. "Are you a family man, Mr. Bennett?"

"I have a daughter."

"Then I guess you know how I'm feeling," he said. He sat silent for a moment, gathering strength to continue. "My son was no angel. I'd be lying if I told you that. But he was my son and now he's dead and I want to know why and who did it."

"The police investigation will find that out, Mr. Grant. You have a good department here. They'll get the guy who did this."

"Maybe they will." He lowered his head for a moment, and stared into his glass, sightlessly. "But now there's a dead woman as well, shot, I'm told, with a gun like Jack's. I'm afraid they're going to use my boy as a scapegoat for her killing."

The thought had occurred to me. Police everywhere love to close files. It looks good the next time you go to the city fathers for money. I discounted it here. The man was in pain. "They're good men. They wouldn't do a thing like that."

He didn't argue, just repeated his fear. "I'm afraid they will. He's dead, the town knows what he was like." He looked at me now out of pale blue eyes. "That's why I've come to see you."

"What can I do? I don't have any powers in this town."

"I hear you're a detective where you come from. Frank Maloney told me."

"That's true," I said carefully.

"I want to ask if I can hire your services." He looked at me with a new keenness, good old Yankee shrewdness, I guessed.

"To do what?"

"To clear my boy's name." He cleared his throat again. "To clear the family name, I guess."

I looked at him in amazement. "You mean that?"

"Yes." He sat there rigidly in his good wool shirt and his buff corduroy slacks, the successful businessman on his day off, his face as keen as a hawk's. "I've discussed this with my wife. She feels the same as me. We've both been very disappointed with the way Jack turned out. He was a wonderful boy but he's never seemed to grow up and get a hold of himself. We both knew he's got enemies in town, people who would nod and say 'uh-huh' if the police made any more accusations against him." He cleared his throat. "I'm sorry to say I'm ashamed of my own son, but I want his name cleared now that he's dead."

I answered very carefully. "Did you know that I tangled with your son and two of his buddies in Brewskis a couple of nights back and that last night they tried to jump me in the parking lot?"

"He's dead," Grant said quietly. "Whatever bad things he's done are over now." I didn't answer and he added, "We don't have anyone else to turn to, Mr. Bennett."

That gave me an opening. I said, "Surely there's a private investigator somewhere close by, somebody with the right licenses for this jurisdiction, someone you can trust."

"If this was a divorce case or about money and nothing else, I'd say yes. But this is a matter that calls for police skills."

Doug came back with a drink for me and I nodded thanks and took it. I was torn. The man was looking to earn his son a nice clean slate to be buried with, only from where I sat it didn't seem that the guy had earned one. But on the other hand, if I went along with this, I could get a look at Grant's room, talk about his involvements, maybe get to the bottom of who his contacts were, who had killed him. I doubted that his father would give as much cooperation to the police.

I settled on diplomacy. "Since I've been here, I've become friends with Mr. Maloney, your lawyer. I think I should get his opinion on this. I didn't get on with your son. Maybe if I'd known him better it would have been different, but I need a referee of some kind to guide me here."

"That sounds like a fair solution." Grant set down his glass and stood up. "Talk to Frank. He's a friend of mine and a fair man. I'll abide by what he advises you."

We shook hands and he thanked Doug for the drink and left. I stayed where I was until Doug had closed the door and come back into the living room. "Weeeeell," he said with a grin I remembered from boot camp. "You got yourself a job offer."

"Hell of an ethical problem," I said. "I just found a pocketknife, probably belonging to his son, right there in the couch at Cindy Laver's apartment."

That took the smile off his face. "You mean that?"

I filled him in and he sat, thoughtfully. "Don't make sense he'd've lounged around on the couch if he'd come to kill her. That don' hold up."

"She say anything about being friends with him?"

"It never came up," Doug said. "We didn't talk about

much except the case. If we'd been an item, I'd been jealous, stuff like that, maybe it would've."

"He must have spent time up there with her. Maybe that adds something to the case. Maybe he knew what she was doing for you," I insisted. "Come on, Doug. How much did you really know about her?"

"Not a whole hell of a lot," he said and there was bitterness in his voice. "And the chance is gone now."

I switched the subject. "Did you ever use the fire escape to visit her?"

"I never went there except with her. I didn't have to sneak around."

"But you know where it is?"

"The kitchen window. I've thought about that. The guy who killed her must've come in that way."

"Maybe not. There's a separate bell for her apartment. He could have buzzed her and she could've come down to let him in."

"Yeah," Doug said. "Or maybe he had a key." He took a slug of his rye. "If guys like Grant were calling on her, maybe she had all kinds of action."

"Maybe he killed her," I suggested.

"And just how the hell we gonna find out?"

"I might do it if I take up his dad's request. I'd have to tell him ahead of time that I'm not going to do any kind of snowjob. I can promise to dig for facts, let the chips fall where they fall."

"Think he'll go for that?"

"I'm not sure. But the best thing to do is ring Maloney and ask him. I have to do that much before I get back to Grant."

"Go for it," Doug said. "I don't think Lieutenant Cassidy will find out as much as you can if you try. He's too busy acting the big wheel detective."

"Can I use the phone?"

"He'p yourself." He waved to the kitchen and I went through and phoned.

Maloney answered on the first ring. "Hi. It's Reid Bennett. Have you heard what's been happening?"

"Yes." A lawyer's precise pronunciation. "I've got the radio on in the kitchen. There's nothing more than you told me. Who killed her? Have you any idea?"

I told him I hadn't learned anything fresh and then moved on to my main reason for calling, Grant's offer.

"How do you feel about that?" he asked.

"Well, let's just say I thought Jack was bad news."

"He was, no doubt about it. But Paul has a point. The police will use that fact to tidy up the death of Ms. Tate. That's if they don't find something that clearly indicates Jack didn't do it."

"Are you implying they might not even look too hard?"

"Oh, they'll look hard but if she's been shot with that gun of Grant's, they won't need much persuasion that he did it."

"They can't prove that until they recover the gun."

"I'd imagine that whoever killed him probably also killed Ms. Tate. If I'd done that I would have left his gun somewhere close by, at the scene probably, or in his car?"

"His car was right there, locked, but he had the keys in his pocket when we searched the body. The killer could have taken them and put the gun inside." He still hadn't given me a clear indication of what he thought so I put the question again. "Do you think I should do this or not? I mean, Grant senior wants me to whitewash his son."

He took a long time answering. Then he said, "I'll talk to Paul, let him know that you won't lie for him. You'll dig out whatever you can, good or bad. Whatever is relevant you'll share with the police. That's your only stipulation." He stopped again. "Did he ask what you'll charge?"

"I hadn't thought about charging him."

He chuckled then, a dry little sound. "Take a little free advice from a lawyer. You have to, Reid. Otherwise he'll think you're doing this just to clear your buddy. No, I think three hundred a day sounds reasonable. Break it out to an hourly rate if you'll be splitting your time on checking into

Officer Ford's case. But Paul Grant can afford that and it keeps everything professional."

"Thank you for the advice. I wonder if you'd be kind enough to call him, tell him I'll come over in about an hour. I'd like to go through his son's things."

"Will do," he said. "Ooops, there's a car coming into the drive. I think it's Ella. I'll talk to you tomorrow."

We hung up and I gave Doug a quick rundown. "Hell, I'd love to come with you," he said wistfully. "But I gotta sit on my hands."

"You can use the time well. Check if Melody left any franks and beans in the larder," I told him. "We'll have ourselves a boot camp supper."

"You going right over?" he asked.

"No. I want to take Sam for a run. He's been cooped up ever since we got here. Won't take me more than half an hour, then shower and over there on schedule."

"I'd like to come with you." He shook his head. "But that's not on. I guess I'll get Angie's skipping rope out and work out in the basement."

I changed into a track suit and running shoes and when I came downstairs, Sam was beside himself with pleasure, squirming and wagging his tail. He knew he'd be along for the run. We set out, running on the left side of the street, clear of the icy sidewalks. The roadway was a little slick but my shoes were designed for bad surfaces so I made good time, clicking off three fast miles with Sam at my heels. On the way I found a piece of open land that wasn't a park or apparently used for walking and Sam breasted his way into the snow and relieved himself there. Then we made our way back to Doug's place with the wind in my face and my mind in neutral.

Like most runs, this one worked its usual magic and I found myself fresher, able to tackle the next stage of the investigation without tension. I showered and put on a good shirt and pants and headed for the Grant place.

Grant came to the door himself. "I'm grateful for this."

"I hope it proves useful to you," I said. "Does Mrs. Grant know I'm coming?"

"She's in the kitchen. Let me take your coat and I'll introduce you." He hung up my coat and led the way through a living room that looked as if all the decorating ideas had come from magazines, and out to the kitchen where his wife was making coffee. She was lean, like her husband, fiftyish and pretty but today her face was drawn and lined with tears.

"This is Mr. Bennett, dear," Grant said. "Mr. Bennett, my wife Jean."

"Mrs. Grant, I'm very sorry about what happened to your son."

She tried to smile but it looked painful. "Thank you. Would you like some coffee?"

"Thank you, ma'am. Black please."

"I'll take Mr. Bennett into the living room," Grant said. "If the phone rings, I'll get it."

She smiled the same flash of pain and turned to the pot. He led me back into the living room. "We've had people here all day," he explained. "First the police, of course. Then friends and well-wishers, the minister. I finally asked him to organize a telephone chain to ask our friends to give us some room until tomorrow. Jean's mother is coming from Florida in the morning. She'll be able to help."

"They mean well," I said. Here, in his home, I could share his distress. To me and the other cops involved in the case, young Grant had been another body and I've seen my share of them. But the hole he had left in this family would never heal.

"Where do you want to start?" he asked.

"First off, did he have any enemies who might have done this?"

"Lieutenant Cassidy asked the same thing. I've been trying to think. Sure he had people mad at him but none who would have killed him."

I phrased the next question very carefully. "Was he in

any kind of money trouble?" I hoped he wouldn't see at once that Maloney had told me about the gambling debts.

"He's had money trouble in the past, we all have. But I don't think he had any pressing problems right now."

"Okay. Now, he was seen at Cat's Cradle in the company of someone from the New York area. Did he have dealings with anyone from there, do you know?"

Now his lean face tightened. "Maloney's been talking, hasn't he?"

I dodged the bullet. "I was with Detective Hinton this morning when he called on Jack's companions from last night. That information came from one of them."

"All right," he said grimly. "That's fair enough, I guess. But just so you know I'm not holding back, let me say this." He set down his coffee, untasted. "My son was a gambler. He got in deep a couple times. I'm not sure who his bookie was but once before he got a call from a slick sonofabitch in a thousand-dollar suit. At the store. Came in there like he owned it. Jack was shaking when he saw the guy come in."

"Did you get a good look at him?"

"As close as I am to you. He said, 'Nice place you got here. Must be worth a bundle.' Then he helped himself to something off the counter and I said, 'Hey, what's going on?' and he said, 'Put it on my tab,' and walked out."

"What was it he took?"

Grant almost exploded. "What does it matter? He acted like he owned the place. Then Jack told me he owed twenty-seven thousand dollars to the man and if he didn't pay they were going to break his legs."

"So you paid?"

"Of course I paid." He got control of himself again and picked up his coffee cup. His hand was trembling.

"What did the man look like?"

"Five-six, thereabouts. Good dark suit, even though this was summertime. He'd be around thirty-five, dark, kind of a moon face."

"Would you recognize him again?"

"After what he cost me?" His voice was a snarl. "You can count on that."

"Did you mention this to the police?"

"Yes. They want me to go in and look at their picture books. I said I would as soon as I can."

"The sooner the better, Mr. Grant. He sounds a lot like the man that was seen with your son yesterday."

He sipped his coffee. It seemed to soothe him. "I'm going this evening. Our neighbor will come in and stay with Jean."

"Good. It could help. If this is the same man, he's got organized crime connections. After the threat he made to your son earlier, he's the prime suspect. And that makes him the prime suspect in the killing of Ms. Tate as well."

He sat there, nodding quietly. "That makes sense."

"Now there's one thing that's more important than it seems. What did he take from your store?"

"A pocketknife," Grant said. "The best little knife we sell. Took it right out of the display case."

"Could you describe it to me?"

He frowned. "What's all this about?"

"Humor me, please. I need to know."

"Okay. It's a bone-handled pocketknife, made by the Apogee company of Detroit. Retails for twenny-nine ninety-five. Two blades. Got a little shield on the side."

"Thank you." I put down my coffee cup. "Could I take a look in your son's room now, please?"

"The police already did," he said with a touch of anger. "They took away a plastic sack of stuff."

"I'd still like to look, if that's okay?"

"Sure. Come on." He led me up the stairs which were wide and lightly painted over the oak, giving a ghostly effect. "I've done a lot of work on this place," he said almost automatically. "It's kind of a hobby and my wife likes new things."

"Your home is beautiful," I said politely. It was a little too modern for my taste, but the work had been done well. He was an excellent craftsman.

He opened the door of a room at the head of the stairs. It was big, about fourteen feet square, and had a bathroom attached. "I built this suite for Jack when it got to the point we figured he was going to be at home for keeps. He spent most of his time here."

"Very nice," I said. I stood in the doorway and looked around. There was a bed which had obviously been stripped by the police searchers, a good sound system and a TV set. There was no bookshelf but a couple of copies of *Sports Illustrated* were lying on the bedside table. There was a small desk under the window.

"Did the police say what they'd taken?"

"They emptied his desk," Grant said flatly. "I don't know why. Cassidy said they were going to check to see if any names turned up that they could check on."

"A good thing to do," I said. "But I'd like to look anyway. Do you want to stay?"

He didn't answer and I thought for a moment he hadn't heard. Then he said, "This used to be two rooms. Jack and I gutted them and built this for him. He worked along with me. Did a lot of the finish work himself. He was a craftsman, my son." He sighed. "No. I don't guess I need to stay. I'll be downstairs with Jean when you're through."

He left, closing the door, and I went over to the desk and opened the top drawer. It was empty and I pulled it completely out, turning it over. There was nothing taped underneath. I did the same with each of the other drawers. They were the same. Then I stooped and looked up inside the open space. Nothing had been taped there either. After that I flickered through both magazines to see if anything had been leafed into them. It hadn't.

Slowly I searched the whole room. I checked the cistern of the toilet, the bathroom medicine cabinet, the whole space. Then I opened the closet and went through all his clothes. Some of them had the pockets inside out, a sure sign that the police had searched before me. There was nothing in any of the pockets except for a couple of tissues in one

jacket. I hadn't known what I was looking for but I felt
flattened by finding nothing at all. So I stood, thinking and
looking around the room.

It was dark outside by now and I went to the window
and turned the venetian blind slats down. As I stood there,
absently considering everything I knew about Grant, I found
myself looking at the trim around the windows, work he had
done with his own hands. His father was right. He had been
a good carpenter. The work reflected it, no gaps anywhere,
smoothly mitered corners on the trim around the windows.
I do some carpentry myself, not too bad for an amateur, but
this work was streets ahead of mine. Out of some kind of
admiration for the dead man's skill I reached down and
tapped the windowsill. And the sound stopped me cold. It
was hollow.

In any work I've done, I've always put the window directly onto the frame I've built underneath. Your new window is always true, and if you get the frame true, you set
the glazed section flat on it, leaving about five-eighths play
at the top to allow for settling. But this sounded hollow.
Slowly I squatted on my heels and looked at it. Under the
windowsill was a piece of molding, four inches wide, stretching to within an inch of the end of the sill on both sides. I
put my fingernails under the bottom edge and gave it a
tentative tug. It slid toward me, revealing a little drawer
about three inches deep by almost the thickness of the wall.
And it was full of papers.

It came right out and I looked inside the gap it had left
to see that nothing remained inside, seeing that Grant had
compensated for the drawer space by notching the sill and
hanging the window on heavy steel brackets. This hidey-hole
had been his own secret. I wondered what he could have
had that was important enough to hide so carefully. I took
the drawer and went to the bed and sat down to find out.

CHAPTER 13

There was a pile of small papers in the drawer and on top of them was a book, the classic little black book that bachelors are expected to keep. I opened it and found it was a sexual diary, full of names, all of them women. With each there were dates and notes on their performance. At the top of each entry was a cumulative number. I shook my head disbelievingly. I've heard of guys who keep a life list, running up numbers like a kid with baseball cards, but I'd never before seen the evidence.

He had scored on an A to F scale although only one woman rated an A+. Her name was Helen Stringer and he had made the note "Good stuff. See you again, H." The others were mostly C's, including Wendy Tate. He had slept with her a month before. But it was the last name on the list that stopped me cold. It was Cindy Laver.

The date was only a week or so ago. And his note was triumphant. "B+. Must have learned something from her big black boyfriend. Well, I showed him! Thanks for the help, good buddy. Mission accomplished."

I copied down the entire note and closed the book

thoughtfully. Who was the good buddy? Was he referring to Doug as some kind of bird dog who had pointed out the sexual importance of a new woman? Or was it someone else? And if so, who, and why?

I leafed through the rest of the papers. They were typed records of his bets, going back a couple of years as far as I could judge. I don't follow sports very much and I couldn't tell whether he had won or lost but I noticed that the sums had increased in the middle of the last year when he'd made one bet for five thousand dollars.

After that there were no more for almost two months and then they had started up again at a more modest level. Two hundred dollars was the average for a while. Then he must have regained his confidence and the amounts increased until they reached two thousand. It was on a hockey game played in Toronto. He had backed Toronto and I did remember that one. Chicago had beaten them in the last minute of play. Without question, Grant had been in debt again to his bookies.

At the bottom of the drawer I found two other papers. They were IOUs in his writing. They were not made out in anybody's name, just IOU for the amount and signed by Grant. I assumed they must have been for betting debts. One was for eleven hundred dollars and it was crossed through and marked "Paid in cash" and signed with a big theatrical squiggle that I couldn't read. The other was for seventeen hundred dollars and was crossed in the same way and marked "Discharged" and signed in the same hand. The date on this one stopped me cold. It was for the previous Thursday, the day after Cindy Laver had been killed. Had that been the price of her murder? Seventeen hundred dollars?

I sat for a few minutes, wondering what to do with my find. I had told Grant that I would not do any whitewashing but he was going to be sad about all of this and I might have to get very firm to take the papers and book away from here. For sure he wouldn't want me doing any more digging after this.

So before I showed him my find I checked the other windowsill, and any other places where Grant might have pulled the same trick with carpentry. I couldn't find anything. Then I put the rest of the stuff back in the secret drawer and replaced it before going downstairs.

Grant and his wife were sitting in the living room, dry-eyed and silent. He got up when he saw me on the stairs. "Did you find anything useful?"

"Jack had a hiding place. I found it," I said. "Would you like to search it with me?"

His wife got up then but he put his hand on her arm. "I'll go, dear." She started to say something but he patted her arm gently and said, "Please."

She sat down and he came back upstairs with me. "Where did you find it? The police searched for two hours."

"I was just lucky. When you told me Jack had done the finish work I checked and found a drawer under the window. There may be other places as well but I didn't find them."

I showed him the place, tapping the windowsill first. "It sounded hollow so I looked underneath." I bent and eased the drawer out. "There."

"Have you looked at this?"

"Yes. It's full of betting slips and there's his black book with girls' names," I said. "They may mean something."

"Let me look," Grant said wearily. He took the drawer and sat with it on the edge of the bed. Surprisingly he checked the betting slips first. "Good God," he said disgustedly. "He was betting thousands of dollars all through '91, while I was struggling to keep my head above water in the recession. How could he have done that?"

"There's a bet for five thousand, last July. Is that when the man came to call on you at the store?"

"July 11. Jean's birthday. I'll never forget that as long as I live," Grant said. He was rigid with anger and disgust, handling the slips as if they were dirty. "Jack promised me he'd never bet anymore. And look at this. Not three months later and he was back at it again."

"Don't be too hard on him. Gambling is an addiction, as bad as drink or drugs. He couldn't help himself."

"And he sure didn't help us," Grant said bitterly. He crumpled the slips and shoved them aside on the covers. Then he took out the book.

"I warn you, that's not going to make you feel any better," I said carefully.

"Right now there's nothing going to make me feel better, Mr. Bennett," he said. "It's no use holding back."

I watched him open the book and glance at the pages, almost blindly. Then he snapped it shut and threw it aside. "Where in God's name did he get his morals? His mother and I raised him the best way we knew. He was in the church choir as a boy, did well in school. And now this." He looked close to tears.

"Did he go away to college?"

"Yes." Answering the question gave Grant some strength back. "Got a business degree. We figured he'd be set to take over the store, expand into another town maybe. But he never amounted to a goddamn thing. Came back and worked at the store, but half-assed, not interested in making improvements, giving us anything back for the money we'd spent on him. He just put in time like a hired hand, spent his nights with his buddies and his women."

There was no way to cancel anything he had said or even to console him so I said only, "Detective Cassidy might find all of this stuff useful. It might give him some new people to question."

"It makes Jack look like shit," Grant said flatly. "A dirty little hard-on, running around town chasing other men's wives and girlfriends just so he could run up a score."

"That won't come out. You can insist on that. You don't even have to hand over the book if you don't want to. You can just make a list of the names and the dates and give it to him."

He picked the book up and his hands tensed around it. I thought he was going to rip it in half but instead he shoved it at me. "Give it to him," he said. "Give it all to him. But tell him I want it kept secret. It's just to be used to help the investigation, that's all."

"You're a good man, Mr. Grant," I said. "I'll do what you say."

"Don't tell Jean," he said. "I'll tell her you found his betting slips. She'll think the cops found the book among his other things."

"Right. I'll get on to it." I slipped the book and the papers into my pocket and we went downstairs. Mrs. Grant was in the kitchen and I was able to get my coat and leave without speaking to her. I was excited by the find, but wary. I wasn't anxious to hand over the book to Cassidy. His attitude bothered me. He had personally charged Doug with Cindy Laver's killing and I figured that even if new evidence came out that changed the case against Doug he would be reluctant to acknowledge it.

In the end I drove to Doug's house. He was in the kitchen, opening cans for supper. "Find anything?" he asked.

"Yeah. The plot thickens," I said. "I found his black book. Looks like he's laid half the women in town."

"That's not exactly news," Doug said. "He was the local stick man. Everybody knew that about him."

"There's one thing that will surprise you."

"You're not going to say that Melody's name is in there, are you?" he asked, carefully tipping beans into a pot.

"Of course not. But he's got Cindy Laver on his life list, a day or so before she was murdered."

Doug's voice didn't change. "The detectives need to know that."

"I've got his father's permission to give it to them, but I didn't want to turn it over to Cassidy, or Schmidt for that matter. I figured it should go to the chief."

"He's an honest man," Doug said. "He'll ask why you

didn't give it to the detectives. I think they'll take care of it. You can safely hand it over to them."

"Then I'd better call right away."

"Okay." He held out his hand. "While you're calling, can I see the book?"

I gave it to him and went to the phone. The man on the desk put me through, after asking my name. Cassidy sounded annoyed. "What's so important?"

"Mr. Grant asked me to go through his son's room. I found a secret drawer under one of the windows. It had some papers and a black book in it with the names of all the women he'd laid, including Cindy Laver, a night or so before she was killed."

"Who gave you permission to go through that room?" As I'd expected, anger first.

"I told you, Lieutenant. Mr. Grant asked me to. Your guys didn't find the drawer, I did. And I think the book would be useful to you. For one thing it says that he slept with Cindy Laver on the seventh. That was the night before she was killed."

"Okay, so bring it in," he said. "May's well look at it."

I resisted the temptation to tell him not to get too excited. He had more to prove than I did. I just said, "Sure," and hung up.

Doug was still leafing through the book. "If the little asshole was telling the truth, he really ran up a score," he said, frowning. "Some of these women are married. A few of them are kind of long in the tooth as well."

"Like how old?" From his interest I could see he had found something significant.

"Like in their fifties, that's twenty years older'n he was. Look, Ella Frazer. He's written, 'Many a sweet tune played on an old fiddle.' "

"Ella Frazer? From the office at Cat's Cradle? When was that?"

"Last fall. He gave her a B."

"That's both of the women who worked in the accounts office at Cat's Cradle. I wonder if that means anything?"

Doug shut the book. "I don't think so. Long's they were warm and willing he was happy." He handed the book to me. "You taking this in to Cassidy?"

"Yeah. Oh, and there's something else." I took out the slips and the IOUs. "These look like they might be betting debts."

Doug leafed through them. "I've never seen any bookie's slip as neat as this. These were all typed, on an electric machine by the look of it. I think this must have been some kind of record he kept for himself."

"Why'd he want to do that?"

Doug shrugged. "Masochist, I guess. Hell, half these were basketball games and that's my sport. I can tell you, he lost these bets." He frowned at them. "Half the time he's bet on the underdog."

"A lot of gamblers do, going for the odds, trying to get out of the hole they're already in." I handed over the last two slips. "These are IOUs. Maybe for gambling, maybe not. Recognize the signature by any chance?"

Doug looked at them both, then went back to the bigger one. "Seventeen hundred bucks, just marked discharged, not paid. And the date is last Thursday. Was this what he got for killing Cindy?"

"Could've been. But unless we can recognize the signature it doesn't give us anywhere to go."

Doug looked at the squiggle. "Could be anything. It looks like the way a guy would sign his name if he was giving autographs."

"That's a thought. Is there anybody in town who might have done that at some time? Any actors, celebrities?"

Doug looked up, thoughtfully. "The only celeb we've got around here is Huckmeyer. He was on the national ski team. Maybe those guys get asked for autographs."

"He's mixed up in this eight ways to breakfast already,"

I said. "I think I'll go talk to him. Hang on to supper for me till I get back."

"Sure. You may find him at Cat's Cradle or Brewskis. That guy never takes a day off."

"Okay then. First the station, then the other places. See you in a couple of hours."

"Good luck," Doug said. He looked at me awkwardly. "And thanks, huh."

I waved at him and left, whistling Sam.

He followed at my heel out to the car and I put him in the passenger seat and then opened the trunk. It was dark now and I knew I couldn't be seen as I took Doug's gun out of its hiding place and slipped it into my pocket. Now that the chief had cleared me to continue investigating Doug's charge, I didn't think I would be searched by the police. And I was liable to run foul of the guy from New York again. This time he wouldn't leave it to locals. He would try to do the job himself.

First I drove to the station. Cassidy and Schmidt were up in the detective office. They must have discussed my call because they both made an effort to be polite. Schmidt tried the harder. "Hell, we should've found this when we searched," he said. "Thanks for doing our job. How come Grant let you in there?"

"He wants me to look into what's been happening. I told him you guys would be the best ones to do it, but you know what it's like when you've lost a family member. He wants the whole world looking." Close enough to the truth that it didn't ruffle feathers.

Schmidt opened the book, glancing at the back page first. "Shit. You're right. He laid that woman the night before somebody offed her."

"His father gave me permission to hand this to you, so it's clean, if it's useful," I told him. "He said he'd like it kept confidential because it makes his son look bad."

"That's for goddamn sure," Schmidt said. "Look at this."

He flourished the book at Cassidy. "He rated all o' these broads like they were competing in the Olympics."

Cassidy gave a knowing chuckle. "Lemme see that. May find some useful names. Know what I mean?"

He and Schmidt looked like a couple of teenagers with their first dirty magazine. I said, "Except for Cindy Laver, the names don't mean anything to me. But there's a chance that he got into bed with the wrong guy's wife. Maybe that's how come he was killed."

"Could be." Cassidy laughed shortly. "We're runnin' around lookin' for some fancy motive and here, a whole bunch of locals had a reason for killing him."

They nodded at one another knowingly, but it was an act, I felt. They had something else. "There's a pile of betting slips as well, and a couple of IOUs. One of them marked discharged the day after the killing."

"Lemme see." Cassidy held out his hand. I gave him the slips and he flipped through them, then stopped at the IOUs. "Who in hell's name's this?" he asked in disgust. "Looks like it's Arabic or some goddamn thing."

Schmidt accepted the paper and frowned. "Beats the hell outa me. But we'll keep it, may come up with a match somewhere."

They looked at one another and said no more, waiting for me to leave. I stood up. "Can I ask what's new on the Tate killing? Did you find the weapon?"

"Yesss." Schmidt almost purred. "Found Grant's gun under the car. His prints all over it. Ballistics are checking it out now but the slugs in her were .22s. We can tie that one up tonight."

"Nice work." I slapped my hands together. "Don't you love happy endings?"

They both laughed but neither of them said anything for a moment, then Schmidt said, "So, thanks for the help. Steve and me will follow up on alla this, see what we can come up with."

"Yeah," Cassidy said. " 'preciate the help."

"You're welcome. I'd like to hear how you make out on this. Would that be okay?"

"Sure. Where you staying? At Doug Ford's?"

I nodded and he made a little shooting motion. "So head on home, have a little taste and we'll be in touch."

I could hear them laughing behind me as I went downstairs, but it didn't bother me. They had cracked the Wendy Tate case. They had reason to feel good.

I drove out to Cat's Cradle. There were three cars in the parking lot, none of them looking as if it belonged to anyone wealthy. The night cleaners were in, I guessed. The place was otherwise deserted. Apparently the lifts closed at dusk on Sundays. I took Sam with me anyway and walked up to the gondola lift, noticing a lone man in the cafeteria swabbing the floor as I passed.

The door of the lift house was locked but it opened to my Visa card, as the chief had predicted, and I clicked on my little penlight and checked the controls. Again as he had said, simplicity itself. There was a big on-off button, nothing more. I didn't touch it but backed out and closed up the shack.

There was nobody around as I went back to the car and I drove out between the high banks of cleared snow and back toward town. Brewskis was on my route and I pulled into the lot which was full. So was the bar, although the noise level was lower tonight, perhaps because it was still early, only six o'clock. All the customers looked relaxed and happy. I noticed that many of them had pale, winter faces, obviously new arrivals, just beginning their week or so outdoors.

Neither of the women I had met was working and I got a beer and looked around, on the off chance that Huckmeyer was present. He wasn't, but I noticed some photographs on the walls. On impulse I picked up my beer and sauntered over to examine them. They were photographs of celebrities, I guessed, skiers that I didn't recognize and in one case a well-known singer, on skis, in front of Cat's Cradle. Most of

them were autographed, the usual florid squiggle that professionals use to save time. And then there was a photo of a
skier in action, caught making a dashing turn, snow flying
from the edge of his skis. I looked at the caption below it.
It read "Cat's Cradle manager, Walter Huckmeyer, member
of the U.S. national team, 1981, 1982." That made me reex-
amine the photograph and what I saw made me cold. It was
signed with the same signature I had found on the IOUs in
young Grant's room.

I studied it carefully, remembering the loops and swirls of
the squiggle on Grant's IOUs. Yes, there was no doubt. The
man who had discharged Grant's debt for seventeen hundred
dollars was Walter Huckmeyer.

I finished my beer and went to the telephone in the lobby.
The detectives were out but I left the information with the
deskman and went back to my car, keeping my eyes open.
Grant had proved that this was a good spot for an ambush
and I didn't want to fall into the same trap again, even now
that I had a gun with me.

I heard Sam keening from thirty yards away. As always
I had left him in the car, with the window down, but I
hadn't set him to keep the area. It wasn't possible when the
innocent owners of cars each side of mine might have wanted
to get in and drive away while I was inside and now he was
letting me know something was amiss.

I whistled and he squeezed through the window and
bounded to me. "Seek," I ordered and he checked in mid-
stride and began casting between the parked cars, looking
for anyone who might be hiding. He didn't turn up anybody
immediately around my car so I went to it and looked
around it carefully. The rear tire was flat. And from Sam's
antics, I knew it had been slashed.

I waited until he had rousted the whole parking lot. It's
not part of his training, there's no way you can convey such
an abstract message to him, but I knew he would also be
remembering the scent of the man who had approached the

car and if the guy was in a car somewhere, he would bark when he found him, but he didn't. The guy had gone.

I walked around the car before I touched anything, checking for other damage. There wasn't any, but there was a slip of paper folded under the driver's side windshield wiper. I pulled it out and looked at it, holding it in my gloved hand. The message was in a childish handwriting. It was short and simple. "Next time it's your throat. Go home," it said.

I set Sam to keep watch while I changed the tire. Then I took a couple of minutes looking under the car, making sure there was nothing there that would go boom when I started up. There didn't seem to be and I went back to Doug's place. It was just after seven when I got there and he greeted me at the door. "Good timing. I've got supper on the stove. D'you find anything?"

"Two things. First, I had my tire slashed and found this on the windshield."

He took the note and frowned over it. "Looks like it was written by a fifth grader," he said. "Or some goon. I guess it could be that soldier of Manatelli's."

"Might be, although I've got a feeling if the guy had been armed he would have shot Sam. He could have done it through the open window. Maybe this was just some local, could be one of Grant's buddies, getting even for what happened last night."

He cocked his head. "You're probably right at that."

"Anyway, like I said, there were two things. The second was I identified the signature on the IOUs."

"How in hell did you do that?"

I told him about the signed photograph and he nodded carefully. "Even if Huckmeyer signed those papers, it proves nothing. I'm still charged with the homicide."

"That's going to change. You're in the clear, Doug."

"Sure," he said shortly. "Let's eat."

While he served, I pulled the blinds down all around. The note had set my nerves on edge. I didn't want to be a target for some guy outside with a rifle.

It was a bachelor meal, franks and beans, a memory of Marine chow. But it went down well and we talked as we ate, working out how we would tackle the investigation if we were working together. Obviously the trick was to lean on Huckmeyer. We already knew he was in the middle of the money scheme and he had some heavy work to do explaining his IOUs from Grant.

Captain Schmidt phoned later, asking what I had meant by my message. He didn't seem pleased with the news but said a grudging thanks and that he would follow up on it.

His attitude was a downer. Doug and I sat and talked about it for a while, then gave up. We turned the TV on and sat in front of it, unseeing, each of us silently churning through the facts we had. Around ten-thirty Doug stood up and yawned. "I'm bushed. I'm going to bed. How about you?"

"I was thinking about that note. I wonder if the guy who wrote it might try something through the night?"

"Figure we should post a watch?" Doug asked carefully.

"Couldn't hurt. I figure I'll sleep down here. Sam'll be outside. He's our perimeter. If he wakes me up I'll take a look."

"I'll spell you out," Doug said, but I shook my head. "No. I've got your gun. If you used it there'd be one hell of a commotion and you'd be back inside by morning. They won't do that to me."

Doug reached out and clicked off the set. "Makes sense," he said, then grinned. "Hell, this is like Nam all over again."

"Yeah." I could see the thought gave him a kind of comfort so I didn't argue. "You go up and crash, I'll put Sam in my car. He'll take care of anybody who comes through the gate."

I put my boots back on and went out of the back door into the unshoveled snow. It was two feet deep and I struggled through it, leading Sam all around the house so he'd know what territory he had to cover. I took a careful look into the street before coming out to where a sniper could have nailed me. There didn't seem to be anyone out there. The only cars on the street looked as if their windows were closed. I gave Sam his instruction to "keep," put him in the car and went back in.

Doug had brought down a couple of blankets and a pillow and I left my boots beside me and settled on the couch, still dressed. I didn't sleep for a long time but eventually the quiet calmed me down enough that I sank away into the deep velvet.

Sam's bark woke me and I was alert instantly. It was still pitch dark. I slipped into my boots, picked up Doug's pistol from the floor beside me and went out of the front door. Sam was on the driveway, struggling with a man holding a gun.

Sam had his arm tight so I took a moment to check up and down the street in a quick glance. I couldn't see anybody else out there so I turned to help Sam, grabbing the man's gun, twisting it easily out of the hand that Sam was gripping. Then I told Sam, "Easy, boy," and tripped the guy so he sprawled on the ground. "Don't move or he'll have your face off," I told him and he lay still.

Behind me the door clattered and Doug ran out. He was fully dressed and I guessed he'd been sleeping in his clothes, like me.

"Get up," I told the guy. It wasn't Lord or his buddy and that surprised me. This man was rougher-looking. And then, as he struggled to his feet, I recognized him. It was Kelly, the drug dealer from the mobile home outside of town.

A couple of doors had opened along the street and I could

see shadowy people on their porches watching us. The cold didn't seem to bother them. This was too exciting.

We didn't need an audience so I said, "Get inside," and prodded Kelly with the muzzle of his gun. It was a heavy automatic, the standard U.S. Army .45 Colt.

"You can't take me anywhere," he protested but I prodded him again and hissed at Sam who growled. Kelly stiffened, then said, "Call the dog off, okay?"

"Easy," I told Sam. He fell silent and Kelly got up and moved past him up the steps to the front door with Doug after him. Behind me, faintly, I heard the sound of a car. I gestured to Doug to go inside and waited for a little while, hoping that the car had Kelly's partner in it and would come back past the house so I could get the number. But it didn't. The sound faded and I gave up and went in, taking Sam with me, fussing him with one hand. "Good boy," I told him.

Kelly was spread-eagled against the wall with Doug frisking him. As I came in Doug tapped him on the back and told him to straighten up. He did, and turned around fearfully. "I made a mistake, is all," he said. "I figured this was Jeannie Cole's house."

"And you brought her a gun instead of flowers. Sweet," Doug said. "Cut the bullshit, Kelly. You got a sheet as long as my arm. I know you."

Kelly was a longtime rounder. He knew how to play innocent. "I just happened to have the gun with me."

"Who sent you?" I asked him as I checked the pistol. It was fully loaded with the safety off and a round in the chamber. I slipped out the magazine and ejected the round, then tossed the gun onto the couch. The magazine I put in my pocket.

"Nobody. Like I told you, I was out to get laid," Kelly said.

"Yeah, sure." Doug sneered. "Now lemme bring you up to speed, punk. I'm not a cop anymore. Nor's this gennleman. We're two guys who woke up and found you sticking a gun in our faces. We had a big fight, which is how you got your teeth knocked out and your nose broken, and we took the gun off you."

"You can't beat me up," Kelly blustered but he was scared.

Doug reached out and gripped his ear, like an old-style schoolmarm. "I didn't hear what you said. Wanna try again?"

"Okay. Okay." Kelly held up his hands. "I talk to you an' you let me go, that okay?"

"You talk, you keep your teeth, that's the deal," Doug said.

Kelly wasn't bright but you could see his street-smart mind ticking over as he started. "This guy came to see me last night. He said he wanted a favor."

"What guy?" Doug hissed it out like a coiled snake.

"Shit. I dunno. Some guy. He said he wanted to pay some guys back. Said they'd ripped him off. Said to take the gun an' come in an' mess the place up."

"You needed a gun to trash a house?" Doug sneered.

"He said to take it. Gave it to me. You seen it. Hell, I don' own no cannon. I got a shotgun home for security, you know. But I don' have no pistol."

"Tell me about this guy," I said. "What did he look like?"

"Just a guy."

"How big? How old? What was he wearing?"

You could see the cogs turning. " 'Bout my size, older. Good coat."

"We'll get back to that," Doug said with soft menace. "What did he say to you? I want the actual words, Kelly. Got that?"

"Sure." Kelly nodded quickly. "Sure. I remember. He said, 'How'd you feel about earning some big bread?' An' I said, sounds interesting. So he said, 'There's a guy in town ripped me off for fifty grand.' He said, 'I want him taught a lesson. Go in there, take this gun. If you get any trouble, knock 'im on the head, shut him up. Then trash the place an' see if you can find my fifty grand. If you can, half of it's yours.' "

Doug laughed scornfully. "Does this look like a place where you'd find fifty grand lying around?"

"This guy said you'd took it off some lady. Said the p'lice on'y got half back what was taken. They got fifty, you kept fifty."

"Tell me what this guy looked like," Doug said. "And I want all the details, right down to his shoe size and the color of his underwear."

"I told you," Kelly whined. "Like it was late. I was asleep an' I didn't take much notice of what he looked like."

"If anybody had woken me up and handed me a .45 and told me to go kill somebody, I'd know what he looked like to my dying day," Doug said. "Now I'm starting to lose my patience, Kelly. You've got ten seconds. Ten. Nine."

Kelly held up his hands. "I never seen this guy before. I told you what he was like. Big's me, maybe fifty-five. Dark hair, fedora, Italian I figured. Round face. He had on a black coat an' a pair o' good shoes. No overshoes, nothin'."

Doug suddenly seemed to lose interest in Kelly. He walked away into the kitchen. Kelly watched him go, then flicked a glance at me, anxiously. I didn't move and Doug came back with a pen and a pad. "Here. Write what I tell you. You can write, can't you?"

"Of course I can goddamn write." Kelly grabbed the pen and paper and Doug started reading out a list of words. They sounded random but I recognized the words of the note I'd found, mixed in with others.

When he had finished Doug took the paper off him and handed it to me. One glance was enough to see that the writing was different from the note but I just nodded to Doug and Kelly asked, "What's goin' on? What's all this about?"

"How much did this mysterious guy give you?" Doug asked. "Or are you a Boy Scout? You figured you'd kill me just to do your good deed for the day?"

"He gave me a grand. Said there'd be four more if the job got wet. Plus I could keep some o' the money I found."

"Five grand your usual charge for a killing? You gotta be rich, all the killing there's been in town this last week," Doug said.

Kelly opened his mouth to argue but I cut him off. "Did this guy come with you?"

"No. I come on my own," he protested, waving his arms.

"Sure. You walked all the way from your place, right?"

"I come in my truck." He looked around at us. "It's the God's truth."

"Where's the truck now?" Doug asked him.

"At the lot in town."

"That's half a mile. You figured you'd walk back there with my TV and video and alla this money you were gonna take home?"

"I wasn't gonna take nothin'," Kelly said, " 'cept the money if I found it."

There was the sound of a car outside, then footsteps on the porch. Then the doorbell rang. Doug opened the door and Pat Hinton stepped in. "Hi, Doug. A neighbor called that you'd caught a prowler."

"Yeah. This asshole, carryin' a .45," Doug said.

Hinton came in, with the same partner I'd met the day before a pace behind him. "Well, Kelly. You got yourself into a whole heap of trouble now, boy."

"I was jus' visitin'," Kelly said but Hinton laughed. "Cuff the bastard, Charlie."

His partner handcuffed Kelly and Hinton picked up the automatic from the couch. "Heavy artillery," he said.

"It was loaded and cocked. Here's the magazine." I handed it over. Hinton took it and grinned. "Well, well, Kelly. Well, well."

"It's not mine." Kelly was snarling now. He'd lost his fear of Doug now the regular troops had arrived. He was pulling a jailhouse act, giving away nothing, acting tough.

"Who'd you steal it off?" Hinton asked casually, then without waiting for an answer told his partner, "Throw him in the car, charged with possession of an unlicensed weapon, and read the sonofabitch his rights."

"Sure." His partner liked the chance to act macho. He prodded Kelly in the back and said, "Let's go, cowboy."

When they'd gone Doug shut the door and said, "Who called in, Pat?"

"Don't know. The dispatcher didn't say. He just said, report of a prowler at this address. I knew it was your place so I came over on the double."

"Can you check with the dispatcher? She'd've taken it down for sure," Doug said.

Hinton said, "Okay," and went to the phone. He spoke for a moment or two, then said, "Thanks," and hung up. "Says it came from Mr. Davenport at 239."

"The Davenports are in Florida," Doug said. "They didn't call. It must've been the same guy who sent Kelly in here."

"You sure?" Hinton frowned.

"Sure's you're born. Knock on the door when you go by. They won't hear. They're in Fort Myers."

"Take your word for it," Hinton said. "An' listen, I hear you came up with Grant's papers, Reid. Nice goin'. Anything worthwhile?"

"Didn't Cassidy tell you?"

"Not in detail. Said you'd found a book and some odd stuff."

Doug and I looked at one another. "I wonder if the bastard's planning to bury it," Doug said.

"Bury what?" Hinton asked.

"Well, Grant's book lists all the women he's slept with, including Cindy Laver, the night before she died. Plus there's two IOUs. One of them is marked paid, the other one discharged," Doug explained. "And it's dated the day after her death. Plus Reid also found out it was signed by young Huckmeyer at Cat's Cradle."

"Have you reported this?" Hinton asked excitedly.

"I told Schmidt around nine o'clock. He said he'd follow up."

Hinton frowned. "He went off duty around eleven. He didn't say anything to me."

"They're trying to shut you out, him and Cassidy," Doug said. "They don't like anybody else taking credit if they can keep it for themselves. Likely they're going to talk to Huckmeyer in the morning, bring him in over the hood of the car like a dead deer."

"What if they're going easy on this? What if they're afraid to turn him in?" I asked.

Hinton jumped on that one. "Are you saying they're on the take?"

"No. I'm wondering if they'll want to involve a prominent citizen in what's going on. They've got the obvious suspect, Grant. He's dead. Nobody's gonna miss him a whole lot. If they pin the Laver killing on him, and the Tate killing, everybody's going to think it was some sex thing. All they have to do is try and find the guy who killed Grant."

"Okay," Hinton said. "Yeah, there's some logic in that."

"So we need to know who killed him," Doug said. "And I figure it was the same guy who sent Kelly here to off me and Reid."

"Who was likely the same guy who called in to report a prowler," I said. "My guess is he was scared we'd work Kelly over and get the truth out of him. He wanted him out of here and in the station where there's Miranda rules and lawyers and all of that stuff."

"We keep a tape of incoming calls," Hinton said. "I'll listen to it when I get to the station house, see if I can identify the voice."

"Must be a local," Doug said. "No out-of-towner would know the name of the people at 239."

"Leave it with me," Hinton said. "If I recognize the voice I'll be on his case so fast his head's gonna spin."

Doug reached out and bumped him on the arm. "Thanks, Pat."

Hinton winked. "What's a partner for?" He nodded and left and Doug shut the door behind him.

"This is getting complicated," I said. "Hell, who'd want to get us two killed?"

"Manatelli," Doug said firmly. "His ass is in a sling. He's not afraid of us but he's afraid of the mud that's getting stirred up. If news of it gets back to his boss, he's for the deep six with the concrete overshoes."

"Yeah, but how would he have known your neighbor's name?"

"Maybe Kelly gave him the name ahead of time," Doug said thoughtfully. "Kelly knew he'd need some backup if we got to him. But it's no use now. He won't tell the police anything."

"Not if he's been arrested enough times to know the rules. And the most he can be charged with is trespass and having that gun."

"You watch," Doug said grimly. "I'll bet there's some fat-ass lawyer down there inside an hour, have him out before he says a word. I'll check with Pat in the morning. You'll see, Garfield will have sprung the guy."

"So let's get some sack time," I said. "We can sleep safely now."

"Yeah." Doug gestured at the couch. "Leave that, come up an' crash in Angie's room."

"This'll be fine. I'll set Sam to keep for us. We can sleep." I yawned. "See you in the morning."

"You sure about that couch?" he asked doubtfully.

"Sure as you're born." I gave him a bump on the arm and he went up to bed. I told Sam to keep and went to sleep. It took a little time to unjangle my head but at last I was gone and didn't wake until Doug came down. It was almost nine o'clock.

He was shaved and fresh and waved hi. Then he put

the coffeepot on and called the station. I heard him talking as I got up and folded the blankets. He came back in as I was heading up to the shower. "Surprise, surprise," he said. "Garfield was waiting at the station when Kelly got there. Had him out before the guys could even talk to him."

I paused at the foot of the stairs. "This is all being organized by someone local."

"Someone with money," Doug said. "And the best bet is Huckmeyer. I think we have to talk to that guy today."

"You can't. I have to," I said. "How about a big breakfast? I figure this is going to be a tough day."

I showered and shaved and came down to bacon and eggs. By the time I'd finished it was almost ten and I took Sam and set out for Cat's Cradle, stopping first at a tire place to have a replacement put on my spare.

The mechanic showed me the damage, a clean slit, an inch long. "Somebody didn't like you parking where you did," he said cheerfully. "I'd watch before I parked there again."

"That's a promise," I told him.

The skiers were out at Cat's Cradle in full strength but I found a parking spot and went to the office. I was still fifty yards away when I saw Captain Schmidt coming out. He was alone and I jogged over to him. "Morning, Captain. What did Huckmeyer say about the IOUs?"

Schmidt had eyes like a bull terrier, sunk deep in the beef of his face. "Oh, it's you," he said and kept walking. I fell in beside him and he spoke without looking at me. "Like I expected. He said yeah, he'd been owed money by Grant. Two times. Both times the guy paid him and he canceled the IOU. That satisfy you?"

"Why did he mark one 'paid' and the other one 'discharged'? Did you ask him that?"

Schmidt checked his stride and turned to face me. "You won't be happy until Huckmeyer's in trouble, will you? What is it with you?"

"Did you ask him?" I repeated.

"Yes. I asked him. He said that the second time he was in a hurry and just scribbled on it."

"If he was in that big a hurry, why not scribble 'paid'? It would've saved him a whole bunch of letters and a second of his valuable time."

Schmidt took a deep breath and looked at me for a moment before answering. "Frankly, Mr. Bennett, you are starting to give me a pain in the ass. Just because you come up with something doesn't make it any more important than anything else we find."

I tried to speak but he held up his hand and kept on talking. "I am satisfied that this man, who I've known since he was a pup, is honest and can be trusted. If he tells me a perfectly valid reason why he did something, that's okay by me."

"How many people does he lend money to? Did he tell you that? Or didn't you bother asking him?"

He looked at me for a moment, then said, "We're through talkin'," and walked away to his car.

I stood and watched as he got in and drove away, spurting snow and gravel from under his wheels in an angry rush. Then I turned and went on to the office.

The same receptionist was at the desk. I told her, "Walt's expecting me," and walked through to Huckmeyer's office.

He was at his desk and he jumped up when I came in. "You can't come in here."

"You don't think so? Phone the chief of police. He's given me permission to follow up on the Cindy Laver killing."

He picked up his phone, watching to see if I was going to chicken out. I just turned my head away, humming a little song, and he hung up and sat down. "I've just been talking to the police," he said.

"I'm aware of that, Mr. Huckmeyer. I spoke to the captain but he didn't ask you a couple of questions which I'd anticipated, so if you don't mind, this will only take a minute."

"That's all the time I've got," he said. "I'm going out to check the operations."

"Fine. First, can you tell me please how many other people you lend sizable sums of money to?"

"I don't have to answer that," he said sharply.

"No, but if you don't, you leave the nasty suspicion that you only lend to rounders who end up getting killed on your property and being charged, posthumously, with another murder."

He stood up. "Talk to my lawyer."

"Who's that? The lovely and talented counselor Garfield? The same guy who sprang Kelly last night after he came to kill me?"

"I don't know what you're talking about." It came out right but he wasn't looking at me.

"The same guy who knew the names of the people on Doug Ford's street, so somebody could use their name and call for the police before we had a chance for a good talk with Kelly?"

"I don't care what the chief has told you. This isn't a police investigation and you're not a cop. I want you out of my office."

I wagged a finger at him. "I'll go, but I have to tell you that Mr. Manatelli isn't going to be pleased. All this fuss at Cat's Cradle is going to get back to him. He may dump another body on your slopes. Only this time it might be yours."

He was white, either from anger or from fear, there was no way of telling. "Get out," he hissed.

"Bye. See you again when you feel more like talking," I told him.

I turned to the door and asked, "Oh, just one more thing. How much cash was in the bag that Cindy Laver took home that night?"

I could see the question had rattled him but he just repeated, "Get out. And stay out. I'm going to put a security man on the door to keep you out."

"Better get two, one to go with you when you visit Brewskis," I said and left.

I looked in at Brewskis but the staff people I knew hadn't come on duty so I drove back, slowly. Kelly's pickup was beside his shack and so was a Cadillac. I pulled in behind it, noting the license. A Vermont plate.

As I walked up to the front with Sam at my heel, Kelly opened the door. He had his shotgun at the ready. "Get offa my property," he said. "Do it now before I shoot that fuckin' dog."

I pulled Doug's pistol out of my pocket. "Pull that trigger and you're one dead rounder."

"You think so?"

"Wanna try?" I kept the gun aimed squarely at his eyes.

He let the muzzle of the gun droop. "We'll talk," I told him. "If not now, after your shyster lawyer's gone home. I'm gonna be in your face until you tell me who sent you."

It was the kind of shoving match you see in schoolyards. We both knew we couldn't do anything but I knew his kind. You have to keep the pressure on or they forget the trouble they're in. He lowered the gun completely and then, surprisingly, looked back into the shack and then stepped aside.

A man came out of the doorway, dark, fifty-five or so, well dressed, Italian. And then another man. The one who had kidnapped Angie Ford.

The first one spoke to Kelly, very low, and Kelly dropped his eyes and went back inside. Then the guy spoke to me, a low voice that let you know he expected to be listened to. "Put the gun away," he said.

I did and he came down the walk toward me. "You got a problem?" he growled. Pure godfather. Marlon Brando has a lot to answer for.

"Not me. But it seems you do."

The bodyguard had his hands in his pockets but I figured there was a gun in one of them. He spoke to his boss first. "That's the guy I told you about, from Canada." He seemed like he wanted to be more respectful, to call his boss Mr.

But he was afraid to say the name where I could hear it. The boss said nothing and the bodyguard spoke to me. "You said you was goin' home."

"I lied. I'll mention it next time I go to confession."

Manatelli grinned at me. "You're a good Catholic boy. I like that." Then the grin dropped away as he went on. "I give the word an' you don't make it to confession. You're dead."

"Like Cindy Laver? Like Grant? Like Wendy Tate?"

He spread his arms. "I don't know anybody with those names."

"So what's your proposition? Or did you come out here to get some fresh air?"

"Tough," he said softly. "Always tough guys. Listen, tough guy. I'm a reasonable man. I see a problem, I fix it. You're too tough to be threatened? Fine. I deal with you another way. What's your price?"

"My price is simple. But it's not money. I want Doug Ford cleared. That too high for you?"

Manatelli grinned again. It didn't look any warmer this time. "What's he charged with?"

"Just to refresh your memory, Murder One, plus theft of fifty grand."

"Go on back to his place and wait," he said. "It's going to be all right. I have connections. Unnerstand?"

"As soon as he's clear, I'm gone. And the talk about your money-laundering goes with me. Everything's sweet."

That made him narrow his eyes. "Go and wait," he said.

"I'll wait one day."

The bodyguard made a growling sound and his coat crunched up as he raised the gun he had in his pocket.

I figured he was the guy who'd cost me a new tire so I sneered at him. "Nice coat. Get the tailor to cut more slack in the next one, or get yourself a smaller gun. The size of your dick would be fine."

His chin dropped and he opened his mouth to reply but

Manatelli looked at him and they both just stood there as I walked away and put Sam into my car.

Doug's next-door neighbor was chipping ice off the sidewalk when I drove in and we exchanged waves as I got out of the car. I went in and found Doug in the basement, cutting a board on a table saw. He switched the saw off and took off his goggles when I came down. "What'd our boy say?"

"Not a lot, but I had a talk with Manatelli." Doug stood and listened while I filled him in and then said, "How's he gonna handle that, get me off the charges? D'he say?"

"No. Maybe he just wants me out of his hair while he pulls some stunt. Like maybe he's moving his money from the bank to Barbados or some place. But that won't stop me going on with the investigation if he hasn't cleared you."

"He's a snake," Doug said. "I don't see how he can get the charges wiped unless he's got clout with the chief. An' that don't wash. The chief's honest."

"So, we'll wait," I said. "Maybe he's planning to pull some stunt but we're armed. We're in the house. He knows he can't get at us. And tomorrow, I'm back on his case."

"Well, okay," Doug said. "If you wanna go by what he said, well, what can I say?"

So we spent the afternoon working together on the bookshelf for Angie's room. Doug cut and I sanded and it came out looking like something from a store. At six o'clock we knocked off for a drink before supper and Doug flipped the TV on for the news.

The usual election stories and foreign wars dominated the national news. Then the local anchor came on and made an announcement that stopped us cold.

"Another violent death has rocked the quiet skiing town of Chambers today." The camera showed a car on a quiet road with police cars around it, doors open, Cassidy and Schmidt and some uniformed men conferring. "An out-of-town visitor, a man who police claim is active in an organized crime family in New Jersey, was found shot to death in this rented car. A gun was found beside him and there are reports that he left a suicide note. Few details yet but we will bring you up to date as we learn more."

Doug turned to me wide-eyed. "That's Manatelli they're talkin' about. Did you kill the sonofabitch?"

I looked at him in disbelief, and he said, "Sorry, Reid. But this whole thing is unbelievable. Guys like Manatelli don't blow themselves away."

"I didn't kill him but somebody else did. I spoke to him before I came back here. He was fat and sassy then. He wasn't planning suicide."

Doug stood up, pacing up and down in front of the TV which was still playing the shot of the crime scene. He reached out absently and switched it off. "Okay. I'm sorry. But who did it?"

"Maybe his bodyguard did. Maybe he was Mucci's man after all and killed him on Mucci's say-so."

"That's the best guess," Doug said, looking at me but not seeing me, his eyes turned inward on his thoughts. "If the bodyguard'd been doin' his job he'd've stopped the guy who pulled the trigger." He stood and considered that for a moment. "But think a minute. If it was a mob killing there wouldn't have been any suicide note." He thrust his arms out. "You know their pattern. They like their message to be loud an' clear."

"Maybe they had a reason for cleaning things up down here. Maybe they're not through with Chambers yet. They want some time and they bought it the best way they could."

Doug sat down, crossing his legs tightly, rubbing his chin. He was tied up tighter than I'd ever seen him, even when things were bad in Nam. When he spoke I knew he hadn't been listening to me.

"I wanted the guy wiped," he said softly. "You heard me say it. But now it's happened I feel like shit. He insulted Melody, sure. An' me an' every brother in the world. But you don't shoot guys for that."

"This isn't your fault."

He waved me off. "I didn't pull the trigger but it's all down to me."

"You didn't kill him. You suspected he was involved in a crime, you checked it out. You're a cop. It's your job."

He didn't answer and I could see he needed some space so I said, "I'll put some coffee on."

It's true. Watched pots never boil. I stayed in the kitchen for what seemed like an hour until the coffee was ready. Then I heard the doorbell ring. Doug answered it. "Well, hi, Captain."

"Can I come in, Doug?" Schmidt was polite but his tone was formal. But not to where he sounded as if he was here to rearrest Doug. I put another couple of mugs on a tray with the coffee and took them through. Schmidt and Cassidy were coming in, keeping their hats on. This was business. "You heard about the mob guy?" Schmidt asked Doug, ignoring me.

"I heard about a killing, the TV didn't say who it was," Doug said carefully.

"Yeah. Well. Was a guy called Manatelli. The chief said you saw him in town here, figured he was pulling something."

"That's right," Doug said. "Manatelli's a honcho in the Mucci family."

"Right now he's so much pork." Schmidt waved one hand. "Ate his gun in his car. Left a note."

"That's what the TV said."

Schmidt looked at me as I set down the coffee. "You been here all day?"

"Most of it. Since around one. Why?"

"Can you prove that?"

"Why do I have to prove things, Captain?"

"Because I don't believe in Santa Claus," Schmidt snarled. "Answer me."

"I came in around one, like I said. The guy next door was clearing his walk. I spoke to him. Haven't been out since."

Schmidt looked at Cassidy who nodded and left without speaking.

"You said he left a note, Captain," Doug said softly. "What did it say, or is that confidential?"

"It's a fake, is what it is," Schmidt said. He looked at the coffee tray. I poured three mugs and handed one to him, one to Doug.

Doug said, "Thanks. ' makes you say it's a fake, Captain?"

Schmidt sipped his coffee. "It was written on the back of an envelope. Now if the envelope had been addressed to Mr. Manatelli, at the guy's home address, fine, that makes it look promising. But this was one o' those junk mail envelopes. Like, congratulations, you may have won a million bucks." He shook his head angrily. "Who the hell takes an envelope like that along with him in his car to the lookout on top of Mount Reach, then writes a note on it—just the envelope, not the stuff that was inside—an' sticks his gun in his mouth?"

"Sure sounds phony. What'd it say?"

Schmidt set down his cup. "It said, and I quote, 'I can't face it. I killed three people and framed the nigger cop with the money. But my boss wants the other fifty K. He'll kill me a worse way than this.' "

"Any idea who his boss is?" Doug asked carefully. "Is it Mucho Mucci?"

"We're checkin'. But the main thing is, you're clear."

"Clear?" Doug stood up, setting down his coffee cup very gently as if it were a primed Claymore mine. "You mean all this is over?"

"Yeah," Schmidt said. "The chief sent me to tell you. Like the only thing I had to do was see that you didn't have any part of this. Where have you been all day?"

"Right here, in the basement. Making a bookcase for my daughter. Wanna see?"

"Naah. The body was found around four. It was still warm. There were tire tracks of another car on the lookout. He was killed three o'clock, thereabouts. And it's been snowing all afternoon. I just checked, there's no track outside your place so I know Reid here is on the level when he said he was back at one. But we had to establish that." He waved his hands, a "what can a guy do" gesture. "Then I have ta take you to see the chief for the press conference."

"Press conference?" Doug was startled. "What in hell's that all about?"

Schmidt covered his embarrassment with a show of cop bonhomie. "Well, in case you haven't checked in the mirror today, you're still a different color from the rest of the department an' the chief felt bad about arresting you. Now he wants to put it right. I hope that sits okay with you, Doug."

"I understand," Doug said. I could see how angry he was but Schmidt didn't know him as well as I did.

"Yeah. Well. I wan'ed to say I never liked the charge and this is a happy day for me. For the whole department. I hope you ain' gonna hold it against us, what happened."

"No," Doug said. "I'm sorry about the people who've been killed. Always will be. But I've got no beef with what happened to me."

His voice was toneless but Schmidt's relief was obvious. He stood up and very tentatively stuck out his hand. Doug shook and Schmidt clasped his wrist with his other hand. "Thanks, Doug. You're a good detective an' a nice guy. Maybe I can buy you and Reid a drink after."

"That would be very nice, Captain. Thank you. I'll tidy up and come on in," Doug said.

"Great." Schmidt let go of Doug's hand and nodded, smiling his bull terrier smile. "I thank you for your professionalism and I'll tell the chief you'll be there, when? 'bout an hour be okay?"

"That's fine," Doug said. "I'll be there, in my best suit for the gentlemen of the press."

"Great," Schmidt said again, then, like a good little guest, "Thanks for the coffee. That a Marine recipe?"

"No saltpeter," I said to break the tension and we all chuckled and he went out.

Doug closed the door and came back to his seat. "They're grabbin' at fresh air," he said. "That note's phony as a three-dollar bill. Schmidt knows it, we all know it. They're just using it to clean up three homicides. Four, if you count Manatelli."

"This isn't the Kennedy assassination," I said. "Quit looking for a conspiracy. Manatelli's gone. Your family's safe, the town of Chambers is back to normal and you're golden."

That finally made him laugh. "Shit. How'd you ever pass the physical? You're blind, man. I ain' never gonna be golden."

I laughed with him, glad of his relief. "Go change and I'll drive you down there."

"Golden?" he said and laughed again. He shook his head and went upstairs.

He came down dressed as if he was going to a wedding. Neat suit, white on white shirt and a blue and red tie. I gave him a thumbs up and he laughed. "Kinda wish I had a red hat an' python boots like a pimp. See what the brass would feel about paradin' me out in that."

"It's all over," I said. "Why don't you call Melody and talk to her, then I'll drive you over. You can sit in the back if you like and I'll open the door for the cameras."

"Get outa here." He waved at me and I left him to telephone while I went and washed up.

When I got back downstairs he was sitting waiting for me. "Melody says to give you her love an' thanks," he said.

"How are they all?"

"Glad to be coming home. I spoke to the kids and everyone's fat an' happy." He smiled. "It's over, Reid."

"I know. Now let's get downtown and let the world know."

The press conference was held in the front office. The chief and Captain Schmidt were center stage with Doug, and Cassidy and Beeman, the uniformed guy on the desk, were beaming in the background, trying to get their pictures on TV. The chief described the suicide and read out Manatelli's note while the cameras rolled. And then everybody shook hands with Doug and he started to talk. He exonerated the department for arresting him. They had acted on the evidence, he said. It was a reminder to all of them of how hard it is to be sure of a case on the evidence.

I saw Schmidt shuffle his feet a little there and figured he was thinking about the phony suicide note but he said nothing.

Doug didn't give anything away about his suspicions of money-laundering but he explained that Ms. Laver had been assisting him in his investigations. Manatelli must have been involved and had killed her and staged the evidence. He didn't know why Grant and the second woman had been killed. Maybe they had found out about the first killing and been killed to shut them up. He said he was deeply saddened by what had happened but glad the case was closed.

The chief was beaming by the time Doug finished and he took a moment to say that he was grateful to Doug for his professionalism in accepting what had happened to him. He repeated his apology to Doug and the fact that Doug was reinstated and the people of Chambers could all rest easy now with the situation back to normal.

The reporters didn't buy everything he offered. They had questions. What was the investigation Doug was working on? Why had Manatelli been involved? Was the case anything to do with Cat's Cradle, where Cindy Laver had worked? There were some sharp minds out there and they weren't gulping down the story the way the chief must have hoped they would.

Then one of them, a woman who had obviously done some digging of her own, asked the sixty-four-dollar question. She had heard that a man who sounded like Manatelli had been seen in Chambers a few times, always with another, younger man who looked as if he might be an associate, maybe a bodyguard. Had anyone seen the man since his boss was killed?

The chief had thought about that one in advance. Yes, he had heard the same stories as they dug into Manatelli's movements since leaving the airport thirty miles away in his rented car. They were still looking for the man to find out what he could tell them, but there were no doubts, from the forensic evidence, no doubts at all that this had been a suicide.

There was a flutter of questions over this but the chief fielded them and slowly the reporters were satisfied.

A radio man and a TV crew stayed behind to talk to Doug and he answered all their questions. He was impressive, polite and attentive. He wasn't nervous and I could see that he had won them all over. Then at last they were finished and he shook hands with the interviewers and they left.

Schmidt had been standing close by, a little jealous of the attention Doug was getting, but now he snapped on his smile and took Doug by the arm. "How about that drink?"

"Be great, Captain. If you're sure you can spare the time."

"Got all the time in the world tonight," Schmidt growled

playfully. "Three homicides wrapped up an' a good man outa jail. Hell, we got a mess o' things to celebrate."

He held up long enough to call Cassidy to join us. Cassidy was equally cheerful but it looked a little forced, I thought. He covered it with a big laugh. "Morgan can take care of business for a spell. He's closin' up files like homicide is goin' out of style."

Schmidt led us to his car and when we were seated he said, "Let's head out to Brewskis. I like the idea of lookin' at pretty women in tight ski pants. Sound okay to you guys?"

"Great," Doug said. He was ill at ease but the others hadn't noticed. Schmidt and Cassidy sat in front and carried the conversation, lots of inside jokes with roars of laughter that sounded mechanical, like the first sputter of a snow vehicle motor starting up. Doug and I chuckled along as indicated but said nothing. It was tense in that car.

We got to Brewskis, which was busy as ever, and Schmidt parked illegally in the fire exit zone beside the door. "So. Let's get at it," he said and led us in.

The usual crowd of skiers was having the usual fun. A few of them must have heard the news. I saw them poking one another and pointing Doug out, trying not to be obvious. Schmidt ignored everyone, striding to the bar and using a mix of heartiness and strength to move a guy out so we could all four sit together.

He didn't check our preferences but ordered Wild Turkey and we toasted Doug and did our best to look like buddies. Carol Henning was on duty at the bar and she shook hands with Doug and took the captain's joshing and managed a word with me in passing. "Big day for you, Reid."

"Big day for justice." A class answer, I thought.

She reached over and covered my left hand with hers. "Glad it worked out the way you wanted."

"Thanks, Carol." I raised my glass to her and Schmidt called out, "Hey, that guy's got a wife and six kids back in Canada. You wanna mind him, Carol."

"Married guys I can handle, Cap." She smiled at him and I guessed he'd made the moves on her himself.

After a while the waitress, Cathy, found us a table and Schmidt ordered a bottle which wasn't bar policy but they'd put us in a corner where we didn't look too obvious so they obliged. Most bars stretch the rules a little for the police. It helps speed up the response time if you ever need A Cop Quick. Schmidt was pushing the drinking, sloshing whisky into all our glasses as soon as we'd taken a sip. It was the kind of drinking you do when you're eighteen and out to prove you're tougher than your old man. I was dogging it as much as possible and Schmidt roared at me to drink up. "That's the trouble with you goddamn Canucks. You can't drink."

Doug had been doing his share of the drinking, not enjoying it any more than me, but glad to be free and glad of the captain's gesture, recognizing it as part of his rehabilitation into the department. But he was still icy sober under the happy face he'd slipped on like a mask for the party. "Reid's a rye man," he explained. "Don't you worry, Cap'n. He'll be the guy drives us all home."

"Rye is it?" Cassidy whirled and shouted to the waitress. "Hey, Cathy."

She came over and he said, "Bring my friend here a double double rye, okay?"

"Sounds dangerous," I said and looked at her.

"Sure thing, Captain," she said to Schmidt and returned my gaze, weighing up the order and the spot I was in. I widened my eyes helplessly and she took the hint. I was in the corner, facing the bar, and I watched her give the order and saw Carol filling it. One part rye, one coffee, two water. Right color, but not a killer. It pays to have friends everywhere.

She brought it back and I raised it to her. "Thank you, Cathy. Your health."

"So down the hatch," Schmidt ordered and I drank three quarters of it in a gulp.

"Perfect," I told Cathy. "If you want to repeat the dose when necessary, I'll be real grateful."

She grinned at me. "No problem."

I'd temporarily shut Schmidt down and he eased up on me, feeling the effects of his own bourbon, starting to ramble about cases they were working on and how badly Doug was needed in the detective office. Doug was loosening up and the situation became easier. Until around ten, when Huckmeyer walked in.

Our booth was three or four down from his usual table and as he crossed the room he saw me and his face darkened. He changed direction and came over.

"Captain," he said to Schmidt who stood up and shook his hand like a lodge brother. Then he shook with Cassidy and finally with Doug. "Congratulations, Detective. I'm glad this business has been cleared up."

Doug made some reply but Huckmeyer wasn't listening. He nodded briefly and turned to me. I beat him to the punch, standing up as a gesture of surrender. "It seems I owe you an apology, Mr. Huckmeyer. I hope you'll excuse my manner earlier today. I was too wrapped up in what I was doing. I know I offended you and I'm very sorry."

It took the wind out of his sails. He'd been set to throw me out but now he would look too ungracious. He just scowled and said, "I'm not a crook, mister. I want you to know that."

Surprisingly Cassidy stood up for me. "We all know that, fer Crissakes, Walt. Hell, the guy was in Nam with Doug. They're buddies. He was makin' waves. He's apologized."

Huckmeyer stood, still looking at me sternly. Then he said, "Okay. I accept the apology." He stooped and picked up the tab from in front of Schmidt and tore it in half. "Have a good time, gentlemen. You're my guests tonight."

We all thanked him and Schmidt prevailed on him to join us. He did, for one drink, a draft beer, and Doug and I took the opportunity to switch along with him. The others went on hammering the Wild Turkey and Cassidy, showing the same surprising tact, got the conversation around to Huckmeyer's skiing career.

He talked about it, modestly enough, for as long as it took to finish his beer, then excused himself. "I've got a young lady to meet. I know a bunch of p'licemen will understand that."

We did an appropriate amount of joshing and he left us, easing the collar of his turtleneck as if he'd been in a wrestling match.

Schmidt was pretty drunk by now and his meanness was showing through. "You figured that guy was crooked?"

I shrugged. "Just stirring the mud a little, Captain. There wasn't much else I could do."

He leaned over the table at me, thrusting at me with his cigar. "I've known that kid since he was knee high. He's a good kid."

"I agree." It's no use arguing with a drunk.

He sneered. "Jesus. You're chickenshit." He laughed raggedly. "The big tough ex-Marine an' you ain' got the guts t'even argue."

Doug said, "You're outa line there, Cap'n." His voice was low but it had enough force in it to shut Schmidt down. He sat back and blew cigar smoke.

"So tell me about this case you got against young Walt."

"This ain't the place. We're drinkin' his booze," Doug said in the same dangerous tone.

"Nowhere better," Schmidt said. "Kinda cuts out the bullshit, seein' that we're his guests an' all."

"It's not a case. It's an observation," Doug said. "An' I'd rather not discuss it in public, Captain. If that's okay."

"Indulge me." Schmidt drained his glass and split what was left in the bottle with Cassidy and then drained his glass again.

Doug looked stubborn. "You know what I told the chief, Cap'n. And I don't want this to turn into a shouting match. We're drinking this man's liquor."

"Talk," Schmidt growled.

Doug shook his head regretfully but spoke. "Somebody here's selling the credit card slips for cash. The cash comes from an unnamed source. It looks to me like a money-laundering operation. And it also looked, given the fact that Manatelli was here, and he wasn't a skier, that it's mob money being washed."

Schmidt spread his hands and made an innocent face. "Well, excuse me, Detective. I guess I'm dumb. I don't see any crime here. Not at this location anyways."

"I said that a'ready," Doug said. "It's not a case. It's an observation. I was checking on it."

"Well, in that case, I'd guess the observation is over," Schmidt said. "Manatelli ain' around anymore."

"You're right," Doug said. "Listen. Can I get you another drink?"

"No need," Schmidt said grandly. "The chief laundryman is pickin' up the tab."

"Not for me, thanks, Captain," I said. "I'm driving home tomorrow and I can't do that if I'm wearing an ice pack."

"Yeah. An' my family's coming home. I don' wanna pick 'em up at the airport with a hangover," Doug said. "Thanks for everything, Cap'n. It's been great and it's great to be back at work."

Schmidt laughed and blustered about what poor drinkers we were but I guess the tension had gotten to him too. He stood up and beckoned to Cathy who came over with her tray. "These guys are crappin' out," he said, and dropped a ten-spot and the torn check on her tray. "Mr. Huckmeyer has very kindly made us his guests tonight. That's for you."

"Well, thank you, Captain." She gave us a big smile. "Come back real soon."

"With you waiting table. Count on it," Schmidt said and we all chuckled obligingly, even her.

We made a quick trip to Huckmeyer's table. He was still alone and he looked at his watch when we approached, then rose to meet us. "Can you beat that? She's stood me up," he said.

We thanked him for the drinks and he shook hands all around, even with me, and we headed out. I checked them. "Hey, I won't be coming back here. I want to say goodbye to the women."

The captain made some crack to Cassidy and they laughed but it wasn't unfriendly and they kept on going while I turned back to the bar and spoke to Cathy and Carol Henning. "Thanks for fixing my drink. I'm going home to-morrow and that guy wanted us all hammered. You were really on the bit, bailing me out that way."

I wanted to tip them but Cathy waved me off. "No thanks, Reid. I could see you were having a bad time. You're welcome."

I thanked them again and shook hands. Cathy gave me a quick kiss on the cheek and Carol, who couldn't reach over the bar, squeezed my hand fondly. It made me feel good.

We said goodbye and I turned to leave. I was halfway to the door when a man came in. It was the same guy I'd seen with Manatelli that morning. He didn't recognize me with-out my parka and toque on. He checked all around, then crossed the room and headed for Huckmeyer's table.

had no choice but to leave. I stayed only long enough to see Huckmeyer stand up at once, nodding almost imperceptibly toward the back. The guy took the hint and moved that way while Huckmeyer walked apart from him toward the office door. The other man took off his hat and shrugged out of his coat as he walked. Before he followed Huckmeyer into the office he checked and looked around. As soon as I saw that I ducked out.

Schmidt had backed his car to the door and they were waiting for me, ready to make the obvious cracks. "Hell," Schmidt said. "You sure took your time. We figured you were just going to kiss 'em goodbye. What happened? They lay you?"

"A man's gotta do what a man's gotta do," I said easily and he guffawed and turned right around from the wheel to look into my face. "For a goddamn Eskimo, you're okay, Reid."

"Thanks, Cap'n. You're okay yourself, well scrubbed."

It was the kind of teenage joshing that goes on when guys drink. Not clever but it does cut the tension and that's what Schmidt had been aiming to do. He drove, not well. He'd had about ten ounces of booze and he pushed too fast and slid wide on turns but at least he stopped for the red lights in town and got us back safely to my car.

Saying goodbye took another minute or so and then Schmidt had to make like the commander and tell Doug to take the rest of the week off to get back with his family. But eventually it was over and Doug and I got into my car. He immediately loosened his tie and sat back. "Thank God that's over," he said.

I didn't waste time. "Huckmeyer did have a date. But not with a girl. Manatelli's bodyguard came to see him. Huckmeyer didn't speak to him. Gave him the eyes and went into the back office. The guy followed him."

Doug whistled softly, a long, surprised note. "Now that's interesting. Makes all this look like a plan."

"Could be. Or maybe the guy has something on Huckmeyer. Like knowing that he did it."

"Either way it don't fit with the nice neat ending the chief figures he's got," Doug said.

"What do we do? Wanna go back out there?"

"And what? Grab the guy when he comes out, talk to him?"

"We could do that."

Doug thought about it. "You could. I couldn't. Not now I'm back on the department. If he squawked, I'd be in a whole mess of trouble." He looked at me anxiously. "Hell, they've already stretched their goodwill far as it'll go. If I start making waves they'll come down on me, both feet."

"The only other thing is to go back and follow the guy. See where he goes."

"Wouldn't hurt, I guess," Doug said doubtfully.

I turned the car around. "He has to be there for a reason. Let's go see. It's better than doing nothing."

Doug didn't answer but I saw him snug up his tie again, the sign that he was back at work.

We got back to Brewskis and parked in the first row of cars, up at the far end, where we could see the door. People came and went and we waited, wishing we'd taken the time to use the men's room. Then, around eleven o'clock, the guy came out, unmistakable in his city clothes.

He walked between the parked cars in front of the door and back into the lot. Doug got out, shutting the door so his silhouette wouldn't show, and stood watching the man. Then he slipped back into his seat. "He's in a car, going around the other end of the line, out toward the road."

"Okay." I started after him, leaving my lights off. "Keep your eyes on him. I'll have to concentrate on keeping out of the ditch."

It wasn't too bad at first, with nothing coming the other way. Then a high truck came up very fast and I had to slow down and work hard to stay out of the snowbank beside the road. The truck driver flashed his lights at me and leaned on the horn as he went by but I hung on, leaving my lights out as Doug followed the taillights ahead of us.

The car ahead picked up speed toward town and I thought I was going to lose him. But then I saw him turn, not signaling, and pull into a driveway. I kept on past the drive, glancing up it.

"That's Kelly's place," Doug said. "He must be staying there."

I drove on another hundred yards and stopped. We both got out and spent a grateful minute against the snowbank at roadside before getting back in to consider our options.

"What now?" I asked.

"Goddamned if I know," Doug said. "I mean, we got nothing to go on. This guy was with Manatelli. He should've stopped him from getting killed. Failing that, you'd have expected him to hightail it outa here when his boss died. Instead of that, he goes to see Huckmeyer. I got no idea why."

We looked at one another in the dark, helplessly. "We need help," I said. "There's two guys we could talk to. Pat Hinton is one. He could fill us in on the details of what happened today."

"He may not know much more'n us," Doug said. "If this

case was wrapped up by Schmidt an' Cassidy, they'd've kept it tight. Pat likely hasn't seen the note.''

"Okay. Then the other possibility is Maloney.''

"The lawyer? What can he do?''

"He wants to be the next judge around here. He's up to speed on what's been happening. He knows everybody and everything about the town. And he's got a good mind. He'll look at it from the legal point of view.''

Doug was doubtful but after a while we compromised. We would wait where we were for half an hour, to see if the man was going to stay at Kelly's place. Then we would head into town and talk to Maloney. "It's late,'' Doug said. "I don't think he's gonna welcome us with open arms.''

In fact it didn't take us half an hour. In twenty minutes the lights went out in Kelly's shack. We hung on for a few minutes more but the man didn't leave and we drove into town.

I rang Maloney from a pay phone. He answered on the second ring, sounding wide awake. "Mr. Maloney. It's Reid Bennett. Sorry to call you so late but there's a lot going on and I wondered if I could come and see you. I've got Doug Ford with me.''

"Of course. Come on over. I'll be waiting.''

I thanked him and hung up and drove to his house. The porch light was on and he came to the door as soon as we drove up. He was wearing a dressing gown over pajamas. "Come on in,'' he said.

We went in. His radio was playing some piano piece and there was an open book facedown on the table beside his favorite chair. He sat down and waved us to the couch. "What's happening?''

Doug filled him in and he sat and listened carefully. When Doug finished he said, "I see what you mean. The death of this man Manatelli raises a lot of questions.''

I'd been listening to Doug just as carefully and one question had occurred to me. I laid it out. "This is so obvious that I guess it's been taken care of. But it's nagging at me.''

"Shoot," Doug said. He seemed a little more relaxed now, slipping back into his role as cop.

"Let me guess, Reid," Maloney said softly. "Because I've got a question as well." I waited for him and he went on. "You're wondering whether anyone has identified the body found in the car."

I looked at him with new respect. "Exactly. The only people in town who know what the guy looks like are myself and Doug and maybe Walter Huckmeyer. Captain Schmidt had never met him or he'd have said so."

Doug looked from one to the other of us. "Jesus H. suffering. You think this is a plant?"

"We can't be sure until one of us has seen the body," I said.

"They must have compared his face with an FBI photograph," Doug said. "Must've done."

"When did Captain Schmidt come to see you?" Maloney asked.

"Six o'clock, just about on the nail," Doug said. "We were watching the six o'clock news."

"And the body had not been found until four, you said." Maloney would be a good judge, I thought. He was calm and thorough.

"You're right." Doug pinched his lips together and shook his head. "They wouldn't have got a picture faxed back from the FBI in that time. They must have been going on the ID they found on the body."

"We can't check until the morning. Cassidy and Schmidt have gone home by now," Doug said.

"The question is . . ." Maloney raised one finger, a courtroom trick, but it worked. We listened and he said, "Why, if this isn't Manatelli's body, would he want people to think it is?"

"He's ducking out on his boss," Doug suggested. "I figure he was skimming Mucci's operation. You can't get away with that. I figure he's skipped, planted some other poor bastard."

"Maybe." I was thinking along a different track, prodded down it by Maloney's attitude. "Maybe it was more than that. Maybe he's moving his money out of the bank. He wanted to close things down here, tidy them up first. So he planted the body."

"Like I said, he's skipping," Doug insisted.

"What Reid says makes sense, when you remember his conversation with Manatelli. The man promised to clear you, today. He must have been planning the death of this impostor, plus planting the suicide note."

Doug stood up. He was always restless. Even when we were in the boonies, worn out by humping eighty-pound packs through the monsoon all day, he could never sit still. "It don't make sense. What's it to him whether I do ten to life in the pen?"

"It was the price Reid demanded for leaving things alone," Maloney said. "I think we have a number of things to do."

"What?" Doug sat, but nervously, on the edge of the couch like a girl on a bad date.

"First." Maloney gripped his left index finger with his right hand. "Get a positive identification of the body. If it's Manatelli, then perhaps everything is kosher, although the note sounds improbable. But if it's not Manatelli who was killed, we move to phase two." He wrapped the next finger. "We check with the bank—I'd better do it—and see if Manatelli withdrew a large sum of money today."

"What about the bodyguard?" I asked.

"The police should talk to him. Perhaps Detective Hinton would be the best man to do it," Maloney said. "Can you talk to him in the morning, Doug?"

"He's gonna be gun-shy," Doug said. "Schmidt has wrapped the case up. He won't want to see it coming unraveled on Pat's say-so."

"Then perhaps I should talk to the chief," Maloney said. "I know him." He paused and added apologetically, "Through the lodge."

Doug grinned for the first time since we got there. "Then you're the right kind of brother to do the talkin'."

"Exactly." Maloney smiled. "I'll call him first thing. He says he's up at six. I'll call at seven."

"He won't be happy," Doug warned. "He'll be fine with you, but he's gonna hate my black ass for stirring this up."

"Then I'll tell him Reid told me," Maloney said. "So don't worry, and don't worry about the bank. I have a similar connection there."

Doug blew out a little puff of relief. "Well, thank you, sir. It's gonna be a lot easier if you take charge."

Maloney stood up. "Well, tomorrow is going to be busy, so let's call it a night. Thank you for coming to me with this."

We left him then and went back to Doug's house. I took Sam out for a walk around the block and came back to find Doug working in the basement, changed into blue jeans, sanding down the bookcase as if it needed the work. "I can't sleep yet," he said apologetically. "You hit the sack. I'll be a while here."

I could see he needed space so I said, "Okay, Doug. See you in the morning," and headed up to bed.

The drinks, plus the light sleep from the night before, had left me more tired than I figured and I was asleep in minutes with Sam curled on the rug beside the bed. I didn't hear Doug come up and was woken up only by the telephone.

It was still dark outside. I heard Doug answering but not the words. From his tone I could tell that it wasn't Melody on the other end. He was brisk and formal and didn't laugh the way he used to do when I last saw the pair of them together.

I swung out of bed and started dressing. It sounded like that kind of call. By the time I had my pants on he was at the bedroom door. "That was the chief. Wants me to go in and look at the body in the morgue, right away. He don't sound happy."

"Should I come?"

"Yeah," Doug said. "You saw Manatelli yesterday. I haven't seen him in a couple months."

I washed up and shaved, wishing there were time for a proper shower, and then dressed while Doug went through the same routine. We stopped briefly at a diner to pick up some coffee and arrived at the morgue at seven-thirty.

"The chief's here," Doug said and flipped his thumb at a parked car. "Let's get at it."

We went in. The chief was in the lobby with a uniformed officer. Doug spoke first. "Morning, Chief, Roger."

"Good morning," the chief said and the patrolman nodded. "Mr. Maloney phoned me this morning. Said he'd been wondering about this man Manatelli. Said that this all sounded a little too pat and asked if anyone who knew Manatelli had identified the body."

"Who found him?" Doug asked.

"I did, Detective," the uniformed man said. "Mount Reach is the limit of area three. I pulled in at the lookout to make my book up before going off duty." And to have a quiet smoke. I thought. The man went on. "There was a car parked there, a Lincoln. I saw what looked like blood on the window of the driver's side so I checked an' found him."

"Good thinking," Doug said. "Shall we take a look?"

The chief was looking at me. "Do we need to take up Mr. Bennett's time?" he asked stiffly.

"I spoke to Manatelli yesterday," I explained. "Doug thought my identification would be the most up to date."

"Very well then." The chief opened the door to the inner office where an orderly in a fawn dustcoat sat sipping coffee. He set down his cup. "Ready now, Chief?"

"Please." The chief was tense as we followed the man through into the big cold room with the stainless steel cabinets down one wall.

"He's in here," the attendant said, indicating a drawer at waist level. "Between the guy an' the girl he killed. Justice, huh?"

"Open it," the chief snapped. The man looked at him, hurt that his comment had been ignored.

The body was covered with a sheet and the attendant flicked it back from the face. Doug and I looked at it, then at one another. "That's not him, sir," Doug said. "I'm sorry, but somebody's pulled a stunt on us. That ain't Manatelli."

glanced at the chief first. His jaw was set and I knew he was working out a plan for damage control. The uniformed man took his cue from his boss, showing no emotion. The only one shocked was the attendant. He stood there with his mouth open. You could see he was thinking, just wait until the guys at the pool hall hear about this. Maybe he could even call the local radio station, win twenty-five bucks for the news tip of the week.

The chief nipped all those plans in the bud. He stuck his finger about an inch from the guy's nose. "Listen up. This is a police investigation. We already knew what this detective has confirmed. We're doing what we're doing to put the man Manatelli off guard. He thinks he's fooled us and that's what we want, while we keep on looking for him." He paused, then demanded, "Do you understand me?"

"I think so, sir."

"Good," the chief said. "Now pay attention to me, because if you don't, you'll be looking for a new job."

That point was loud and clear. The man cleared his throat and asked, "What d'ya want me to do, Chief?"

"You say nothing. If any word of this gets out it will hamper our investigation and you are out of this job or any other city job as long as you live."

"I know about being confidential." The man's face was red. "I can see what's happenin', Chief. I won't say nothing to anybody."

"Not even Dr. Weichel," the chief warned. "He already knows. But that's all. We don't want anyone else to know. Not your wife. Not your neighbors. Not even your god-damn dog."

"I gotcha." The guy was hoarse now.

"Right. Close this up." The chief turned and swept out. We followed him. He stopped in the lobby and said, "My office. Follow me down there."

"Right," Doug said and we went out and got into the car.

Doug didn't speak until the chief's car had started away and we followed. Then he said, "He's gotta feel like a god-damn moron."

"The question is, where does this leave you?"

Doug picked up the pace, following the chief's driver who was breaking the speed limit back to the station. "If it falls apart, I'm back inside and all bets are off. But he won't want that to happen. He'd look too stupid." Doug grinned without amusement. "After those swell speeches yesterday about what a righteous boy I am, if he has to send me back inside he's got egg all over him."

"That's the good news. The bad news is that Manatelli's had almost a day to do what he planned."

"Outside of business hours," Doug said as we pulled into the parking lot behind the police building. "If he was plan-ning something at the bank, it ain't done yet."

We went in. Roger, the cop who had driven the chief, was in the front office waiting for us. "The chief says to go right in, Detective."

"Thanks." Doug nodded to him and the cop looked grate-ful for the recognition. I guessed he'd felt the rough side of the chief's tongue on the way back, had heard the same speech as the morgue attendant.

The chief was standing at the window. He turned and went to his chair. "Siddown," he said. We sat and he looked at me. "I don't see how you can help us here, Mr. Bennett."

"With all respect, I think I can, Chief. If you're keeping the information confidential, you can use me instead of spreading the news any further."

He thought about it in silence for a moment, then said, "Yeah. You're right." He opened his desk drawer and rummaged, then came out with a badge. "I don't have a Bible here. You a religious man?"

"No. But I mean it when I swear an oath."

"Good. Do you swear to uphold the laws of the United States and the State of Vermont during your tenure as a special officer with the Chambers Police Department?"

"I do." I raised my right hand for him and he passed me the badge.

"You're in," he said. "It's confidential but until this thing is wrapped up, you're a member of the department. I'll see what I can do about pay an' all when this is over."

"Good." I didn't waste time. "Let me tell you what I saw last night. At around ten-thirty Manatelli's bodyguard visited Walter Huckmeyer in Brewskis. They went into Huckmeyer's office. Then I followed the guy and saw that he went to the mobile home of Mike Kelly, the biker who deals grass, the guy who came after Doug and me two nights back. You know about him."

The chief waved one hand. "Of course. Right. Get over there and find out what you can. Do you have a weapon?"

"Just my dog."

"That's a start. But take this." He dug into his drawer again and came up with a police .38 in a shoulder holster. He broke protocol by passing it to me without opening the cylinder but I took it and checked the load. Six shots. I took my coat off and slipped the holster on. "You want the guy in here?"

"I want the truth," the chief said ominously. "If you have to charge him with the murder of the guy in the morgue that's fine. But find out what Manatelli's doing and where the sonofabitch is."

"Will do." I turned to Doug. "Can I get a house key? I want to take Sam." To the chief I added, "It's on my way, won't take more than a minute."

"Under the window box at the left side," Doug said. "Good luck."

I picked up Sam and pushed my car to the limit out to Kelly's shack. The car we'd followed the night before was still there and there was a light on inside. I went up to the door and banged on it. Sam was at my heel, silent and ominous.

Kelly came to the door in long johns. He was just out of bed, eyes gritty. He didn't even have the moxie to reach up for his gun. I shoved him aside. "Where's your buddy?"

He was still blustering and I took a moment to grab his shotgun and turn and fling it away by the barrel, sending it cartwheeling over the driveway, into the snow on the other side. I knew he'd never go out that far, dressed as he was.

"You can't do that," he roared but Sam and I went by to the back room of the shack. The bodyguard was sitting up in bed, feeling under his pillow. I told Sam, "Fight," and he jumped on the bed, snarling in the man's face.

"Get him offa me," the man screamed but he didn't reach any farther.

"Hands on your head," I said, then to Sam, "Easy, boy."

The guy put his hands on his head and I felt under his pillow and took out his gun, a Walther. I stuck it in my coat pocket. "Where's Manatelli?"

"He's dead. Where you bin? It was on the news last night."

"That's my second question. Who's the guy in the morgue and who shot him? You or Manatelli? But first I want the truth. Where's Manatelli?"

"He's dead," he said again. I reached for his hand and

folded his fingers backward. The pressure was too much and he sprawled face first on the covers, his hand up behind him. "You're breakin' my hand."

"I know," I said. It wouldn't break until I cranked the pressure way up above where I had it, but he didn't know. He had soft hands with no real strength in them.

"Fer Crissakes! I don' know," he said and I turned up his fingers a little farther. He screamed. I ignored him, glancing around to check on Kelly. He was dressed now in denims and a work shirt.

"Sit," I told him. "On the floor, where I can see you. Move and the dog'll have your face off."

He sat. I pointed to him with my free hand and told Sam, "Keep." Sam ran over to him, making him cower back, covering his face, then stood in front of him, his big head a few inches from Kelly's face. Scratch Kelly as a threat. I turned my attention back to the man on the bed. "I couldn't hear you," I said softly. "Remember. I asked where your boss is."

"He's with the kid from the ski lodge," he hissed. "Please. Please leggo o' my hand."

I threw his hand away. "Get dressed."

He lay for a moment, nursing his fingers, breathing in a low sob. "I'll kill you," he said softly. "I'll shoot your god-damn balls off."

"Forget it. You're inside for life," I told him. "Get dressed and hurry."

He sat up, sullenly. He was wearing a blue silk undershirt and boxer shorts. "You look sweet," I told him. "You'll be a big hit in the joint in those shorts. Get dressed."

He didn't move immediately and I slapped him hard across the face. It's not my style but there was no time to play games. I wanted him at the station and I had no hand-cuffs. I had to cow him completely.

The slap broke his machismo. He scrambled into his clothes and I ushered him out into the main room of the tiny shack. Kelly's topcoat lay on the couch, added to the blanket he had used to cover himself through the night. I checked the pockets for a weapon. There was nothing there and I tossed the coat to Kelly. "You too. You're coming in. Now, where's your phone?"

"I ain't got one." A sneer. That's how tough he was. No phone! Wow!

"Get your boots on."

He swore and protested but I hissed at Sam who went into a savage bark that instantly had him scrambling into his coat and cowboy boots. Then I took both guys out and put them in the back seat of my car, setting Sam facing them from the front seat with the instruction to keep. "One move out of either of you and you're gone," I warned.

They didn't move. I backed quickly out of the drive and howled back down to the station. A uniformed man was coming down the steps, heading for his car. I called out to him. "I have the man the chief is looking for, here in my car. Help me bring him in, please."

I'd seen the cop around, so I guessed he knew who I was. He didn't ask questions, just came to the car door and opened it. I told Sam, "Easy," and he relaxed while the two men got out. "Inside, please, officer," I said and followed them in.

The chief was out of his office, standing at the telephone. He held up one finger when he saw me, then quickly finished his conversation and hung up. "This the guy?"

"Yes. He says the guy we're looking for is with young Huckmeyer."

"Get over there," he said. "Ford's upstairs. Take him with you. He knows where to go." He lifted the counter flap. "You two, this way."

I left him and ran up the stairs. Doug was sitting with Pat Hinton and they looked up. "Manatelli's staying with young Huckmeyer. The chief says to pick him up."

They both sprang up. Doug said, "Take the detective car, Pat. I'll go with Reid."

We sprinted downstairs and out to my car. I opened the

door and told Sam, "In the back," and he hopped over the seat so that Doug could get in.

"He's on Maple. Go up Water Street, that's three blocks up on the left," he told me and I backed out and raced away up the street. It was eight-fifteen now, just light. Traffic was moving, mostly cars with ski racks. I saw the drivers glancing at me nervously as I roared by and turned onto Water Street.

"Right on Maple. It's a big white house," Doug said. His voice was soft and excited. "We've got him," he said. "We've got the bastard."

"Not yet," I said. "Not until he's got handcuffs on his wrists."

"Huckmeyer. Huckmeyer. Be there, you smooth-talkin', smooth-skiin' devil, you," Doug crooned. Then he said, "In there."

I whisked into the driveway. It was empty.

"He's gone," Doug said. "He always drives a Blazer, leaves it in the drive, summer an' winter."

Pat Hinton pulled in behind us. "He's gone," he said as he got out. "I bet he's at work, Cat's Cradle."

"Let's check the house," Doug said. "Maybe he's left Manatelli at home."

"Cover the back," Hinton said. "I'll bang on the front door."

"Come on, Sam." I clambered over the snowbank beside the walk to the front door and plowed through the knee-high snow to the back of the house. There were no tracks back there. Nobody had made a run for the fence when we arrived, and there was no sign of life in the house.

I stood there, with Sam, until Doug appeared at the side. "No answer," he said. "Don't mean Manatelli's not there, but he's not answering if he is."

"Let me check these windows," I said and I made the rounds. It was no good. All of them were covered by aluminum storm windows with screens, all shut tight. It meant breaking two panes of glass and the screen to get in.

"Maybe he's got a slip lock on the front," Doug said.

We trudged back through the snow, which was filtering down over the top of my boots and chilling my legs to the bone. When I got to the porch I took the boots off and shook out the snow.

Doug checked the lock. "Dead bolt," he said. "We can't get in without a key or a wrecking bar."

"Check around for a key," Hinton suggested. He lifted the mat and Doug and I checked under anything else movable but we found nothing.

"You better stay, Pat," Doug said. "Get on the horn and tell the chief what's happening. Me an' Reid'll head out to Cat's Cradle."

"I'd like to be there," Hinton said longingly.

"Manatelli's the guy we're after," Doug said. "We have to cover this place."

"Yeah. Okay." Hinton slumped a little but went back to the police car and sat inside. We saw him talking on the radio as I backed out around him and headed for the ski hills.

Traffic was stopped on the road out of town and it took twenty minutes to get to the cause of the problem. A car with New York plates had slid off the road into the snowbank and a bunch of hearty ski types were trying to push it out. We slowed long enough for Doug to check that none of the people looked like anything but skiers, then spurted on to Cat's Cradle.

It was already busy. The hills were dotted with the brightly colored outfits of skiers carving their way down the slopes and the parking lot was still filling up with carloads of newcomers, fit-looking people, a few children, carrying skis over their shoulders, making for the tows.

"Let's hustle," Doug said. "If he gets on the slopes we'll never find him."

The office staff was just arriving and Doug paused only for directions to Huckmeyer's office. It was empty and there was no coat hanging there. We ducked back to the front and asked the receptionist where he was.

"I haven't seen him. If he's in, he may be on the slopes. Are his skis in there?"

"Didn't see them," Doug said. "Is there a phone in the lift shacks?"

The girl frowned. "No. Why?"

"Never mind," Doug said. "Which one would he use?"

"The gondola lift. It goes to the top of Devil's Fingers. Those are the hard runs, the ones he likes."

"Thanks," Doug said. "Let's go."

We ran out and up the slope to the gondola lift. There were skiers in the line, fit and full of fun. They laughed when we plowed past them into the lift house. "Has Walter Huckmeyer gone up here?" Doug demanded.

The kid in charge was around nineteen, young and efficient and insolent. "Who wants him?"

Doug reached out and pulled the big lever next to the kid. "The police, son. Now tell me, is he on this lift?"

"Hey. You can't stop the lift. We on'y stop it for emergencies," the kid blustered.

"P'lice emergency." Doug pulled out his badge case and flopped it open. "Now. Tell me. Is Huckmeyer on the lift?"

"Wen' up around five minutes ago," the kid said. "He could be at the top by now."

"Do you have a line to the guy at the top?"

"No, off'cer." The boy was finally getting the message. "We can start and stop it from either end if somethin' goes wrong, or to let people on and off, that's all. And we've got a signal bell."

"Leave it shut and use the signal to tell the top guy to leave it off until I tell you to turn it back on. Understand?" Doug said.

"Shit. I guess so." He was lost now, his authority stripped away. Doug turned to me. "How do we get up there?"

"There's a couple of skidoos in the ski patrol chalet. I'll take one up there."

"Are they hard to ride?"

"Like a motorbike, kind of. But you're needed down here.

Get some more guys out to cover the foot of the slopes in case he's on his way down. And go and immobilize his car. The staff'll know which it is."

"Good thinking," Doug said. "Take these." He flicked out his handcuffs and I slipped them into my pocket and told him, "You'd better take Sam. You know his commands. I'll turn him over to you."

"Right. Good." Doug stood still while I ran through the handover procedure. Then Doug ran back down to the office with Sam at his heel.

I clumped up to the ski patrol office and showed them my badge. The woman in charge was bright and sensible. She gave me a skidoo without question and pointed out the easiest way to get up the slope. It was steep, the kind of grade you see in the Winter Olympics, and there was a section of moguls about a hundred yards long close to the top. The few skiers who were taking them were shocked to see me, but none of them fell. I drove around the area, hugging the edge of the trees where the ground was fairly even, although still steep. And then, above it, I came to a ten-foot precipice.

A skier came over it, above me, like a bird, to land on the short, smooth section that led to the moguls. Like the kid had said in the office, one hell of a challenging run.

The ground sloped up to the trees on either side of the ski slope and the precipice bowed at the ends to meet it so I was able to pick my way through the trees and find a grade I could climb. I covered the last fifty yards to the top of the gondola lift and got off the machine, leaving it facing back toward the slope.

The boy in charge was waiting for me, and beyond him, hovering above the treetops, was the closest gondola with a bouquet of faces peering at the glass toward me.

"What's goin' on? I got people stranded," he said.

"Has Walter Huckmeyer got here yet?"

"Haven't seen him."

"Okay. Start up and bring the car to within six feet of the dock."

"You mean in, don't ya?"

"No. I mean where the people can't get out until I've checked them."

"Now, listen, Mac," he started. He was cut from the same cloth as his buddy at the other end.

I took off my glove and flashed the badge the chief had given me. "Chambers police," I said. "Do like I said, please."

"Okay. You're the boss." He started the car and I saw relief in the trapped faces, then exasperation as the car stopped short of the pad.

I studied all the faces, making sure Huckmeyer wasn't among them, then stood where the door would come and waved the kid to finish bringing it in. He did and the people poured off, angry and questioning. The delay had wiped out their skiing spirit and turned them back into city people, frustrated and argumentative.

I stood there, ignoring their questions, until they moved away, snapping on their skis. Then I signaled the operator again and he brought up the next car in the same two stages.

Three cars came up before I detected the one that Huckmeyer was in. I couldn't see him, but I could tell from the way some of the faces were turned away from me, looking down, that he was crouching there, hiding from me.

I called to the operator to bring it right in. The stopping point I'd chosen, six feet out, was only twelve feet above the snow and I figured a fit young skier like Huckmeyer might drop out and head down the slope, leaving me with my face hanging out.

I'd guessed right. I heard shrieks from the women in the car and two skis flopped out to land heel down and stick in the snow. Then Huckmeyer sat on the edge of the doorway, turned and gripped the floor, looked down once and dropped as the car kept moving.

He landed, rolling like a paratrooper and reaching for his skis, and I turned and ran for the snowmobile.

The machine started first pop and I headed back down

the hill, forty yards behind him, with him gaining on me as he headed for the precipice. I'd scouted it before I climbed through the trees and knew where it was only four feet high. I turned the machine and headed straight down at the shallowest point. It was a risk but I was hunting mad and I leaned as far back as I could on the machine and wound it up. He went over the edge, twenty yards to my right and fifty yards in front of me. I lined up straight to cut the risk as far as I could, then braced myself up off the seat, arms and legs slightly bent, clutching the saddle with my knees.

The machine hung in the air for hours, it seemed, but my speed kept the nose from dipping and I landed flat with a jolt that crunched my stiffened spine and made my head sing. But I was still up and I could see Huckmeyer hammering away at the moguls, doing his best to keep his lead.

I had him. The machine whisked around the edge of the mogul field and I was level with him within ten feet of the end. He gave a convulsive pump with his arms, trying to lift himself into maximum speed, but I was there, five yards to one side and outrunning him.

I aimed for the back of his skis, knowing what would happen when I hit them. It did. The track of the machine passed over the backs of both skis, checking him so that both bindings snapped, sending him sprawling forward down the slope. I whipped around in front of him and jumped off the machine. He was game as hell and tried to run but I caught one hand and twisted it up his back, fiddling in my pocket for the handcuffs. He almost broke away and I stuck my foot between his and tripped him, facedown.

That was the final straw. He lay there, panting into the snow, and I unsnapped the catch on his right ski boot and yanked it off. He yelled at me, "Hey. What d'you think you're doing?" I ignored him and handcuffed his right hand to his right ankle.

"Get on the machine in front of me," I told him and he got up and hobbled through the deep snow to the snowmobile. "In front," I said. "And don't try anything cute or I'll pull your other boot off and make you walk down."

He got on, bent low over the restriction of the handcuffs, and held on to the handlebars with his left hand. I got on behind him, dropping his ski boot between us, and drove slowly down the slope. Skiers passed me, swinging their heads to see the action. I ignored them and they went on, picking up speed, racing to get back to their friends with the most exciting news of the day. One ski patroller passed, with a spare pair of skis in one hand. Huckmeyer's, I guessed, but the man gave no indication, just went on down the slope, carving his turns with the easy grace of a lifetime's skiing.

I drove back to the ski patrol chalet and stopped. "Inside, Walter." He sat there a moment. "Do I have to stay this way? Couldn't you put the handcuffs on my wrists?"

"Lean forward. Put your head flat down," I ordered and he looked at me bitterly but did as I said. I sat on his back while I unlocked his ankle, using the cuff key from my own key ring. Then I grabbed his left wrist and cuffed his arms behind his back.

I got off him. "That better?" He said nothing but swung his leg over the saddle and sat there. I dropped his other boot in front of him. "Shove your foot into that and get into the shack," I told him and he did it without a word.

There were two patrollers in the shack, the woman in charge and the man who'd picked up Huckmeyer's skis. The woman said, "What's going on? Why's Walter in handcuffs?"

"It's a police matter. Do you have a phone, please?"

"Sure." She pointed and I nodded thanks and pushed Huckmeyer gently toward a chair.

He sat, as well as he could with his hands behind him, and I phoned the police and reported what I'd done. They said they'd contact the radio car at the scene and let Doug know. He would join me.

I thanked the dispatcher and hung up. "I need to talk to Mr. Huckmeyer in private, please," I said.

The woman stood up. "You're not going to hurt him?"

"No, ma'am. I'm a police officer, temporarily assigned to the Chambers department. I just want to talk. But it has to be in private."

She looked at Huckmeyer, nervously. "That all right with you, Walter?"

He nodded dumbly and she reached for a parka. "I have to be near the phone," she told me. "I'll be outside. Call me if it rings."

"Will do, and thank you." I was beginning to realize what a jolt I'd taken. My whole body ached and my head felt as if it would like to fall off and roll across the ground. I eased my neck gently with my right hand. The male patroller spoke then. "Hurt yourself, did you? Jesus. You gotta be a head case. I saw you go over that jump."

"Special circumstances," I said. "Your machine's okay."

"How about you?" the woman asked.

"I'll be fine, thank you. But I do have to talk to Mr. Huckmeyer."

They looked at one another and then left. I swung my chair to face Huckmeyer. "Where were you going?"

"Skiing," he said tightly. "Why the hell else would I be on the gondola? I work here. I have the right to ski when I want to."

"We were at your house. Manatelli's gone. D'you know where?"

"I don't know what you're talking about. I don't know anybody called Manatelli."

"Walt, believe me. His bodyguard is down with the police chief, singing like a bird. He told us Manatelli was with you last night. So don't waste time. It's him we want. Not you. He's the guy who killed those people. Or set it up for his flunky to do it."

"I don't know why you came after me. I don't know anything. I want to speak to my lawyer. I'm going to sue you for everything you've got."

"That's fine. We'll take you downtown. Then you can get your shyster in. But by then it'll be too late. Once Manatelli's gone, your chance of making any deals is over."

"I'm saying nothing," he said. "Except to protest the humiliation you've caused me."

"Fine. Sit there and wait. See how slowly the time goes. Then think about spending ten, fifteen years the same way."

I got up and went to the door. "You can come in now, thank you."

The ski patrol supervisor came back in. She didn't say anything but looked at Huckmeyer nervously. He said, "This is a bad mistake, Jennifer. I'm going to sue this man for what he's done."

"Do you want me to call anybody for you?" she asked.

"Please. Call Mr. Garfield at Garfield and Wallace in town, could you. Ask him to come out and clear this thing up."

"Will do," she said. She glanced at me, a look of pure contempt, and picked up the phone. I stepped outside, still easing my neck. Doug Ford was jogging up the slope from the office. He had Sam at his heels and he was beaming a yard wide.

I went forward to meet him and he stuck out his hand, raised high. I slipped back a barrelful of years and gave him the dap we'd worked out in the platoon. High slap, low slap, clap hands, both hands clap the other man's. We were like kids playing patty cake.

"Got the bastard. Got him," he said.

"That's good news. But he's just phoning for Garfield. Wants to sue my ass."

"Fear not," Doug said. "I just been talking to Ms. Frazer. Our friend from last night had her checking the books for irregularities. She says the kid's been squirreling money away like there's no tomorrow. She's found forty-seven grand already and that's just this year."

"Great. He's playing innocent in there and I don't have a hell of a lot to hold him on."

"The chief says we can charge him with conspiracy to commit murder. The guy you brought in wants to testify, go on the witness protection program."

"Has he spoken to a lawyer?"

"The lawyer set it up. Slippery Sam Garfield himself came in right away, talked to the guy in private and then begged the chief for the chance to let the guy talk."

"That was bloody quick. The guy must've been busting a gut to roll over."

"Could be. Could just be," Doug said jovially. "But I get the feeling that Garfield knew what was going down. He didn't want any of it getting on him, so he gave the guy a nudge to clear it up."

"Sounds good to me." I rubbed my neck again and Doug asked me what happened. When I told him he laughed.

"You wild sonofabitch. You coulda killed yourself."

"I think maybe I hastened the process some. You wanna talk to Smilin' Jack?"

"Sure. Why not?" Doug put his hand on my back, but gently. "Let's go give him the glad tidings."

We went back inside. The ski patroller was standing with the phone in her hand, looking at Huckmeyer who had his head down, defeated.

"Morning, Jennifer," Doug said cheerfully. "Morning, Walter. If you're calling Garfield, save your money. He's at headquarters, giving singing lessons to Manatelli's bodyguard. You wanna join him?"

"I'm not saying anything," Huckmeyer said huskily.

"No problem," Doug said. "The guy down there is doing enough talking for everybody. Come on now. Let's go join them."

Huckmeyer looked up. He was close to tears. "Do I have to wear handcuffs? Those people down there know me."

I took the initiative. He was close to cracking. It was time to play good cop. "No. I'll take them off if you'll come with us nice and easy."

Doug glanced at me but I ignored him. He had too much

residual anger from the time he'd spent in the lockup. This was my call.

"Thanks," Huckmeyer said. "I appreciate it."

Doug took his cue from me. He unlocked the cuffs and opened his coat to put them back in the case on his belt. "Shall we go?"

We went out and walked down the slope with Sam behind us, at Doug's left heel, as per his instructions, but glancing at me.

We didn't speak and nobody paid much attention as we walked back to my car. The skiers were too busy getting ready for their day's fun to take note of non-skiers.

When we got to the car I put Huckmeyer in the front. He seemed to appreciate the privilege. Doug and Sam got in the back, Doug still not speaking. I started the motor and let it idle for a few moments until warmth started spreading through the heat vents. Then I made my pitch. "Walter. You're caught up in something nasty here. I know you're not that kind of guy and I want to make it easy for you."

He didn't look at me but I could see he was buying it. "Garfield is allowing Manatelli's bodyguard to cop out. That means they're after the big fish. Manatelli. I need to know where he is. If you tell me, Detective Ford and I will do everything we can to get you off lightly."

Now he turned to me and his face was anguished. "It's too late. He's gone back to New York."

I glanced back at Doug who shook his head silently. He wanted me to go on. "When did he leave? I was talking to him around noon yesterday."

"He went to the airport this morning," Huckmeyer said and his voice faltered. "I drove him. He caught the seven-thirty flight."

Doug opened the car door. I held up one finger to check him while Huckmeyer went on.

"It's too late now to stop him," Huckmeyer said grimly. He glanced at his wristwatch, a Rolex. "He'll be there now, I guess."

That didn't sit right with me. "He's not planning to stay in New York. I'll bet he's flying to some place to pick up the money he's taking out of your bank here," I said.

"I'll call the chief, let him know what's goin' down. Maybe he can check the bank, find where they're transferring the money an' get the planes watched at New York. He'll change planes there," Doug said. He got out and ran for the office with Sam bounding after him.

"Why will you stop him?" Huckmeyer asked. "It's a free country. He can go where he likes."

"Not with a Murder One charge against him. He killed whoever it was in his car yesterday. We don't have an ID yet but we will. We know it was a murder, that's certain."

Huckmeyer turned to look at me. "I didn't know about the murder." He sounded as if he was telling the truth. "Not until last night. That's when Alfredo came to see me at Brewskis. He told me Manatelli was alive and needed a place to stay."

"How much more did he tell you?"

"He said that it was all over. Everything was cleared up. I wouldn't have to sell the credit card slips anymore. They were moving out of town."

"You knew it was Manatelli's money buying those slips?"

He nodded. "It wasn't illegal, what I did. And I needed the money. I had debts."

"What kind of debts? Gambling debts?"

He shrugged. "Does it matter now?"

"No, I guess not, Walter. But can you answer me one more question?"

He nodded, looking ahead again. "Okay."

"Where were you going this morning? You weren't going skiing, were you? You were going up that hill for a reason. Is the money hidden there? The fifty thousand you skimmed from what you planted on Doug Ford?"

"It's under the floorboards in the lift house. That's where I arranged for it to be put. Jack Grant put it there. I was going to get it out and pay back the company now that everything's over."

"We'll go and get it once you've talked to the chief," I said. "But he's going to want to know where it came from. Like did you kill Ms. Laver and take it?"

"No." He was shocked. "I've done some bad things this year. But I've never hurt anybody. Not anybody."

He was jolted. I could see he wasn't able to say anything more so I used the chance to be the good guy and closed the questioning down. "I believe you. Now just take it easy and we'll wait for Officer Ford." He took out a handkerchief and blew his nose, wiping his eyes when he thought I wasn't looking. And we waited.

Doug was back a minute later. "The chief's on the phone to New York. He's got a warrant for Manatelli on Murder One. He's getting them to check all flights out to tax havens." He paused to take a breath. "He's on the phone to the bank now, to find out if and where the money's being moved." He sat back and Sam jumped into the car and over him to sit on the vacant seat. Doug groaned. "Fer Crissakes, Reid. Can you take Sam back? I'm not used to havin' a goddamn shadow."

"Tell him, 'Easy,' then 'Go with Reid,' and tap me on the shoulder."

"Shit. Like gettin' an award," Doug said. But he was laughing and he carried out the command and Sam relaxed while I fussed him.

"Good boy," I told him. "Sit. Easy."

He curled himself in the seat next to Doug and I drove back to the station.

We didn't cuff Huckmeyer to walk him inside. It was a break for him because the first of the reporters had arrived and they were snapping pictures and hollering questions at us. We ignored them, Doug and I smiling politely, Huckmeyer stone-faced. We took him inside and straight through to an interrogation room. Doug sat him down and I asked him, "Anything you need, Walter? A cup of coffee? To use the men's room?"

"No, thank you. I want to get this over." He was under control but ready to talk. I sat with him while Doug went and notified the chief.

They came back together and the chief stood in the doorway, looking stern. "It's a sad day for me, seeing you in here on such terrible charges," he said.

"I'm trying to help," Huckmeyer said miserably. "I didn't kill anybody. I admit I've been taking money from the company. I admit I've been doing business with Mr. Manatelli, but the business was legitimate."

"It may be. He isn't," the chief said. "And we know that

he's the man behind the killing of Ms. Laver and the other people. But you're still involved up to your neck."

"What can I do, chief?" Huckmeyer was close to tears.

"You can tell us everything you know," the chief said. "I'm going to have Detective Ford charge you with the theft of money from your employer. Then he'll read you your rights. I know you work for your dad and probably that charge will be dropped, but it's a criminal offense and we don't want you to say later that we coerced you in any way."

Huckmeyer nodded dumbly and Doug took out a card and read the charges formally, adding the Miranda message. The chief hooked his head at me and led me out of the room.

"I want to thank you for everything you've done. I think we can handle it now. The bank president says the money is being transferred to the Cayman Islands. I've got the New York police looking for Manatelli everywhere there's a connecting flight."

"What's he charged with?"

"The murder of the John Doe in the car yesterday. In fact he's not John Doe anymore. We have an ID."

"Good work. From the FBI?"

"Yes." The chief nodded briskly. "They sent us a mug shot. The man is a member of the Mucci family. His name is Romeo Ciulla. He worked with Manatelli, some kind of numbers man, bookkeeper, something like that. Captain Schmidt's at the airport with his picture to see if he flew in yesterday. We figure that's what happened. He came in, Manatelli offed him and left the note to make us think everything was closed up."

"So what would you like me to do next?"

"Well, there isn't very much. I'd rather keep you out of the interrogation if you don't mind. I think the kid'll be freer with me than he would with you."

"That's fine with me. But there is one thing. He says he's got fifty grand from the night Doug was killed, squirreled away under the floor of his gondola lift, at the top of the slope."

"Can you go out and bring it in?"

"Well, I could, but I've been thinking about that. If Manatelli knew where it was, there's a good chance it's been tampered with. Maybe the money's gone. In which case, Huckmeyer himself should recover the box so he knows the department didn't take it. And secondly, given Manatelli's way of settling problems, maybe he's booby-trapped it. That way he could count on Huckmeyer being out of the picture as well."

The chief stroked his nose thoughtfully. "That makes sense. The guy's got no more conscience than Eichmann. I'll try to round up a bomb guy."

"Do that. But if you need help, my dog is trained to sniff explosives."

The chief puffed out a respectful sigh. "I'm going to have to seriously consider getting a K9 unit for the department," he said. "Okay. When we've talked to Huckmeyer, maybe you and your dog will go with him to get his money back. Can you wait somewhere until then?"

"Will do. I'll go across the street for some breakfast."

"Good. Keep the receipt." He smiled, dismissing me, and I headed out for pancakes and good Vermont maple syrup. Not the greatest. I'm from Ontario and my neighbors make the very best, but what the hell, it wasn't corn syrup.

I was on my second cup of coffee when Doug came in. "Nice goin'," he said. "I'm in there workin', so goddamn hungry my stomach thinks my throat's been cut, and you're here with the knife and fork."

"The chief's paying. How's that make you feel?"

He laughed and ordered toast and coffee to go and led me back to the station, munching. "The kid's talked," he said. "He didn't arrange the killing, but he planned to charge Cindy Laver with theft. He'd shorted the cash deposit by forty-eight big ones. That's why he didn't make the deposit with her."

"Nice guy. What'd he do with the money?"

"That's where it gets kind of cute," Doug said. He

crammed the last of his toast into his mouth and couldn't talk for a while. "He was paying for AIDS treatments for his brother. The brother's gay an' the father won't speak to him or help him. So young Huckmeyer's been skimming." I shook my head sadly. "Then he's the white knight. No jury will convict him with that as a motive."

"You're right. I don't think it'll even come to trial," Doug said. "It's been two years of medication and treatments and the costs were sky-high. Like I said, it makes him look like Prince Valiant. I don't see how they'll make the money charges stick."

"So what now? 're we going for the box?"

"Yeah. He says he was scared and didn't want to put the money right back into the bank. Wanted to talk to his dad. So he hid it until the old guy comes back from golfing in Florida."

"If Manatelli knew about it, he's likely still out his fifty," I said. "Let's go see. Did the bomb guy get here?"

"Yeah. There's a guy from Burlington inside. Got enough gear with him to handle an A-bomb."

"Good. I don't want to get blown up again. Once was enough."

"Shit. I'll never forget that day," Doug said seriously. "I figured you were going to lose your hands."

"Good as new." Impulsively I pulled up my sleeves and showed him my scars, through and through on both forearms. "You done good, Bro, getting me on that chopper so fast."

He didn't speak, just put one hand on my neck and squeezed.

The bomb man was waiting for us inside the station, a trim little guy, around thirty, erect, as most short cops are, and officious, with a bristly little moustache. Doug introduced us and I told him about Sam.

"You sure he's good enough for this work?"

"I'd bet my life on it. He's better than any parts per million air sampler you've got in your bag of tricks."

He shrugged. "It's your ass. An' this is your bomb, if there is one."

He went in his own car. Huckmeyer came with Doug and me. He looked pale and teary but he held his head up as we passed through the same reporters and drove back to Cat's Cradle.

I took Sam with us and we all went up on the lift, the four of us and Sam. At the top, Huckmeyer sent the operator out of the lift house and stopped the lift. Then he knelt down in one corner and lifted out a piece of baseboard, a plank of pine held only by two nails which he pried out easily by easing the board forward.

"It's under that board," he said, pointing. "There's screws in it but they aren't fastened."

The bomb guy had put on his protective clothing in the lift. Now he told us all to step outside. I watched him work, through the open door, my palms pressed over my ears, mouth open, just in case.

He lifted the board, moving very carefully and checking underneath. After he'd made sure it was safe he lifted it all the way out and called us back in, speaking softly. We tiptoed in and looked down. In the space under the floor there was a children's lunch pail with a picture of Superman on the front.

"Okay. Stand back," I said. "I'll have Sam sniff."

Doug shook his head. "Man. I gotta get you workin' on my kids. That dog is the best-trained thing I ever saw."

"The training doesn't stick with anything that doesn't eat kibble," I joked and I sat Sam down and prepared him to take on the sniffing assignment. The bomb man was watching, disdainfully.

"I thought they need a special collar for sniffing work," Doug said. He was exuberant, elated, like we were on R and R together in Bangkok.

"He needs a cue. It could be a collar. I use a word," I said. "Think back to the worst word you know."

Doug laughed and swore but I shook my head. "No, think Nam. Think Ho Chi Minh." I said the name slowly, holding one finger in front of Sam's nose. Instantly he barked. His head went down to the box but he didn't touch it, just barked furiously.

"Easy, boy," I told him, and stood back, patting his head. "Good dog," I said again and waited for Huckmeyer to speak.

At last he found a voice. "You mean there's explosives in there?"

"That's the kind of guy you were doing business with. Now let's get outside and let this gentleman do his job."

We stood back, down the back side of the slope from the lift house. It seemed like forever and Huckmeyer kept looking at his watch which didn't help.

Finally the man came out, carrying the box. He set it down gently on the snow and took out a drill. "This is the hard part," he said, his voice muffled through his head cover.

We watched as he drilled a hole in one side of the box, well down from the lid. He let the drill go in only the thickness of the metal. I was sweating as I watched him. He bent and peered through the hole, then drilled again. I was still sweating and I backed off another step, reliving the day when the guy in front of me on the trail stepped on an enemy mine. It wiped him out and peppered me. I remembered the pain of my smashed arms and waited, muscles clenched.

It took him half an hour. An endless half hour. Then he folded back the flap he'd made and reached inside with a pair of pliers. I heard the snip of a wire and fell flat instinctively, but this time there was no explosion. I got up slowly, seeing that Doug was also picking himself up. Huckmeyer was looking at us wide-eyed. The bomb man was taking his headpiece off.

"Okay, heroes. It's safe now." He was sneering.

Doug was coldly furious. He walked up and grabbed the guy by the shoulder. "Lissen up, asshole. You ever seen anybody blown away?"

"No." The guy's voice went up angrily. "Of course not."

"Well, we have," Doug said. "Show him your goddamn arms, Reid."

"There's no need."

"Do it," Doug thundered, and I did. The bomb man and Huckmeyer stared in wonder at the white marks on my forearms. They didn't speak and to break the tension I said, "These wounds had I on Crispin's Day. Remember, *Henry Fifth?* Maybe you saw the movie."

"Shit." The bomb man rubbed his chin with a gloved hand. "I'm sorry, guys. I didn't mean anything."

"Reid was ten yards from the guy who hit the booby trap," Doug said. "That poor bastard was blown in half. His guts were draped all around the trees like a line 'f dirty laundry. Now just open the goddamn box."

He was chastened. "Sorry, guys," he said again, then opened the box. There was no money in it. Just four sticks of dynamite and the triggering device, the kind of contacts you find in security systems on house windows.

"You sure it's safe now?" Doug asked.

"Safe as it can be. I don't like dynamite, it sweats gelignite, but I've got shock-resistant packing in my cooler chest."

"Then stow it and let's go," Doug said. "And don't touch anything. We gotta check for prints."

The man quickly lowered the box into his cooler, on top of a layer of sponge rubber. Then he packed it around with more rubber and closed the cooler. "Okay now," he said.

Huckmeyer called the lift operator back from the place off in the woods where he'd been watching us. He was full of questions but Huckmeyer shut him up. "Somebody boobytrapped the place," he said. "They were trying to extort money from me. It's safe now."

The kid whistled in horror, then Huckmeyer instructed him to get us back on the car and move us directly to the bottom of the hill, ignoring the other cars that came up as we did so.

"They'll be madder'n snakes. But okay, Mr. Huckmeyer." The kid did as he was told and we were down at the bottom of the hill in five non-stop minutes.

The kid in the lower lift house had more questions, and the lineup of skiers was furious, but Huckmeyer ignored them all and we went back to the car and drove into town. Nobody spoke on the way.

We got to the station and went in. The bomb man came in behind us, carrying his box of tricks. The chief summoned me. "What did you find?"

"A bomb. Homemade but it would have done the job. The Burlington guy did a great job. He's got the bomb with him. It needs fingerprinting and maybe you can trace where the dynamite came from."

"We know where it came from." The chief was angry. "Manatelli planted it. That's where it came from."

"He flew in from New York, or Newark, wherever. He didn't bring explosives in his luggage." I was weary and angry. The long wait in the cold had stiffened my sore back and I wanted to stand under a hot shower until my rigid muscles slackened. I guess my impatience was showing. The chief was polite.

"I see what you mean. We'll work on it." He paused and put the polite question. "You okay?"

"I hurt my back chasing Huckmeyer on the skidoo. I need some heat on it. Sorry if it shows."

"You need a sauna." The chief pulled out his wallet quickly, like a bargain hunter grabbing for cash to snap something up. "Here, this is my membership at the health club. Take it. The address is on it." He handed me the card and I took it gratefully.

"Appreciate that. I'll return it with the badge and gun when I've got the kinks out of my spine."

"Good. Do that. And thank you." He shook my hand, too hard. "Oh, and there was a message for you. Mr. Maloney wants to talk to you. He's at his office. You know where that is?"

"No. Only his house."

"Here. Let me write it down." He turned and took a pen from the desk and wrote on the edge of a flier about car theft.

"Thank, Chief. I'll go see him first."

"Good." He beamed at me like a headwaiter and then turned away to talk to the cop at the desk.

I went out to my car, slowing down now, favoring my back. The hot shower, maybe even a sauna, loomed ahead of me like a vacation in the sun. After that I would phone my wife and head back into my own world.

An elderly woman was working a computer in the reception area of Maloney's office. She stopped work and showed me through. Maloney was in his office with a clutter of documents on his desk.

He stood up, smiling. "Thanks for coming in, Reid. I have a couple of things to share with you."

"Good. Everything's falling into place."

He waved me to a chair and indicated the coffee maker that was sitting on the side cabinet. I shook my head and he said, "Ella has been checking the books at Cat's Cradle, along lines I suggested. She finds discrepancies."

"How was it done?"

"It's complex. It's a question of season memberships. They cost about twelve hundred dollars. Your Walter was hiding some of them from his bookkeeper. He had a number of passes made up outside the usual procedures and passed them along directly to members. He's been able to hide the deficiencies so far because his father thinks the bad economic situation has kept people away. In fact, his son has been robbing him."

"The chief told me he had. No details, but he also told me the reason," I said. "Apparently young Huckmeyer's brother, the actor, has AIDS. Walter's been skimming to pay for the medical treatments. The father had disowned the other son and wouldn't pay."

"I'd heard rumors," Maloney said. "That's quite commendable of Walter, when you think about it. I'm sure his father will come around when he hears the whole story."

"So what else is happening?"

"The bank." He put both hands flat on the documents and leaned toward me. "I spoke to Eric Lawson this morning. He wasn't anxious to talk about it but he's in the process of arranging a transfer of funds to the Cayman Islands. It's in excess of a million dollars."

"I heard that. I guess that's where Manatelli is heading. He flew out this morning. We've got the police looking for him in New York and New Jersey, at Newark. The chief got a warrant for Murder One."

"There's more." His eyes were shining with excitement. "About the money transfer, I mean. I was able to prevail on him to let me take a look at the transaction and we found that the amount going out had a slight clerical error in it. It was one decimal point out."

"You mean he was set to transfer ten million instead of one?"

"Yes." Maloney sat back. "The new woman at the bank, the one I told you about, is handling the move. The documents were all in order but when we dug into the computer we found that Manatelli's account had been inflated. They were going to strip the bank."

"But surely there are checks, safeguards. They couldn't get away with that?"

"Not within the country, but by the time the cash was received, even electronically, in the Caymans, it couldn't be retrieved." He waved one hand. "Oh, technically it could, but it would take years to sort out the rights and wrongs of it all. In the meantime, the bank would be closed out. All its assets would be frozen. And Manatelli would be spending it all.

"Has the woman been arrested?"

"Not yet."

"Not yet? She should be in the station house asking to see her lawyer."

"So far there's no real crime. She could claim it was a clerical error."

"So you have to go through with this?"

"Not completely." He smiled a tight little smile. "Computers are so wonderful. They have a young teller at the bank, a boy called Jenkins. He's a hacker. He spent the early part of the day with Eric revising his program for him."

"To do what?" Computers are a blind spot with me.

"It will respond to the command to send the money to the foreign bank, responding to the transfer numbers on cue, but in fact the money will be rerouted to a new account, Eric has opened today in the bank's name, within the branch."

"So she sends it, sits there rubbing her hands. And the money's never left the bank?"

"Exactly." He allowed himself a smile.

"So that's what all this was about. Manatelli started the business of buying credit slips just to get into the bank so he could take it over."

Maloney nodded. "That's how I read it."

"But why here? There's all kinds of banks closer to his home than this."

"That was part of its attraction, I'd imagine. He was far enough from his own sphere of action that he could operate without fear of his employer's knowing what he was doing. Remember, he has a million dollars of his own money in this sting. That almost certainly came from his employer and just as certainly his employer did not know."

"Yes, but why here? Why Chambers of all places?"

"The only connection I can see is Jack Grant's gambling."

"That's a possibility. But the amounts he lost are just spit to these guys. I saw his slips. His biggest loss was five grand at one time. That's not enough to bring a big fish like Manatelli out of New Jersey."

"Maybe that's where it started." Maloney held up one finger. "Atlantic City. There's gambling there. Grant went at least once, about a year ago. I remember his father telling me. He had a very good time there, came back with money in his pocket."

"And you think someone scouted him down there in New Jersey and followed him back here to check this place out?"

"We'll never know unless Manatelli tells us when he's arrested, and I doubt he'll say anything he doesn't have to," Maloney said. He checked his watch. "Paul Grant is due in to see me." He glanced up. "If you like, I can make arrangements for him to settle whatever indebtedness he's incurred with you."

I thought for a moment. "No. That's okay. I was only over at his place an hour or so. Forget it. But there's one thing he could help me with, if you could spare a couple of minutes before you get down to business."

"Sure." He checked his watch again. "He's always very punctual. I'll see if he's here yet."

He went to the door and opened it. I heard him say, "Good morning, Paul, come on in."

Grant came in. He looked as if he hadn't slept at all. His face was gray and the circles under his eyes seemed to rest on his cheekbones. He nodded at me and grimaced, as close as he could come to a smile.

I stood up. "Good morning, Mr. Grant. I was just leaving but I wondered if you could help me on something before I go."

"I'll try." He sat and Maloney went to the coffee server and poured him a cup. He took it without a word and tilted his face up to me politely. Let's get this over with, his expression said. I have a life to return to after you've gone.

I started carefully, not wanting to cause him any extra pain. "This has nothing to do with your son's death. The police think it's a whole separate case."

"What is it?" It had worked. He was relaxed.

"They found an explosive device this morning. They're checking it of course for fingerprints and so on, but I wondered if you might know, from running a hardware and building supply outlet, where in Chambers you could get the materials to make a bomb. The trigger device and the explosive? I wouldn't know where to look.''

He seemed relieved at the question. It hadn't involved his son. He set down his coffee cup in the saucer and leaned back. He might have been sitting in a lodge meeting. "Even in a town as law-abiding at this it's no problem to get your hands on four sticks of dynamite.''

His words hit me like the shock wave from an explosion. And in the sudden horror on his face I could see he had realized the significance of his words.

"No. It wouldn't have been,'' I said. "Not for you.''

He stood up, blustering. "What's this man saying? Frank?''

Maloney looked at me but didn't speak.

"Four sticks of dynamite. Plus the kind of five-buck security system window latch you sell.'' I shook my head at him. "Really, Paul. I wasn't sure until you said that. What happened? Did Jack tell you about the money? Is that why you knifed him? And threw him off the chair lift on the way up there?''

Perhaps a month or even a week later he would have risen above the accusation. He hadn't said anything incriminating. Some cops might even have missed the clue he'd dropped. A good lawyer could have laughed the case out of court. But too much had happened to him in the last week. He sat down wearily and spoke to Maloney. "Frank, I want to retain you on this,'' he said.

Maloney reached out and rested one hand on his shoulder. "Count on me, Paul." Then he turned to me, his face filled with sadness. "Have Mary call Chief Williams to come over, would you please?"

I did, then waited on the street until the chief turned up, with Pat Hinton beside him in the car. The chief got out and strode up to me. "What made him open up? Did you pressure him?"

"No, sir. I asked about the bomb and he said, right away, it would be no problem, even in a town as law-abiding as this, for a man to get his hands on four sticks of dynamite."

The chief rubbed his chin. "That's not a case."

"I know. But it seemed obvious to me that he knew about the bomb and I went on. I suggested that he'd killed his own son, to reclaim the money from the shack. That's when he turned to Maloney and asked him to represent him."

"If Maloney tells him to dummy up, we've got nothing," Hinton snapped.

"I know. But Maloney was the one who suggested I call the chief. I think he wants his client to cooperate."

"Jesus Christ," the chief said. "Come on, Pat. Let's go check what's happening."

I watched them go, then let Sam out of my car and walked down the street to a phone. My wife answered on the second ring. Her voice was music.

"Hi, Fred. It's your wandering boy."

"Reid. Lovely to hear your voice. I was beginning to think you'd found yourself a bouncy little ski bunny and settled in for the winter."

"I had to beat them away with a stick, but no sweat. How's Louise?"

"The world's most incredible infant. Mensa material, I'm sure. Plus she's going to be an Olympic athlete. She's beautiful, Reid."

"So are you," I said. "I'll be home tonight, late and weary but all yours."

"I'll prepare a warm welcome." She laughed. "Two warm welcomes, if you include a late dinner."

"You can skip the dinner. It's not meals I've been missing."

She laughed again. "Can't say too much, old spot. Peter Horn's here, talking to Mom, playing with Lulu, drinking coffee. He's been dropping in a lot the last few days."

"I asked him to. Wanted to keep all the marauding Murphy's Harbour bachelors away from your door."

"They're staying away in droves."

"Well, that's good. Everything's going well here. Doug is free and clear. The case is all wrapped up. I'll tell you about it when it's not long distance."

"I can't wait. Drive carefully. I want you here in one big oversexed piece."

"Be there around midnight, I'd say."

"Fine. You can change your daughter when she wakes up at one."

"Be glad to. Bye, love."

"Tell Doug I'm glad it's over. Bye, dear."

She hung up and I did the same and paced slowly back

to Maloney's office. The chief's car was still there so I sat
in my own and cranked up the heater for a while. It eased
the stiffness in my back and I was half dozing when the chief
and Hinton came out with Grant walking between them. I
got out of my car and stood there until Pat ducked away to
have a quick word with me.

"I think Maloney's going for an insanity plea. He let
Grant ramble away without stopping. And when Grant said
he didn't want him to come to the station he said 'Okay'
and sat down."

"Grant say anything worth listening to?"

"Did he? Christ! I've never seen such a can of worms. He
killed the girl because she got in the way when she heard
what he wanted his son to do, which was to dig up the
money for him. Then he took his son up the hill. The kid
said he would squeal to us about Wendy Tate being killed
so he knifed him."

"Who killed Cindy Laver?"

"Jack did, and planted the money in Doug's car." Hinton
glanced over to where the chief was letting Grant into the
back seat of the car. "I've got to go."

"Quick question. Just for my satisfaction. What's Grant
senior using for an excuse? Does he say he was avenging
Cindy Laver, or what?"

"Pretty much." The chief had got into the passenger side
and was beckoning to Hinton who pulled himself away from
me. "Sounds like a crock to me. I figure he did it because
the kid wouldn't stop gambling and was still involved with
Manatelli. He came at you that night in the parking lot on
Manatelli's say-so."

The chief waved again, this time angrily, and Hinton ran
to the car. I watched them drive off and went upstairs to
talk to Maloney.

He was sitting in his office with a Bible open in front of
him. He looked old and sad. "Matthew 7:1. The King James
Version," he said, and I could see tears in his eyes. "Judge
not, that ye be not judged." He left his finger on the text as

he spoke to me. "Ironic, isn't it. I want to be a judge but I can never get that text out of my mind."

"I guess it means we shouldn't judge people by our own standards. The Indians put it differently. They say 'Never judge a man until you've walked a mile in his moccasins.' "

"It's so hard to sympathize, you know," he said. "Money was at the back of all of it. Cindy Laver? Killed out of greed. Jack Grant told his father that he felt so bad killing her he cleaned up the mess and laid her out on the bed. But he did it, nevertheless. For money. To settle a thirty-thousand-dollar gambling debt with Manatelli."

"There weren't any betting slips that big in his papers."

"I know," he said. "Paul and I had a long talk while we were waiting for the police to arrive. He told me he pulled out all the heavy betting slips before he let the police search the room. He wanted enough evidence that they would think Jack had a motive, but not enough to make anybody think that he himself had a reason for killing his son."

"That doesn't sound like a crazy man talking. Sounds like a businessman."

"That's what he is," Maloney said. He closed the Bible and put it back into his desk drawer. "I'll be pressed to make an insanity plea stick. He was clever enough to call on you when the police didn't find the secret drawer. He thought you'd be more thorough than they were."

"It's a tangle," I said.

"It's untangled now. The chief took a call while he was here. They've arrested Ms. Corelli at the bank. She put the transaction through and was heading out to her car when they picked her up."

"So it's all wrapped up," I said. "Doug's free and clear. The bank's safe. There's a warrant out for Manatelli and Grant's inside. Time for me to go home."

He stood up and thrust out his hand. "Thank you for coming here. Without you, this would have gone very differently."

"Maybe." I shook hands with him. "I think you've got a

pretty good department here. A guy like Pat Hinton wouldn't have let things rest. Especially after the bank folded. That would have got everybody reopening the case. They'd have cleared Doug."

"That would have been after the fact of the bank collapse. This way is much better, for the town, for everyone." He came around the desk to pat me on the shoulder and walk me to the outer door. He was a good man, courteous, compassionate. I hoped he made it to judge.

I went back to the station house to turn in my badge and gun and talk to Doug Ford. The chief was still busy with Grant but Doug was free. He seemed flat, overwhelmed by the pace of things, I guessed, but he got us a couple of coffees and we went into the detective office.

"There's a new development," he said soberly.

"If you mean the bank, I heard, from Maloney."

"Yeah, that too," he said. "More than that. This was a flash from New York."

"They've picked up Manatelli?"

"They picked up a stiff, from the first-class lounge at Kennedy. Middle-aged Latin-looking businessman. Keeled over while he was waiting for the flight to the Caymans."

"Manatelli?"

"That wasn't the name on his ticket and passport. But the cop was sharp. He dug through the guy's pockets and came up with his real passport. Manatelli. He just happened to stop in for a coffee. Just happened to drop dead. Waddya make of it?"

"I don't believe in divine justice. Sounds to me like there's a leak in the New York police organization and our friend Mucci got wind of what's been happening."

Doug pursed his lips thoughtfully. "Not their trademark, is it? Bullet in the head is more their speed."

"That's the old way. They're in a lot of legitimate business now. Bloodstains are messy. They could have dropped something in his drink." I shrugged. "He's just as dead."

We sat down and looked at one another, but without focusing, the thousand-meter stare of combat fatigue. Doug spoke first. "That makes five killings."

"You're not feeling sad about Manatelli?"

He looked away and blew his nose before he turned back. I got busy examining my coffee cup until he spoke again. "I wanted a peaceful life when I got back from Nam," he said softly. "I tried other jobs but it was hard in the seventies. A vet was a goddamn outcast then. I couldn't get anything worthwhile. I was laboring on a building site with a bunch of assholes who couldn't even read. Melody didn't mind. She was finishing up her degree. She never put me down. But I needed something I could take pride in. So the parish priest pulled some strings for me. I took the exam and joined the police department. And from then on it was the war all over again."

"It was pretty much the same way with me, Doug. Face it. We're a couple of soldier ants. Other people do other things. We protect them. It's what we do. What we are."

"I guess you're right." He set down his cup and stood up. "Hey. You heard Cap'n Schmidt give me the week off. I'm goin' home, clean up before Melody and the kids get back."

"Good thinking." I stood up. "Soon's I've seen the chief I'm gone."

"You coming by the house before you go?"

"Yeah. To grab my bag. Then I gotta go. It's a long drive home."

"Yeah," he said. He came around the table. "Thanks, Logger." My nickname from the Marines. Canadian, therefore a lumberjack, as far as my fellow grunts were concerned. Nobody had called me "Logger" in years.

"You're welcome, Bro." His own nickname, in a largely white platoon.

He reached out to shake my hand and we gave one another an impulsive hug.

We disengaged and I said, "See you at the house."

"Right," he said and went downstairs.

I stood at the window and watched him walk to his car. He was carrying a burden. I knew that, but he walked proud. No one else was going to know. Me, and Melody when she got home. But he was in command again.

The chief summoned me downstairs a little later. He was brisk and businesslike. I listened while he gave me the same news I'd heard from Maloney and Doug. I didn't interrupt. He was too happy about it, although he was trying not to let it show. It took only a couple of minutes and I could see he was rehearsing for the reporters who would be pouring in when the bank story got out.

When he'd finished he sat back. "So it's all wrapped up. Long and bloody, but it's over."

"Well done, Chief," I said. Everyone likes to be stroked. He was no exception.

"Thank you. And I have to return the compliment." He looked at me levelly. If I'd been a member of his department I would have been holding my breath, waiting for the other shoe to drop. He went on. "Without your assistance, this case could have dragged on. It might even have been too late to save the damage to the bank. This town is in your debt."

"I came here to look out for Doug Ford. He's reinstated with no blots on his record. That's all the thanks I was looking for."

"It's not enough," he said quickly. Then he realized his tension was peeping out so he tried a smile. "And besides, I want to keep everything in the family."

I waited and he opened his drawer and took out a piece of paper. "Read this please, and sign it."

It was short but had been drafted by somebody who knew some law. It was on Chambers PD letterhead and said, as I remember it, "In acknowledgment of remuneration received I herewith absolve the town of Chambers from any further financial liabilities to me. Further, as a sworn member of the Chambers Police Department, I will keep confidential all knowledge of procedures and events within the department's jurisdiction before and during my tenure." My name was typed below, along with a date and time and a space for a witness.

"Fine by me, Chief. Do you have a pen?"

He handed one to me and I checked the clock and wrote down the time and the date, signed it and handed it over. He witnessed it and put it back in the drawer, bringing out a check.

"This will be satisfactory, I hope."

I glanced at it, expecting a few bucks. It was made out for one thousand. Not a fortune but out of a police budget, something that would create questions among the city fathers. "This is very generous, Chief," I said.

"You've probably saved us ten times that much in overtime pay. I wish it could be more, but you know how it is in a small town."

"I surely do. Thank you. And I'll give you back your gun and badge. And your gym card." I laid them all on his desk.

"I just need the gun and the card," he said. He pushed the badge back across the desk to me. "We'd like to have you as an honorary member of the department." He smiled tightly. "Unpaid, of course."

"Of course," I said and we laughed and shook hands and I left.

When I got to Doug's house, I found him vacuuming. He had a pile of girlie magazines on the hall stand. "Found these in Ben's room. He's starting to grow up." He was grinning.

"Nothing changes," I said and he laughed.

" 'the hell am I going to do with him?"

"Don't embarrass him. Put these back where you found them and keep him busy playing sports."

"He's a'ready in every damn thing in the school."

"Then buy him a cornet and a couple of Wynton Marsalis records."

Doug slapped his knee. "Well, damn. Yeah. If he's horny, buy him a horn. Good thinkin'."

I picked up my stuff and came downstairs. He had my

bottle of rye on the table. We had done a fair bit of damage to it. "Here, take this." He handed it to me.

"Nah. I'll pick up a whole one at duty-free. Get something nice for Fred."

"Good thinking." He fell silent. We were getting down to the hard part, saying goodbye, while demonstrating what big tough guys we both were.

"Listen. Pickerel season opens May 15. Why'n't you bring Ben up, the whole crowd if Melody can get away? Fred would love that."

"I'll try," he said. "Depends on Melody's work."

I hoisted my bag into my left hand. "Okay. So, I'm on my horse."

"Right." He came with me to the car. I let Sam out for a minute and Doug fussed him. "You done good, old buddy," he said.

Then he stood up. "You too, Logger."

"What are friends for?" We stood and looked at one another for a moment. Then Doug held up his right hand and we did our dap and laughed like nineteen-year-olds. An old lady was walking by with her dog and she paused to watch us. She looked like she might be frosted by our high jinks but she surprised me, calling out, "Nice to see you, Doug. When's Melody getting home?"

"Nice to see you, Brenda. Melody's home tonight. I'm picking her up at the airport at ten."

"Then you'll need some dinner," she said firmly. "George is home at six. Come on over then. Otherwise you'll have some dreadful hamburger or something. And bring your friend."

"This is Reid Bennett. He's on his way home. But thank you. I'll be there."

I smiled at the old lady and we told one another we were pleased to meet and she waved and walked on.

"Looks like you're back in the social register," I said.

"Sure does," Doug said. "And I want you to know that lady's one awesome cook."

"Then enjoy." I got in the car. "Take care, eh."

"Yeah. Drive careful." Doug stood and waved while I backed out and turned down the street, honking as I passed the old lady and her dog.

I was lucky with the weather. It was overcast but it didn't snow and I drove into the flatter country in New York State and headed north on Highway 81 toward the Thousand Islands bridge and the last couple of hundred miles home.

I was in that comfortable driving trance, cruising just above the limit with the radio tuned to some country station and my mind in neutral. It fell dark around five and I put my lights on. I'd planned to pull off the highway at Watertown for dinner and a cup of hundred-mile coffee before crossing the bridge into Canada.

There wasn't much traffic and most of it was local, trailing along at the posted limit. I passed all of them. Not in a cloud of dust, but creeping up until I had to slacken speed or go by. I figured the state troopers wouldn't stop me for my extra five miles an hour. If they did I could always pull the brother officer stunt. It works.

Then, just south of the Watertown exit an unmarked car passed me. It slowed ahead and a hand came out of the passenger side and put a red flasher on the top. An unmarked patrol car. I slowed obediently, preparing to make fellow-cop noises. It slowed further and a big light shone out of the rear window into my eyes. I blinked and saw the car's turn signal flicking, pulling me over.

So I stopped, like a good little citizen, and got out of the car. That's a tip, by the way. Always get out of the car. In a law-abiding place like Canada, anyway. It shows the cop that you respect his authority. It's a gesture of surrender, the way a weaker dog will cower instead of fighting. Usually it will get you off with a warning instead of a ticket.

I was expecting cops. So I'd left Sam in the front seat and shut the door. I was alone and helpless when I saw the front-seat passenger get out. He was a civilian and he opened the rear door of the car and let a man out. This one was short and in the light from my headlights I could see he was middle-aged and Italian-looking. I backed off a step toward my own car and the aid Sam could give me. But he held his hand up. "Mr. Bennett, please."

He didn't sound threatening and nobody else came with him. The other guy had gotten back into his car. There were just the two of us and I figured I could roll out of the line of fire before he could shoot me.

So I stood. A car came up behind me and I waited for it to stop and complete the ambush but it went right by.

The man came within two paces of me. He was around five-two but had more authority than a million taller men in high positions.

"Mr. Bennett," he said. His voice sounded pleasant and musical. "My name is Antonio Mucci."

"Have we met, Mr. Mucci?"

"Not until now," he said. His hands were at his sides. He was wearing gloves. His men were in his car. He was trying to put me at my ease.

I didn't speak and he waved one hand, the Italian prelude to words. "You're wondering why now. Am I right?"

"Yes, as a matter of fact."

"I was in Syracuse," he said. "And this morning I got some news about a man who works for me. Angelo Manatelli." He waited for an answer but when I stayed quiet he went on. "I find that this man has been cheating me. I find he has killed another man who works for me."

"He did. A man called Ciulla."

"Right. Right." He didn't want conversation, I could tell. Politeness aside, this was intended to be a monologue.

"So I ask who found out about Angelo. And I hear that you did. You and some small-town cops." He laughed now. "These small-town guys, they didn't do it alone. They brought in an expert from Canada, I hear. Without you, nobody finds out about Angelo cheating me."

"They'd have found out sometime."

"Maybe. But by then it's too late. My money has gone. Angelo's gone and Curly Ciulla is just as dead."

I could see where he was going now but was wondering why. Why here? Why me?

"So it seems I owe you a debt, Mr. Bennett. I'm a man who pays his debts."

"You don't owe me anything, Mr. Mucci. A friend of mine was in trouble. Now he's cleared. That's all that matters."

"To you, maybe," he said. "Me, I see things differently."

It could still get sticky, I realized. He might be planning to pay me off with a bullet in the head. He had been exposed as blind to what Manatelli was doing. I was one of the few people who knew.

"So. I'm close to this highway. I have friends who watch for your car. They tell me where you are. I come to talk to you."

It was time to show some strength, I realized. No more deferring to him as "Mr. Mucci." "I appreciate your courtesy. But there's no debt involved."

"You're sure?" He sounded amused. "Like you'll excuse my saying so, that car you're driving is getting old." He gestured to my car but I didn't turn around. I'm too old for tricks as easy as that.

"It's two years old, good for another five, easy."

He started tugging at his right glove. While he was doing it I glanced behind me. Nobody visible. But it was dark outside the cone of my headlights. I was wishing I'd turned them off when I got out. But he only took off his glove and extended his hand. He did it the way a cardinal might so you could kiss his ring. "I heard tell you were straight," he said. "I'd like to shake the hand of an honest man."

If he was going to double-cross me, this was his moment but I had no choice. "Thanks for the compliment, Mr. Mucci. A pleasure to meet you."

I shook his hand. It was soft, but empty. He didn't have a C-note or two clasped in it.

"So. We've met." He released my hand. "A pleasure like-
wise, Mr. Bennett."

"Then I'll say goodnight. I've got a long drive ahead of
me still."

"Drive safely," he said and stood there as I got back into
my car. He stood where he was as I passed him and I
pushed my lights off and then back on. He raised his hand
and walked back to his car.

I was scared for the next eight miles, to Watertown. They
had taken the red light off their roof but they stayed with
me, thirty yards back, all the way to the exit. Then they
pulled off and I pressed the gas a little harder, all the way
to the border.

It was a relief to be under the bright lights and in the
bustle of the crossing point. I picked up a liter of Black
Velvet and a bottle of Chloe at the duty-free and drove over
both bridges to the Canadian side. Here I had to tell white
lies to the woman in the immigration booth. I'd been in the
United States for a vacation. I hadn't acquired anything.

On the 401 across southern Ontario, the facilities are right
on the highway itself. They're all soulless franchises with
standard food and full-service gas stations. The fillup cost
me twice what it would have done in Watertown and the
hamburger was blah but I was ravenous. The hunger of fear.
The same fear made me ring home, tingling with concern
while I waited for the phone to be picked up.

Fred answered, sounding cheerful and normal.

"Hi, love. Just wanted to let you know I'm just east of
Kingston, right on schedule."

"Well, good. But listen. Who the Sam Hill is A.M.? Is it
some rich widow from the ski slopes of old Vermont?" Her
voice was teasing but she wanted to know, badly.

"No, it's a Mafia heavy called Antonio Mucci. I just had
a most interesting talk to him on Highway 81 in New York
State."

"Well, he must have broken the bank," she said. "You'll
never believe the roses he's sent."

"To you?"

"To all of us. 'Mr. and Mrs. Reid Bennett and family. With thanks. A.M.' There's four dozen of them. They came from Parry Sound. The woman said the order cleaned out the store."

I was standing with my forehead pressed against the side of the phone partition. A woman passing by with food on a cardboard tray looked at me oddly and I straightened up.

"That's good news," I said. "It means he's out of my debt which is the way it should be. He's heavy."

Her voice had puzzlement all through it. "I don't understand."

"You will. I'll explain it all when I get home."

She laughed. "First things first."

We said goodbye and I hung up and headed back to my car, carrying a raw burger for Sam. In my mind it was some kind of sacrificial offering. He took it carefully from my fingers and swallowed it in two gulps. His reaction cheered me up. "Looks like everything's back to normal," I told him and drove off west up the 401.